CAUGHT

Also by Lisa Moore

Open
Alligator
February

Caught
Lisa Moore

Chatto & Windus
LONDON

Published by Chatto & Windus 2014
First published in Canada by House of Anansi Press in 2013

2 4 6 8 10 9 7 5 3 1

Copyright © Lisa Moore 2013

Lisa Moore has asserted her right under the Copyright, Designs
and Patents Act 1988 to be identified as the author of this work.

First published in Great Britain in 2014 by
Chatto & Windus
Random House, 20 Vauxhall Bridge Road,
London SW1V 2SA

www.vintage-books.co.uk

Addresses for companies within The Random House Group Limited can be found at:
www.randomhouse.co.uk/offices.htm

The Random House Group Limited Reg. No. 954009

A CIP catalogue record for this book
is available from the British Library

ISBN 9780701188542

The Random House Group Limited supports the Forest Stewardship
Council® (FSC®), the leading international forest-certification organisation.
Our books carrying the FSC label are printed on FSC®-certified paper.
FSC is the only forest-certification scheme supported by the
leading environmental organisations, including Greenpeace.
Our paper procurement policy can be found at:

For Steve

Caught

The
Break

Searchlight

Slaney broke out of the woods and skidded down a soft embankment to the side of the road. There was nothing but forest on both sides of the asphalt as far as he could see. He thought it might be three in the morning and he was about two miles from the prison. It had taken an hour to get through the woods.

He had crawled under the chain-link fence around the yard and through the long grass on the other side. He had run hunched over and he'd crawled on his elbows and knees, pulling himself across the ground, and he'd stayed still, with his face in the earth, while the searchlight arced over him. At the end of the field was a steep hill of loose shale and the rocks had clattered away from his shoes.

The soles of Slaney's shoes were tan-coloured and slippery. The tan had worn off and a smooth patch of black rubber showed on the bottom of each shoe. He'd imagined the soles lit up as the searchlight hit them. He had on the orange coveralls. They had always been orange, but when everybody was wearing them they were less orange.

For an instant the perfect oval of hard light had contained him like the shell of an egg and then he'd gone animal numb and cringing, a counterintuitive move, the prison psychotherapist might have said, if they were back in her office discussing the break — she talked slips and displacement, sublimation and counter-intuition, and allowed for an inner mechanism he could not see or touch but had to account for — then the oval slid him back into darkness and he charged up the hill again.

Near the top, the shale had given way to a curve of reddish topsoil with an overhang of ragged grass and shrub. There was a cracked yellow beef bucket and a wringer washer turned on its side, a bald white.

Slaney had grabbed at a tangled clot of branches but it came loose in his hand. Then he'd dug the toe of his shoe in deep and hefted his chest over the prickly grass overhang and rolled on top of it.

He lay there, flat on his back, chest hammering, looking at the stars. It was as far as he had been from the Springhill penitentiary since the doors of that institution admitted him four years before. It was not far enough.

He'd heaved himself off the ground and started running.

This was Nova Scotia and it was June 14, 1978. Slaney would be twenty-five years old the next day.

The night of his escape would come back to him, moments of lit intensity, for the rest of his life. He saw himself on that hill in the brilliant spot of the swinging searchlight, the orange of his back as it might have appeared to the guards in the watchtower, had they glanced that way.

The Long Night

Slaney stood on the highway and the stillness of the moonlit
night settled over him. The evening thumped down and then
Slaney ran for all he was worth because it seemed foolhardy
to stand still.

Then it seemed foolhardy not to be still.

He felt he had to be still in order to listen. He was listening
with all his might. He knew the squad cars were coming and
there would be dogs. He accepted that there was nothing he
could do now but wait.

A fellow prisoner named Harold had arranged a place for
him. It was a room over a bar, several hours from the penitentiary, if Slaney happened to get that far.

Harold said that the bar belonged to his grandmother.
They had a horsehair dance floor and served the best fish and
chips in Nova Scotia. They had rock bands passing through
and strippers once a week and they sponsored a school
basketball team.

Harold's place was in Guysborough. The cops would be
expecting Slaney to be going west. But Slaney was lighting out
in the opposite direction. A trucker would be heading for the
ferry in North Sydney, bringing a shipment of Lay's potato
chips to Newfoundland.

Slaney could get a ride with him as far as Harold's place in
Guysborough, then backtrack the next day when things had
cooled down a little.

He bent over on the side of the highway with his hands on
his knees and caught his breath. He whispered to himself. He
spoke a stream of profanity and he said a prayer to the Virgin
Mary, in whom he half believed. Mosquitoes touched him all

over. They settled on his skin and put their fine things into him and they were lulled and bloated and thought themselves sexy and near death.

They got in his mouth and he spit and they dotted his saliva. They were in the crease of his left eyelid. He wiped one out of his eye and found he was weeping. He was snot-smeared and tears dropped off his eyelashes. He could hear the whine of just one mosquito above the rest.

It was tears or sweat, he didn't know.

He'd broken out of prison and he was going back to Colombia. He'd learned from the first trip down there, the trip that had landed him in jail, that the most serious mistakes are the easiest to make. There are mistakes that stand in the centre of an empty field and cry out for love.

The largest mistake, that time, was that Slaney and Hearn had underestimated the Newfoundland fishermen of Capelin Cove. The fishermen had known about the caves the boys had dug for stashing the weed. They'd seen the guys with their long hair and shovels and picks drive in from town and set up tents in an empty field. They'd watched them down at the beach all day, heard them at night with their guitars around the bonfire. The fishermen had called the cops.

Slaney and the boys had mistaken the fishermen's idle calculation for a blind eye and they had been turned in.

And they'd mistaken the fog for cover but it was an unveiling. Slaney and Hearn had lost their bearings in a dense fog, after sailing home from Colombia. They were just a half-mile off shore with two tons of marijuana on board and they'd required assistance.

There were mistakes and there was a dearth of luck when they had needed just a little. A little luck would have seen them through the first trip despite their dumb moves.

Now Slaney was out again and he knew the nature of mistakes. They were detectable but you had to read all the signs backwards or inside out. Those first mistakes had cost him. They meant he could never go home. He'd never see Newfoundland again.

Everything will happen from here, he thought. This time they would do it right. He could feel luck like an animal presence, feral and watchful. He would have to coax it into the open. Grab it by the throat.

Slaney had broken out of prison and beat his way through the forest. He'd stumbled into a ditch of lupins. The searchlight must have seeped into his skin back there, just outside the prison fence, a radioactive buzz that left him with something extra. He wasn't himself; he was himself with something added.

Or the light had bleached away everything he was except the need not to be attacked by police dogs.

There was the scent of the lupins as he bashed through, the wet stalks grabbing at his shins. Cold raindrops scattering from the leaves. Then he was up on the shoulder of the road. He batted his hands around his head, girly swings at the swarms of mosquitoes.

The prayers he said between gusts of filthy language were polite and he had honed down his petition to a single word: the word was *please*. He had an idea about the Virgin Mary in ordinary clothes, jeans and a T-shirt. She was complicated but placid, more human than divine. He did not think *virgin*, he thought ordinary and smart. A girl with a blade of grass between her thumbs that she blew on to make a trilling noise. He called out for her now.

His prayers were meant to stave off the dread he felt and a shame that had nothing to do with the crime he'd committed or the fact that he was standing on the side of the road, under the moon, covered in mud, at the mercy of an ex-convict with a transport truck.

It was a rootless and fickle shame. It might have been someone else's shame, a storm touching down, or a shame belonging to no one, knocking against everything in its path.

His curses were an incantation against too much humility and the prayers pleaded with the Virgin to make the mosquitoes go away.

Then the earth revved and thrummed. He jumped back into the ditch. He lay down flat with the lupins trembling over him. The sirens were loud, even at a distance, baritone whoops that scaled up to clear metallic bleats. The hoops of hollow, tin-bright noise overlapped and the torrent of squeal echoed off the hills. Slaney counted five cars. There were five of them.

Red and blue bands of light sliced through the lupin stalks and the heads of the flowers tipped and swung in the backdraft as the cars roared past. The siren of each car was so shrill that it pierced the bones of his skull, and the tiny hammer in his ear banged out a message of calibrated terror and the rocks his cheek rested on in the ditch were full of vibration and then the sirens, one at a time, receded, and the echoes dissipated and silence followed.

It was not silence. Slaney mistook it for silence but there was a wind that had come a long distance and it jostled every tree. Some branches rubbed against one another, squeaking. The leaves of the lupins chussled like the turning pages of a glossy magazine.

Five cars. They would go another three or four miles and

then they'd let the dogs out. They had taken this long because they'd had to gather up the dogs. Slaney listened for the barking, which would be carried on the wind.

He crawled out of the ditch to meet the next vehicle and he stood straight and brushed his hands over his chest and tugged the collar of the coveralls. He couldn't wait for the truck that had been arranged. Anything could have happened to that truck.

He was getting the hell out of there before the dogs showed up.

A station wagon went by with one headlight and he could see in the pale yellow shaft that it had begun to rain. The station wagon had a mattress tied to the roof. It had slowed to a crawl. There was a woman smoking a cigarette in the passenger seat. She turned all the way around to get a good look at him as they rolled to a stop.

Slaney would remember her face for a long time. An amber dashlight lit her brown hair. The reflection of his own face slid over hers on the window and stopped when the car stopped, so that for the briefest instant the two faces became one grotesque face with two noses and four eyes, and there was an elongated forehead and a stretched mannish chin under her full mouth and maybe she saw the same thing on her side of the glass.

The cop cars must have passed her already and she would have known that they were looking for someone. She exhaled the smoke and he saw it waggle up lazily. She reached over and touched the lock on the passenger door with a finger. They paused there, looking at him, though Slaney could not see the driver of the car, and then they sped up with a spray of gravel hitting his thighs.

Slaney had become aware of how small he was in relation

to the highway and to the hills of trees and the sky. He felt the unspooling of time.

Time had been pulled up tight as if with a winch and somebody had flicked a switch and it was unspooling with blurry speed. He expected it to snag. If it snagged, it would not unsnag.

Four years and two days. Time moved evenly in prison without ever hurrying or slowing down. It was jellied and unthinking. He had timed the break so he could be out of prison for his birthday.

Slaney's sister had visited him in prison over the last year, and they'd spoken about the break, using general terms and a kind of code they made up as they went along.

She'd let him know that Hearn was planning a new trip and was expecting him. His sister was in contact with Hearn. And she was the one who told him the transport truck would pick him up on the side of the road.

The gist of it was that there would be a ride for him at the appointed time. Most escaped prisoners get caught on the first night out. Slaney had to get himself through the first night, and then he'd head west, across the country, to Vancouver, where he'd meet up with Hearn. He was heading back to Colombia from there and he would return with enough pot to make them both millionaires.

Easy Rider

There were two pinpoints of light in the distance that dipped down and disappeared and bobbed back up. Slaney prayed to the Virgin that these were the lights of the transport truck with the driver who had turned his life around and had accepted Jesus into his heart, and had attended Alcoholics Anonymous, believing in the twelve-step program and the ancient, sinister advice of one day at a time.

This trucker had, according to Slaney's sister, gone to work in a diner on Duckworth Street where ex-cons were welcome because the owner was also an ex-con, and he'd met a nurse there and they'd married and had a child and bought a new house on the mainland.

Slaney's sister had put in a call and the trucker said he would be passing through and he would pick up Slaney if he saw him and drop him at Harold's.

The lupins on the side of the road were spilling forward, rushing through the ditch in the reaching headlights as if a dam had broken. Spilling all the way down the sides of the vast dark highway in a lit-up river of sloshing purple, trying to outrace the reach of the pummelling lights. Then the transport truck was upon him, deafening; the long silver flank dirty and close enough that Slaney could have touched it. Behind the truck the lupins tumbled back into darkness, unspilling, snuffed out.

The truck had passed him and Slaney was covered in a film of wet grit. The exhaust smelled sharp in the ozone-laden air. He wiped his face with his sleeve. Slaney knew the minute he had seen the headlights in the distance that if it didn't stop he would be caught. Two possible lives formed and unformed and one of them had to do with the truck stopping and the other had to do with being caught within the next hour.

There would be the walk back down the corridor to his cell. He could summon the image of a crack in the concrete floor near his cot, or it came to him unbidden. This was a sign that the prison had got inside him. When he opened his eyes he saw the red tail lights of the truck stopped a ways down the road.

He ran hard; he was afraid the driver would change his mind and take off. Slaney opened the door of the truck and climbed up into the cab. The vibration of the idling engine passed through the seat under Slaney into his thighs and ass and shoulder blades. There was a Virgin Mary statuette on the dash. She was ivory-coloured, her arms were held out, tiny palms upward. Her pale longish face tipped down, eyes closed.

The driver put the truck into gear and he waited, his face set toward the side mirror. He just sat there, looking behind them as if he had all the time in the world. Finally, a yellow convertible flared past them and was gone.

Thank you for stopping, Slaney said. The driver reached up to the ceiling and touched a light that snapped on and he looked Slaney over. A few mosquitoes became visible near the white ceiling light, and the two men were reflected in the wide black windshield, the broken white line of the highway shooting up between them. The trucker took in Slaney's orange coveralls.

The mosquitoes were collecting on the inside of the windshield; the light made them glitter like splinters of glass. Slaney leaned forward and put his thumb against one. He looked at his thumb and there was the tiny squished insect, the wings crushed, and a touch of blood, probably Slaney's own.

Out for a midnight stroll? the trucker asked. Slaney rubbed his thumb against a seam in his coveralls.

Something like that, Slaney said. The driver looked at his watch. He said he'd been told Slaney would be farther up the road.

I thought I had a ways to go before I run into you, the driver said. You're lucky I never went on past. You come out in the wrong spot.

It was hard to judge where I was, Slaney said.

You didn't have directions?

I never had nothing.

You're lucky, the driver said.

I hope I am, Slaney said.

It comes and goes, the trucker said. Comes and goes.

The driver had a full black beard and moustache and thick greased hair that held the marks of the comb near his temple and hung in wet-looking ringlets over the back of his lumber jacket. He touched the ceiling light and it went off. He pulled the rig out onto the highway. Each wheel hitched itself up onto the asphalt with an arthritic lurch and the quivering machine became smooth and they took off.

Almost at once, three more cop cars with the lights on passed the truck and Slaney hunched down under the dash.

There's some dry clothes back there, the trucker said. He jerked his head toward a red blanket he'd nailed over the bunk behind them. Slaney saw the blue Samsonite overnight bag that belonged to his mother. Slaney's sister must have packed the bag for him.

He flicked the chrome locks with his thumbs and the suitcase popped up. There was a brown envelope with three hundred dollars and a slip of paper that had a phone number. It would be the number for Hearn. He memorized the number and crumpled the piece of paper and looked around for how to dispose of it. There was an ashtray in the armrest but it was blocked with butts. He balled up the paper and swallowed it.

The three hundred would have been every cent his sister had.

Three pairs of jeans, underwear, socks, a jean jacket, and a cake tin with a Norman Rockwell illustration of a hobo fleeing with a stolen pie, a hound dog snapping at his trousers. He lifted the lid and there were chocolate chip cookies.

He took out one of the five plaid shirts and it was covered in cellophane and folded around a piece of cardboard, held in place with a number of straight pins. He took the pins out and laid them on the armrest where they shivered and rolled.

Slaney changed on the bunk. Then he felt around in the bottom of the case to see if his sister had packed a joint or two. There was a rent in the blue lining near the seam and something was caught in the threads. Slaney wiggled two fingers into the tear in the lining beneath the zippered pockets.

It was a ring. He pulled it free.

His mother's old engagement ring. His mother had lost the ring years ago during a hospital stay and they'd thought stolen. But no — it had fallen between the hard casing and the torn fabric. Slaney put the ring in the pocket of his new jeans and sat back down in the passenger seat and he and the trucker watched the empty highway before them.

We're going to take a little detour, the trucker said. He turned down a dirt road with dusty alder bushes grown so close the branches scraped at the truck. The wheels sank into deep potholes and climbed up over stones and they proceeded at a crawling pace, rocking from side to side, jerking up and down, all eighteen wheels, until the lane seemed so overgrown they might not be able to proceed or reverse. The trucker turned off the lights and killed the engine.

What's going on? Slaney asked.

I'm going to wait here for a bit, the trucker said. Take a little snooze. Let the cops do their thing.

He stood and hefted his jeans up over his belly and disappeared behind the red blanket. Slaney heard him flap the sheets and he heard the trucker's boots fall to the floor and his head hit the pillow.

Nothing stirred outside the cab except the twigs and branches scraping against the steel sides of the truck. The trucker's breathing became deep and steady, a long deep reeling in of air and a phlegmy whistle of exhalation that couldn't quite be called a snore.

Slaney heard a woodpecker knocking close by, deft and humourless. It was a beautiful noise. The windshield steamed up. He sat still for two hours and ten minutes.

The trucker finally let out a groan and he stumbled out from behind the blanket and seemed surprised to see Slaney, as if he'd forgotten all about him.

Oh, hello, he said. He got back into the driver's seat and felt around in his pockets for some gum and he offered Slaney a piece and Slaney said, No thanks.

The trucker removed the paper and the silver foil from a stick of gum and tossed them out the window and folded the stick into his mouth. Then he started up the truck. Slaney rolled down his window and tossed out his orange coveralls.

The truck broke out of the alder bushes onto the highway. Slaney reached back behind his chair for the cookie tin that had been in his mother's suitcase and removed the lid and the trucker took a cookie when it was offered and said it was good.

Slaney ate seven cookies. After a time the trucker reached under his legs and drew out a bucket of Kentucky Fried

Chicken and said that Slaney was welcome to all that was left. He handed the bucket over without taking his eyes off the road and Slaney took off the cardboard cover and inside there were several drumsticks and a bunch of paper napkins. Slaney cleaned the meat off the bones of each drumstick.

The whole bucket, the trucker said. Didn't they feed you in there?

It was a mystery to me, Slaney said, how they could call it food.

A while past dawn Slaney realized he had dozed off but he'd felt the driver suddenly become alert beside him.

There was something in the road.

A dayglo lime green object the size and shape of a tortoise.

It was phosphorescent and insubstantial and poisonous-looking; it had the jellyfish waver of something dreamt.

Slaney slammed his foot as if he had a brake on the passenger side. They hit the object. A crackling little *pock*.

It was a plastic spaghetti strainer. It smashed to bits under the tires and Slaney saw the pieces blow around through his side mirror. Luminous flecks of green plastic. The pieces remained aloft in the backdraft of the truck, spinning in a vortex, then fluttering down all over the asphalt.

Vigilance

Get the key to the room at the bar, Harold had told him. Say hello to my half-sister Sue Ellen.

The strip bar was on the highway with not much around it except a bungalow set way back from the road. There had been a garage but the gas pumps were removed and the dirty window had been hit by a bullet. A sun-silvered hole the size of a quarter, a web of cracks that spread in concentric rings outward to the peeling window frame.

There were demolished cars in the field near the garage, all missing wheels and doors and the hoods were up, the engines were gone. A crippled school bus up to the axles in grass had a sodden Union Jack hanging out one of the windows. Beyond the garage stretched a field and there was the grandmother's bungalow with a tethered horse on the lawn. The horse was white and trotted in circles, flicking its head, slapping its tail.

Slaney could see Harold's grandmother out on her back porch hanging up the laundry. The line squeaked each time she flung it out over the field below.

He thanked the truck driver but they both just sat without moving.

I didn't expect to get this far, Slaney said. As soon as he said it, Slaney recognized the statement was true. He had believed he would get caught.

Right now four years in prison seems like a long time, the driver said. You'll lose that feeling. Then he said he hadn't wanted to get involved.

Aiding and abetting, he said. Slaney looked down at the late-morning fog on the road. The sun had already shrunk the shadows and was pelting down a warm, muggy heat. He wanted to find out if the room was available.

I got a new wife, the driver said.

You try to see what's coming but it shifts on you, Slaney said.

My wife wouldn't have condoned this, the trucker answered. She would have put her foot down.

They had been together in the cab through the night and Slaney had listened to the calls over the CB radio and there was a lot of talk about his break. There were bears all over the road, the truckers said. Slaney had heard the broken late-night banter, half lost in bursts of static and jargon about sirens and the cops, about wives with cancer and a little girl named Nancy who had lost her first tooth and what the weather was like and he had learned the trucker went by the handle Woolie because of his beard. But Slaney and the trucker had hardly spoken at all.

Now that they had arrived the trucker wanted to talk. He spoke to Slaney about what he'd heard.

Slaney and his friend Hearn had lost more than a million dollars' worth of weed when they were busted and there were people in Montreal who had invested and they were looking for their money back.

I'm telling you this because I like your sister, the trucker said. Slaney thanked him and he assured the trucker he'd be careful and he said goodbye but the guy kept talking.

You walk away with a couple of busted kneecaps, consider yourself lucky. I knew a guy, they came at him with a mallet. Another guy lost an eye out of it.

How well do you know my sister? Slaney asked.

What the hell are you talking about, the trucker said. I'm married.

You said you liked her.

Jesus, not like that. I'm telling you this because your sister is a good kid. Doing social work, she helped me out. Nice young woman.

You don't need to tell me, Slaney said. The trucker scowled out the window. He jiggled the gearshift.

I stop for you in the middle of nowhere and you come up with this about your sister.

You're right, Slaney said. I'm sorry.

Another guy they put in a wheelchair, the trucker said. Slaney nodded.

The trucker spoke again: Another guy. Never mind about the other guy.

Well, thank you for the ride, Slaney said.

My wife and me only been together two years, the trucker said.

Maybe you don't need to mention to her, Slaney said. About all this.

The trucker said that not saying what happened was another variation of lying, but it was less damning. He told Slaney that he had learned how easy it was to tell a lie relatively late in his life, and found he'd had an aptitude for it. But as a child he had gravitated toward honesty.

Maybe everybody starts out that way, Slaney said.

It's just a matter of looking someone in the eye, the trucker said, and speaking as if you could hardly be bothered recounting the facts.

A woman came out of the front door of the bar with a red plastic bucket that slopped as she walked. She had a long skirt that flapped around her sandals with every step she took. She crossed the parking lot to the ditch and flung the water out and walked back with her head down. She seemed to be singing to herself.

Look them in the eye, Slaney said.

You look them in the eye or you look to the middle distance, the trucker said. He put on an expression, the expression he used when he was lying, to illustrate his point. It was a belligerent look, solemn and tinged with equanimity. Slaney saw it was the same expression the trucker used when he wasn't lying. It might have been the only expression at his disposal.

Nobody doubts me, the trucker said. He shook his head a little as if this were a disappointment.

You're friendly, Slaney said. Everybody takes a shine.

I can lie as easily as I can butter a piece of bread, he said. But I tell you what. If I were you I'd keep my ears open. Even a lie you can learn something.

The trucker had a drive ahead of him but he still seemed reluctant to get back on the road. He'd been in prison a long time, he told Slaney. A lot longer than four years. He gave Slaney the look again.

I was in for a crime I didn't commit, he said. He did a drum roll on the steering wheel with two fingers. Slaney didn't know whether to believe him or not.

If you're young when you go in, you don't stay that way, the trucker said. He admitted that he didn't believe in God, though he'd tried for his wife's sake. She worked long shifts in an emergency ward as a nurse.

It's not the other prisoners or even the guards, he said. It's something else, prison is.

It's something else again, Slaney said. The trucker's face took on an open-eyed softness. He seemed to be looking at something that he could not believe. He flicked his hand through the air in Slaney's direction, batting away everything he'd just said.

Across the field Harold's grandmother picked up her laundry basket and went through the screen door and it closed behind her with a click that Slaney could hear from the parking lot of the bar. It was an intimate sound, carried on the breeze over the fields to the bone in his jaw.

You won't get very far, the trucker said. I'll tell you that.

I'm going to try, Slaney answered. He opened the door of the cab and jumped down and closed it. He stood back on the shoulder with his hands on his hips. The truck crept back onto the road and was gone down the highway.

A Room with a View

Slaney walked up the wheelchair ramp that led to the side entrance of the bar. From there he had a view of rows of cabbages and fields of hay. The clouds tumbled backwards in folds and billows all the way to the horizon.

The door was held open a crack with a stone and it was very dark inside and stank of beer and cigarettes. Someone had been smoking weed. There was a yellow cone of light over the pool table at the far end of the room.

The bartender was a scrawny woman with long silver braids tied at the ends with red glass bobbles. Her skin was tanned dark and her eyes were pale blue. She wore bibbed overalls and had a pack of cigarettes rolled up in the cuff of her white T-shirt. Two pairs of eyeglasses hung from chains around her neck. She was emptying ashtrays from the night before.

If you're here for the dart tournament it was yesterday, she said.

Harold sent me, Slaney said. He said maybe there was a room I could crash.

Harold say anything about child support for his three youngsters by two different mothers? the woman asked.

He never mentioned, Slaney said. She reached under the bar and shoved some things around on a shelf and came back up with a key on a wooden fob. She sent it sliding down the bar toward him.

You got the room on the end, top of the stairs, left-hand side, she said. Someone called out to her from the back, asking about a delivery of potatoes.

The potatoes, she said to Slaney. Do I look like I give a good goddamn about the potatoes?

The upstairs hall was lit mostly by a red Exit sign over a back door. Slaney's room turned out to be a whole apartment with a fire escape that went down the back of the building and there was a little hibachi out there and a dried-up geranium in a cracked terra-cotta pot.

Slaney found some hot dog wieners in the mini-fridge of the kitchenette.

A small white Styrofoam bowl sat next to the wieners with the word *small* written on the side in blue marker. There were some packets of ketchup and mustard and relish in the bowl.

Liquid dripped out of the foil package onto Slaney's hand and he smelled the hot dogs and licked his fingers. The flesh tone of the wieners seemed off, and the best-before date was a week gone. He pulled a cord over the sink and a fluorescent tube hummed and flickered and came on. There were a hundred dead houseflies on the windowsill, but the hot dogs looked fine under the light.

Slaney took the wieners and the bowl of condiments out onto the fire escape. He tipped out the lumps of coal and a cloud of glittery black dust puffed up.

He squirted starter fluid onto the coals and let it soak in. Then he squirted some over his hands to get the sap off them from beating his way through the bushes the night before though it felt like one continuous night without definition or metre. His fingers were still sticking together.

Slaney went into the kitchen and used the Sunlight soap

and turned the tap and put his hands under and then he tore off a few squares of paper towel and dried them. He hadn't had access to white paper towel in four years. This stuff must have been the best grade going. Double-ply or Fluffy or Satin Finish, he didn't know what. He saw there were things he had allowed himself to get used to, and he planned to get unused to them.

Slaney went into the bedroom and pulled back the quilted polyester bedspread. He'd seen the pattern of the spread somewhere before, mauve roses, but he couldn't think where. The sheets beneath had been worn through in patches but smelled of fresh air.

He lay down and the world was snuffed out, a dreamless, suffocating sleep that turned out to be more exhausting than restful.

When he woke, hours later, it was as if he hadn't slept at all. The evening sun shone through the tear-shaped windows in the door to the fire escape and left three orange drops of light on the tiles. The door was weather swollen and he had to tug it hard. It made a loud screech. The sun was setting, a boiling red. The sky was streaked pink and the white sheets on the old lady's line were amber-tinged.

The flanks of the white horse were golden pink and Slaney was crying because even if he didn't make it very far, even if they caught him tonight, this was worth it. The horse was worth it.

He was plagued by a premonition of being caught. As if his capture belonged to him, a responsibility he'd been born into, like a title or a crown.

Someone had mowed the grass and there was the smell of cut grass and gasoline from the lawn mower and mint hanging in the warm air. There must have been a patch of mint that got under the mower and this was worth it.

He thought of himself running through the woods and only then did he acknowledge how afraid he had been, of the dogs and the cops and going back to jail.

Slaney had lost four years to the deepest kind of solitude and sorrow and boredom. Of those three torments boredom was the worst. Four years had been taken from him and he would not get them back and he could hardly draw breath seeing what he had been missing.

He wanted a phone. He couldn't call anybody yet, but he wanted a phone. Slaney wanted to call Jennifer is what he wanted.

Slaney wanted to touch her. See her face. He couldn't believe how much he wanted that. He wanted her to rest her chin on his knuckle. Smooth his thumb over her cheek. Kiss her eyelids, her mouth.

He had wanted her all the while he was in jail but being on the fire escape with the sun and the horse — someone smashed a bottle downstairs — Slaney wanted her more. The meadows stretching as far as the eye could see cranked his senses open. All of who he was dilated. It hurt. He'd been so afraid that prison had stolen this for good, but it was coming back.

He gave himself a shake and horked over the railing. Then he hunched down near the barbecue and had to bounce a bit on the balls of his feet to unwedge the matches from the pocket of the tight new jeans and he struck a match and dropped it on the hibachi and the fire leapt up in tatters and lay flat and filmed over the coals, blue and green.

The flames pattered over each black glittery lump. He went back inside and turned the TV on with the sound down and dropped into the armchair and put his feet up on the humpty.

It was an old leather humpty with a pattern of embossed elephants parading around the side, each elephant holding the tail of the elephant before it in its trunk, a foreleg raised in anticipation of the next step. The stitching had given way and beneath the leather was a burlap sack and that had a tear in the side and golden sawdust spilled out onto the tiles, disembowelling one of the elephants.

Slaney slept in the chair and woke to a hard knocking on the door.

He leapt up and stood with his heart galloping in his chest. He had no idea where he was; the room had different dimensions than his cell. It was gaping and shapeless and gutted in the dark. He could not place the room and then knew exactly where he was. His insides turned to water and cramped and there was a great spilling inside him. A loss of balance and a fear so suffocating and profound he could not move.

Slaney was staring at the floor tiles; there was the tab of a pop can near the toe of his shoe. He looked at it but didn't see it. He knew he wasn't seeing it. What he saw was his body flung to the floor, a knee on his back, hands cuffed behind. There was a second round of knocking. Whoever it was kicked the door so it boomed.

He had been caught.

Or he had not been caught.

These were two truths that lived under shells in a shell game that was the filthy, unloved room above the bar where he had given in to sleep. Falling asleep had been a mistake. Sleep had overtaken him even while he was vigilant against the idea of succumbing to it.

Things had transpired while he slept and the roof had blown off his life and he'd missed it. The dormant houseflies on the kitchen windowsill had revived under the fluorescent light and he could hear them buzzing. Or the fluorescent light over the sink was buzzing. A low-watt buzz had begun in his sleep and infiltrated his dreams and now it was the roar of a chainsaw touching down on his skull, ripping through.

Slaney walked to the door soundlessly and touched his hand to it. He listened and heard a foot scuff on the tile outside the door. He had his ear straining toward the tiny sound. The knock came again and it made him jerk nearly out of his skin and then he opened the door.

Celeste and Annette

You got a barbecue going? the girl asked.

I'm Annette and she's Celeste, the other girl said. They were the exotic dancers from the bar.

Slaney had fallen asleep to the lewd whoops of the men in the audience downstairs. They'd started a chant that had infiltrated his dream; the clapping and stamping feet had been charging elephants, thunderclouds of dust.

Strippers, Slaney said. Come in.

Annette lifted the wine bottle she had in her hand as a kind of salute, wagging it back and forth by the neck. Then she sidled in past him.

Nice place you got here, she said. She snapped on a light and stood with her hands on her hips, kind of mock nodding as if she could see the decorating possibilities.

The test pattern was on the television. An Indian chief with feathered headgear, his profile of bone and forbearance. There was a bookshelf with miniature figurines of woodland animals, perhaps two hundred of them that had been collected from boxes of Red Rose tea. The figurines sat on the peeling vinyl skin of the pressboard shelf as if they were climbing hills and descending into valleys in a great exodus.

Celeste tilted her head.

That clock is right twice a day, she said. Next to the bookshelf was a sunburst clock with a bronze face and gold roman numerals and long pointy shafts of metal sticking out on all sides like rays of sunshine. It was stopped at three forty-five and below it was a hole in the wall the size of a fist.

Slaney had the wieners he'd taken from the fridge and the three of them sat out on the fire escape. The flames had died away and the coals were coated in thick pale ash, but they pulsed orange at their core when the breeze lifted. Slaney put his hand over the coals and felt a small wavering heat and put the wieners on, turning them with a plastic fork.

Annette took a joint from her purse and lit it up and they passed it along. Slaney said that he thought being right twice a day was a good average. He made up a theory that there were gradations of accuracy but wrongness was a tolling bell that came out of nowhere. Slaney had thought the girls were the cops and he had touched his hand to the door.

Gradations, Celeste said. She was frowning at the end of the joint. She licked her finger and touched a drop of spittle to the side of the paper.

You can be partway right, Slaney said. But wrong is wrong.

Like with a pregnancy test, Annette said. You're either pregnant or you're not.

She means no such thing as a false positive, Celeste said. But you can get a false negative.

This is very good dope, Slaney said. Colombian Gold,

right? He was thinking the words *false negative* were achingly beautiful. He wished he could get his mind around them. He thought of his English teacher in grade seven. Miss Benson with her heels and the dress with big flowers and her cleavage and her mouth.

No such thing as a double negative either, he said. And he thought it meant things couldn't go wrong twice.

Slaney had heard the knocking and he'd thought *caught* but instead they were having a kind of party, Slaney and two beautiful, very stoned, crazy strippers, while overlooking the fields of swishing grass.

I thought you were the cops, Slaney said. But you're from the other end of the spectrum.

What spectrum, asked Celeste. Slaney had taken the joint from her and he'd held the smoke down in his lungs, letting it billow out as he spoke.

The spectrum that has cops on one end, Slaney said. He moved the orange tip of the joint in a curve through the dark to illustrate how far away they might be from all of that.

You opened the door and there we were, Celeste said. It occurred to him that for a long time, perhaps the rest of his life, a closed door would be a threat. It was why he needed to do the next trip right away, get it over with. He needed the money. He needed a new identity and money to live on. He needed to pay off what happened before.

The big payoff, Slaney said. He'd left the courtroom in shackles, flashbulbs bursting all around him, four years and three days ago. There had been phone calls and visits over those years and this night was part of a larger plan that was coming together on the outside.

Hearn was making things unfold. Slaney and Hearn were partners. The job required Hearn's imagination and a faith that things would turn out.

The first trip had gone wrong because they had not trusted their intuition. Hearn was a great believer in a private, inborn wisdom. Ever since they were kids, when Hearn needed to make a decision, he would close his eyes and hold up a hand to stop all outside motion and sound, just for a brief moment, so he could listen to his own deepest thoughts.

Slaney stuck a fork into a hot dog that was burnt black on one side and rolled it over. Annette said she didn't care how burnt it was. She said it looked good enough to eat.

Celeste went into the kitchen and they could hear her opening the drawers and cupboards and slamming them shut.

You got your eyeliner all smudged, Slaney said to Annette. It's like someone gave you a couple of black eyes.

I was crying before, Annette said. They were leaning with their backs against the clapboard but she turned to him.

Fix it, she said. Slaney licked the side of his thumb and rubbed beneath her eye a couple of times until the smudge was gone. She had an iridescent peacock blue eyeshadow that went up to her eyebrows.

Stupid bastard in the front row, she said. She was glancing upward and her mouth was open and when he was done she blinked several times. Then he did the other eye.

Pretty good there now, he said. Celeste came back with the corkscrew and held the bottle between her knees. The cork made glassy squeaks and it popped and Celeste took a long swig and the bottle glugged and she tipped it back down and wiped the germs off with her hand. She ran the back of her hand across her mouth. Slaney handed around the condiments. They ate the wieners, still cold at the centre, off the plastic forks, looking up at the stars.

In the southern hemisphere they're all askew, Slaney said.

Does the toilet water go the other way down there? said Celeste.

I didn't see too many flush toilets, Slaney said.

What were you doing down there? Annette asked.

I'd say he was up to no good, Celeste said. Then they each said what they wanted most. Celeste wanted to be a certified beautician and Annette wanted to do her upgrading and Slaney wanted another wiener. Then he said he wanted to be rich.

La-de-da, said Annette. Excuse us.

I'd like to get on that horse down there and gallop away, Celeste said. The horse was standing still in the moonlight with its head hanging low. It was abject or it was asleep.

Slaney looked at his watch and said it was his birthday. He didn't tell them he'd broken out of jail for the occasion but he felt sure they knew. At first he thought he might sleep with one or the other of them, but it became clear they were each going off to bed alone and they would wake up alone, and Slaney would never see either of them again.

Pair of Kings

Slaney had slept all day. He made the bed and switched off the lights before locking the door of the apartment behind him.

He entered the gloom of the dance hall downstairs at four in the afternoon and waited for the bartender to come out from the back so he could return the key and say thank you.

It was the same woman from the day before but her silver hair was fanned out over her shoulders and she was wearing a jean jacket with a happy-face button on the lapel. There didn't seem to be anything else happy about her. She gave Slaney a once-over and asked how Harold was doing in prison.

What's it like in there? she said. Is it bad? Slaney ducked a little to the side as if she'd tried to cuff him on the chin.

She said Harold had got off on the wrong foot in life. She was Harold's eldest sister. Sue Ellen Molloy, her name was, she said, and she'd tried to look out for him but she'd had a lot on her plate when Harold was growing up.

There's twenty-one in our family, she said. It was hard on our mother's teeth. Leached off the enamel. They turned to dust in her mouth. Her bones got soft. Took the good out of her. Our father died all of a sudden and Harold came after that. Nobody knows from where. He's only my half-brother. That never made any difference to me. I tried as hard with Harold as I did with the rest of them after our mother passed on.

Slaney said Harold had asked for him to say hello to her and thank her for all she had done for him.

Sue Ellen rang in the price of Slaney's room on the cash register and then rang it in again so the numbers rolled up and reappeared in the little window at the back of the machine with a minus sign in front of them. She tore off the receipt and handed it to him with the amount owed saying zero. He took it from her and tucked it in his pocket.

He was born during a hurricane, Harold was, she said. I woke up that morning and there wasn't a breath of wind. Next thing the trees were lifting out of the ground, stumbling around like drunks in a brawl. Harold was a colicky baby and it went downhill from there.

Harold keeps busy, wheeling and dealing, Slaney said.

He's of a smaller build, she said. Her lips pursed up tight

as though she had broken a confidence and regretted it. Then she said she was afraid for Harold and that a day didn't go by without him crossing her mind.

I have ulcers the size of pennies just thinking about him, she said. That's why I'm so drawn. She put her hands to her face, pressing in on her cheeks, pulling back the wrinkled skin around her temples so she looked like she was walking in a big wind, her eyes glassy slits. Then she ran her hands under her hair, lifting the curtain of silver so it glinted all over in the light, and let it drop again.

You can avoid a lot of trouble in the pen just by looking the other way, Slaney said.

This is what I'm telling you, she said. Harold has a knack for wading into the middle of one cesspool after another. He comes out of there every couple of years or so and it's like he can't get back in fast enough. She opened a cooler under the bar and the bottles tinkled against one another and she took the cap off a beer bottle and handed it to him.

Then the side door was kicked open. The golden afternoon sun, already sinking, blazed through a man's legs and over his shoulders, between his elbows. He was carrying something in his outstretched arms about the size of a small child.

When the door closed behind him the bar was very dark, and as the man came forward, Slaney began to make out something coiled and python-thick around the man's neck. He heard something slithering and snicking over the tiles.

What have you got there? Harold's sister asked.

This here is hardly used, the man said.

That's somebody's vacuum, she said.

A brand-new Electrolux, the man said. And I've all the doohickeys that attach to it.

He told Slaney and Harold's sister that he'd lost his couch and matching recliner in an all-night game of poker and he hadn't been to bed.

It came down to the furniture, he said. He was looking right into Slaney's eyes but he seemed to be watching the moment before he lost the couch play out before him.

A pair of kings, he said. For a moment Slaney thought he was talking about the two of them.

I'm looking for someone to make me a nice offer, he said. Sue Ellen picked up her newspaper where she had started to work a crossword and gave it a snap.

You look like a guy could use a vacuum cleaner, the man said to Slaney. He had stepped up close to the bar and in the band of light hanging over the cash register Slaney could see the man's face yellow-lit and crackled like a varnished painting. He had a high colour in his burst-veined cheeks and purpled nose and his eyes were bloodshot and the whites were lizard yellow. There was a crust stuck to his colourless lower eyelashes. Whatever he was on had him in a fevered grip. There was a glaze of snot over his upper lip, and he glistened with sweat. Below his full wet mouth there was a goatee.

Slaney said he didn't need a vacuum. If he'd told the man he was a victim of leprosy the comment might have had the same effect. The man was overcome with nervous trembling. A shake that came up his body from his right knee to the top of his head.

He put the vacuum down on the floor and cranked his neck to the left side several times to get a hold of himself. He gripped one of his bony shoulders with the opposite hand and rotated it in slow circles.

Everybody vacuums, the man said. His stare penetrated Slaney through and through.

Jesus, the man said. Am I right? Everybody vacuums? Slaney put his beer bottle down on the bar without making a noise.

What kind of guy doesn't keep his house tidy, the man asked. That's what I'd like to know.

The whiff of violence stirred like a draft around Slaney's ankles. It felt as though an unleashing might occur, the bolt of mythical strength that weakened people can summon just before they give out. The man's eyes had a homicidal ferocity but he spoke with something approaching a singsong quality, an effeminate wheedling, like a fortune teller grabbing a passing spirit's voice from the air.

A man's house is his kingdom, the guy said. What are you, some kind of pig? Sue Ellen put down her pencil. She asked the man for the vacuum plug. He passed it to her without taking his eyes off Slaney or breaking his speech at all.

Some filthy pig of a man who doesn't clean up, the man said. Wouldn't know one end of a vacuum from the other. Your mother was a pig. A filthy swine who didn't clean up after herself, nor did she pass on to her son the value of cleanliness.

Let's see if this thing works, Harold's sister said. She drew the cord out hand over hand.

A good vacuum is an investment, she said. I learned the hard way, bought cheap. What I found, the cheap ones only picked up half of what's on the floor. You got to go over it twice. Next thing I said to myself, you want something of value, you have to pay for it.

She plugged it in and the vacuum roared up and she yelled at him to demonstrate.

Pardon me, the man said. Whatever had possessed him had suddenly fled. He had put a finger in the belt loop of his jeans and cocked a hip, trying for something like a Sears catalogue pose, but he couldn't sustain it. His knee started up again.

Let's see what this baby can do, the bartender said. The man vacuumed the floor of the bar for three strokes and stopped to look up at the bartender but she rolled her hand in the air, telling him to keep going.

Look at that machine, she yelled. That's a good vacuum. Look at how it picks up the dirt.

He started vacuuming with harnessed concentration and the engine was loud and Slaney finished the beer and she got him another one and hooked the opener over it and the cap popped off and danced around until she put her hand over it. Then she became absorbed in her crossword puzzle. She had a ring with a speck of a diamond. The diamond and the little band of gold tin that held the eraser onto the top of the pencil sparkled in the oval of light on the bar as she jotted letters.

The man had done the indoor-outdoor carpeting and now switched appendages on the nozzle and did the dance floor and the stage. He pulled out chairs and turned them upside down on the tables and then put them back on the floor when he was done.

He finally touched the button on the Electrolux with his foot and the machine went off. Slaney had just finished his second beer and he stood and got out his money and put a bill down on the bar.

That includes a tip, Slaney said.

Big spender, Sue Ellen said. She picked up the bill and stuck it in a tin can without the label next to the register. Then she unplugged the vacuum and gave the cord a sharp tug and let go and the plug snaked over the bar and across the floor and snapped tightly back into the belly of the machine.

Your wife is going to be none too pleased she finds that gone, the waitress said. Now get home and put that back in the closet before she goes looking for it.

Pretend I never took it, the man said.

Put it back.

I lost a fortune, he said. They took me for all I was worth.

You can't undo what you done, Sue Ellen said. She was tapping the pencil end over end on the bar, considering the man with a hard eye.

People want to turn back the clock, she said. Bloody bastards took advantage of you, Gerald, when you were fresh out of the hospital.

I lost the couch, Sue Ellen, he said. Now I come home from work I got nothing to sit down on.

Gerald's a custodian at the mall, aren't you, Gerald, Sue Ellen said.

I applied, he said. That's the position I landed.

But he's good with engines too, she said. I can't tell you the number of cars he's fixed for nothing around here. He'll work for a bloody song. I couldn't get my car started there, last winter, was it, Gerald?

Spark plug, the man said.

Worst kind of weather, Harold's sister said.

Replaced the spark plug, he said.

Good as gold when you're feeling well, Sue Ellen said. You're just lucky you still have that vacuum cleaner.

Put it back where I got it, Gerald said. Sue Ellen turned the newspaper over and counted more blocks with the tip of a pencil.

That's right, she said. The man gathered up the vacuum and the appendages that went with it and left through the door that clicked shut behind him.

Ten Reasons To Go On

Slaney hit the road after the beer at the bar and this time he was heading west. He'd had two rides and then nothing came or went for more than an hour.

He thought about walking away.

Reviewed his options.

This was the advice of his prison psychotherapist. Review and calculate. Employ reason. Adjust your position.

Why didn't he walk away? The idea of going back to prison made the elastic give out in his socks. His socks were loose and rubbed and his guts were like his worn-out socks when he gave thought to it. He could walk away and work under the table and live a quiet life under a false name and be forgotten. The law would forget him.

But there were reasons to go on:

1. They'd be millionaires inside a couple of months, him and Hearn.

2. He wanted to be on the water. The wide-open openness of that. The exultation and dolphins and flying fish. The swashbuckling glamour of fucking going for it. The wind on the water and beaches and not knowing if they'd make it. Adrenalin and heat.

3. If he quit, it would mean they'd broken him.

4. He would not betray the innermost thing. He didn't know exactly what the innermost thing was, except it hadn't been touched in the four years of incarceration. Come and get me. They couldn't get him. It fluttered in and out of view, the innermost thing, consequential and delicate.

5. He wanted to believe he couldn't be broken.

6. They had a modicum of luck. Whatever unit of measurement

they employ to quantify luck. They had more of it than before. An iota more luck, and it might be enough to get them through. They had experience. What he'd learned could fill a book.

7. He wanted Jennifer to fall in love with him again. He wanted to experience an ordinary moment. A room in a house full of TV murmur and sigh, leafy shadow and the whir of laundry in the dryer. Copper pots hung over the range, pink-orange and faux antique.

He wanted to be half awake in the kitchen of a new house with Jennifer. He practised the phrase: Let me show you around the property.

Saturday morning, a little hungover and horny.

Jennifer in his plaid flannel housecoat, her hair mussed up from bed, pressing half an orange down on the glass juicer she had, twisting it back and forth so the juice ran over the fluted glass dome into the lip beneath and the seeds slipped out. The intent, becalmed look she wore making breakfast.

8. The little glass of orange juice.

9. Her ass as she bent over the toaster to light a smoke. She had candles all over the place. You could be having a conversation and she'd slink off the chair to the floor and start doing yoga. She'd be on her hands and knees, focused and lost, and her legs would straighten out and her ass up in the air and she'd keep on talking.

He wanted her spaghetti.

Nobody could stop him once he got on the water, heading back to Colombia.

If he could hear Hearn's voice, he'd feel better. Four years, maybe Hearn had changed.

Slaney needed someone who knew him from before, a

human X-ray machine that could get through bone and scar tissue and say: not malignant, not morphed, not monstrous. You are the same, Slaney, as you were before. Only better. An iota of luck lodged like a splinter.

10. There's a butterfly under your rib cage: the innermost thing.

A butterfly or comet or silver bullet. Something untouched, inviolate, capable of velocity, flight. He was willing to put it to the test. Take it out for a spin.

He sat on a lichen-scabbed boulder with his head in his hands and he tried to resummon a brotherly trust for Hearn.

The Betrayals

It was almost dusk by the time a pickup pulled over and Slaney leapt off the boulder and he tossed his mother's blue suitcase in the back and opened the door. There was a guy about Slaney's age and an English setter in the passenger seat.

The dog was mostly white and had lit-up brown eyes and shiny black ears and it began to quiver all over. It stood when Slaney opened the door and turned a tight circle, though it didn't make a sound.

Don't mind him, the guy said. There's plenty of room. The dog sank down on its haunches and draped its front paws over Slaney's legs. Its white coat was run through with black speckles, and there was a black patch over each eye and a frayed yellow rope with a slipknot around its neck.

Slaney said, Who's a good boy? The dog lolled out a long tongue and licked Slaney's lips. The driver looked and looked again.

You got a kiss, he said.

Jesus, Slaney said. The guy had a wood chipper in the back of the truck and he said he had a farm and grew flowers that he sold to hotels and restaurants in the area. He had bees, he said, which were an experiment.

Then he told Slaney to open the glovebox.

There in front of you, he said. Open her up.

There was the torn corner of an old Shreddies cereal box with part of a honeycomb sitting on it. Each tiny, perfectly formed cave of wax oozed thick, sticky honey. The dog's nose lifted with a paroxysm of tiny huffs, craning toward the dampened cardboard, but Slaney elbowed him to the side and then trapped the dog's snout under his arm. The dog went still and then wrestled hard.

Try it out, the guy said. Slaney took up some of the honey on his fingers and tasted it. He'd never had honey that hadn't come from a squeeze bottle before. It tasted musky and mineral, a grass-gold sweetness.

The guy said he bred setters, and made a few dollars off it. He had a kennel full of them and his dogs did not bark because he didn't put up with it.

I don't like the noise, he said.

Slaney licked the stickiness off his fingers and he touched the glovebox closed and rubbed the little latch with the cuff of his shirt. He'd been thinking about fingerprints since he got out.

He didn't think; he was aware.

The dog had settled down and his chin was resting on Slaney's leg.

Not a sound out of him, the man said. You notice that? Not a peep, sir.

Here, fella, Slaney said. What do you call this guy?

The wife calls him Handsome, the man said. People always think she's calling out for me.

Hello, Handsome, Slaney said, taking the dog by both ears and resting his forehead against the dog's nose.

Hello, handsome fella.

A guy can't be calling that out in the woods, the man said.

Here, Handsome, Slaney sang out. Then the man told Slaney he'd had to put down a dog last week. He'd had the dog for twelve years and it was the saddest thing he'd ever had to do and he was only now starting to feel like himself again.

Brought him in to the vet, he said. And he shook his head at the thought of it.

I'm sorry to hear it, Slaney said.

Ever done anything like that? he asked.

Slaney said he hadn't.

Put something down?

No, Slaney said.

Looking up at me, the man said. My hand was on his heart when it stopped. I felt it stop. No sooner do they put that needle in than it's over. The body fell against me and he was gone. That dog went everywhere with me. Slept on my bed. You get used to a dog. Becomes a part of you. I don't know if I'm over it yet.

There was nothing on the side of the road but dusty trees, for miles and miles, with just a few houses, here and there, buried in the woods. It was beginning to get dark.

You don't want them to suffer, the man said. He wiped viciously at the corner of his eye with his shirtsleeve and drew snot back up into his nose with one long haul of snagging breath. He'd begun to cry about the dead dog and it made Slaney feel afraid. The situation seemed volatile and unhinged.

I asked the vet, could you close his eyes, he said. You can't close their eyes. The eyes stay open. Isn't that something? There's nothing in them. People say it's like turning off a light. It isn't a light. I'm telling you. Whatever left him came out through those eyes. I saw it go. You never seen it?

Slaney said he'd never seen anything die up close except fish and once a rat in a trap.

You got any kids? the man asked. Speaking of traps. Slaney said his girlfriend had a daughter.

I got twins, the guy said. He reached over and snapped down Slaney's sun visor and there was a picture of two infants in the arms of a department store Santa.

They were a surprise, he said. Slaney asked if they were identical.

Identical enough.

Identical there's supposed to be some kind of connection, Slaney said.

Just as one falls asleep, the other one starts bawling, the guy said. That's the connection. Goes on all night without let-up. People talk about syncing up their naps. I've yet to see them with their eyes closed at the same time. We are trying to make a go of it but their mother never worked a day in her life. I come home and she's mail-ordered half the Avon catalogue.

Slaney patted the dog and he took a silky black ear in his hand and let it slide through his loose fist several times and the dog's eyes opened partway and for a brief instant they were lit a mercurial green, an alien animal glow deep in the dog's eyes, a possession that came and went in a blink, and Slaney thought that nothing was as it seemed, not ever, and it was better to be on the alert.

Trust was just another form of laziness and he would not give in to it. He would do what Hearn told him to do for now because he had no choice. But he would not call it trust. He would stay alert to the parallel universes of dark paths and wrong turns. He would calculate *if this then that* a thousand times a day. Take into account the weakness in every man's character that could make him swerve or sidestep.

The dog's eyes closed again and it nuzzled its head against its owner's fist.

You should see him go, the guy said. When he gets in the woods. I get afraid he won't come back.

He asked Slaney where he was heading. Slaney told him Alberta.

Mecca, the guy said. Then he slowed down and pulled over to the side of the empty road and got out of the truck, leaving his door open. He stood in the centre of the road and clapped his hands twice.

The dog made attempts to jump down from the truck but couldn't. It was shivering all over. Slaney gave it a little shove and the dog toppled down to the ground with a froggy waggle and shot off to the edge of the road. The driver closed the door of the truck.

The dog stood absolutely still, lifted its hind leg, and pissed solemnly, its tail out straight and its head lowered as though he understood the ignominy of having been domesticated hundreds of years ago.

The guy stood at the edge of the road next to his dog with his back to Slaney and pissed along with the dog and shifted, getting himself back together, and he walked into the ditch. He picked up a stick and tossed it into the woods and the dog was gone.

Then the man stepped into the bushes after the dog. The branches swished and flopped to let him in and closed behind him.

Just as Slaney realized the man was gone another vehicle came toward the truck, moving at a crawl. It came out of nowhere.

The last bit of sun flared across the other car's windshield and Slaney tingled all over with a prescient knowledge that the car would stop a couple of yards away from the truck. It stopped exactly where Slaney had known it would.

The engine idled and the car didn't move. Slaney thought of the talk about death and the trapped rat and the man crying without real cause. Even the sharp metal tang in the honey under all the sweetness seemed full of foreboding now.

Slaney couldn't see who was driving, or how many there were in the car or even the make. The headlights were white with pink and blue coronas splintering up in the dark and showing the slanting moisture in the air. The darkness clamped around the two yellow aureoles like a vise.

Slaney had a sense that three or four men would get out with baseball bats and bludgeon him to death.

What a feeling: to be duped. There's no mistaking it once the aftermath is upon you. Always a trap of this magnitude is something you step toward. There's an element of will and submission. But you can't see it coming. A series of steps that eat each other up like the steps of an escalator, churning forwards and backwards at the same time.

He glanced behind and there was nothing for miles. The tree branches joined over the dirt road to form a tunnel of brown, granular light.

Slaney knew at once that he would rather die than go back to jail. That's what came to him.

He checked the ignition and saw that the guy had taken the keys. Between the driver's seat and the emergency brake he noticed a newspaper. He worked it out and flopped it open and there was his own picture taking up half the front page. The flash had made his eyes look black and empty.

The headline read *Escaped Convict David Slaney on the Run.*

Going on about the bloody dead dog, Slaney said to himself. Crying about the dog. He was talking to himself now, speaking out loud without knowing he was doing it.

Slaney grabbed at the door handle.

If I were honest with myself, he said. He had known they'd been travelling toward a reckoning ever since he got in the truck.

This is it, he said. And he said, I'll never see her. That's a shame. That's a goddamn shame. These were all things he said without knowing he had spoken out loud. He was ready to take off and run as hard as he could but he also found he couldn't move.

They would beat him to death, kicking in his skull with their steel-toed boots, they'd smash his kidneys with their fists, or they would bring him back to prison or they'd kill him and put his head on a stick. Of these possibilities he hoped the latter would unfold. Anything but prison.

If something was going to happen he wanted it to happen right away.

Then the man broke out of the trees and strode up from the roadside ditch to the window of the waiting vehicle. He leaned in and spoke for a long time to whoever was in there.

Slaney could make out the man's silhouette against the graininess of the forest beyond. The guy rested one arm against the roof of the car and his forehead against the arm.

He was leaning into the window to speak. He stepped back and held his hands out, offering everything or weighing the odds. Then he leaned in again. It was some kind of argument.

Finally the man patted the hood over the idling engine. The car lurched forward, spitting gravel, and Slaney saw the driver was a young woman in a white blouse. She didn't so much as glance his way as she drove past. She looked relieved or maligned.

The man stood out there in the middle of the road with his hands in the back pockets of his jeans, bathed in her tail lights.

When the car was long gone the man whistled. The sound blasted out over the trees. The guy got back in the truck and turned it on and touched the horn twice.

After a wait, the dog rustled through the underbrush and trotted in front of the idling truck and the guy opened the door and the dog scrambled over his lap, stinking of something so vile and strong it made them crank the windows down fast.

Jesus Christ, the man said. What the hell?

Must have rolled in something dead, Slaney said. There were nettles tangled in the silk of its ears and belly. The guy shoved the dog away from the gearshift and gunned her. The sharp stink came and went and Slaney realized they'd got used to it in a matter of minutes.

Got a look at the paper, did you? the guy said. I figured that was you when I saw a fellow standing on the side of the road. Tall as a long, cold glass of water.

Who was that in the car? Slaney said.

That was an old girlfriend, the man said.

She didn't look that old, Slaney said.

Things were left up in the air, he said. My name is John Gulliver and I guess you're David Slaney.

Why'd you stop for me? Slaney said.

There's pigs all over the road, Gulliver said. I like a toke as much as the next guy. Nothing wrong with it.

Jesus, Slaney said. Then Gulliver said about dishes on the counter at home, piled to the ceiling. He said his wife had never done a load of laundry as long as he'd known her.

I can't hack it, he said.

And that girl in the car, Slaney said.

These babies were one night's work, Gulliver said. I made a mistake. He said the girl in the car was a singer. He said he believed you get one love in this life. One love, and that's it. Lucky to get that.

The voice on her, he said. He'd had to beg her to come meet him.

I wanted to hear her say it in her own words, he said. That it was over.

Did she say it? Slaney asked.

What you witnessed there, Gulliver said. That was goodbye. She doesn't want to lay eyes on me ever again. He drove on without speaking. Then he slammed his fist down on the dash.

Anybody can make a mistake, he said. Am I right? Slaney said it was true.

But you pay for your mistakes, sure as shit, the man said. Next thing comes the information from my now-wife telling me twins. Not one but two. Rochelle, that was Rochelle in the car. She heard twins and she never looked back. We were all at a bar and my now-wife came up and told us. Told Rochelle and me right in front of everybody. Made a scene. Brought up did I want these kids to have a father. In front of everybody she told us twins.

I was married two months later. We're trying to make a go of it, the mother and me. But I'll tell you what. He just shook his head.

Slaney didn't answer him. But the dog shuffled around and dropped its jaw on the man's lap.

There's a nationwide search, John Gulliver said. You're big news, my friend. Billy the Fucking Kid, excuse my French.

Slaney didn't answer.

The bees escaped, he said. Last summer. They get it in their heads.

You got them back? Slaney said.

I just had to wait for them to settle down somewhere, he said. Then I snuck up on them with a net.

Slaney thought again about trust, the comfort it afforded. The opposite of trust was doubt. They were the two choices.

He imagined trust and doubt as twins joined by a fused skull, eye to eye, the two of them, trust and doubt, in the dark forest yelling at each other: Put up your dukes.

Or trust was a door in your head you let fly. You came to a decision.

Whatever is out there: bring it on.

And doubt was the wind that slammed everything shut. Don't stay in one place. Don't settle. That was the doubt. Hearn had not gone to prison. He had jumped bail.

Four years for Slaney, Hearn had lit out. And Hearn was having a good time. He'd made some false ID for himself and gone to university. He was studying English literature with the intent of becoming a professor. It'd taken four years for him to get the second trip together. Hearn was certain the cops had no idea where he was.

There's the phrase they say in court: *element of doubt.* Slaney remembered the definition of *element* from his grade nine chemistry book. It meant something pure.

Doubt was a pure and indestructible thing. The cops had been waiting. The whole bloody town had been waiting for them when they came in off the water, four years ago, with two tons of weed on board.

This time, Hearn had implied, there would be no cops.

All of this had come to Slaney second-hand. Harold had an old girlfriend who knew someone who had passed word on from Hearn. Unbeknownst to Harold's sister, Sue Ellen, Harold was in for the long haul. Forever. He could get information in and get it out and that made his stays there profitable despite the fact that he was of a smaller build.

Slaney had to believe there was a connection between people. He had to believe trust was pure too. It was worth fighting for. He trusted Hearn. He could say that out loud. It would be better that way. And he had no choice. Trust lit up on its own sometimes without cause, and there was no way to extinguish that kind of trust.

John Gulliver stopped for gas and some snacks for the road. He said he was going all the way to Montreal and he was happy enough to take Slaney with him. Said he even knew a place in Montreal where Slaney could stay. He'd drive through the night. He filled the tank and went into the convenience store to pay and when he came out Slaney was gone.

Patterson

Patterson sweat. He was clammy in the creases of his skin, an ill-smelling dampness where his clothes grabbed at him. At the end of the day a mild stink enveloped and appalled him. Once, one of the secretaries had crinkled her nose.

His shirts strained, a tiny bird-beak around each button. The knees of his pants twisted up, cutting off circulation. The arms of his jacket like the blood pressure cuffs they used in hospitals. His blood pressure was through the roof.

His sweat had a smell so singular he half loved it and was, at the same time, felled by the shame.

Patterson had flown into Nova Scotia that morning and rented a car, checked into a Holiday Inn. He'd seen a men's clothing store on the way to the bar. The sign said QUALITY APPAREL FOR GENTLEMEN. He'd thought a few new shirts when he was on the way back. He was perspiring profusely.

You wouldn't think a thing like that could make or break. But he was certain it was why he hadn't been promoted. Look at Nixon, sweat ruined him. Patterson was a staff-sergeant in the Toronto Drug Section but they'd given him to understand promotion was pending. Promotion hinged on getting to Brian Hearn.

There was a size in shirts he would not go above. They brought him shirts bigger than a certain size, he said no. Patterson didn't want to grow into the size.

He'd ordered a scotch and the bartender put it in front of him on a paper napkin.

You from around here? the bartender asked.

Passing through, Patterson said. There was a row of pinball machines and a man in a leather bomber jacket was slamming against one of them. Three of his friends stood around him cheering and he was thrusting his hips and banging the chrome knobs. The bells pealed and pinged, balls snap-kicked, shot up and rolled back. Lime green light glowed up from the glass top and lit his friends' faces so their eyes were zombie sockets.

Patterson raised his glass to drink and he tried it out quietly: Inspector Patterson. Said it to himself, a minor incantation.

A group of women came in through the door, full of racket. One of them let loose a cackle and hit another one on the shoulder with her purse. She trotted up to the bar and squeezed in next to Patterson, waving a bill between two fingers. Her wet-look pantsuit shone bright red and the zipper was low enough to show cleavage.

For a moment their eyes met and she was full of fun and naked innocence, but whatever she saw in Patterson's face caused her to close down. She looked back over her shoulder toward her friends. He knew she had seen the stealth and eager accommodation in him and it had made her feel tawdry.

The bartender asked what he could do for her and she was instantly jazzed up again, Patterson forgotten. She ordered up a table full of cocktails, bringing her fist down on the bar after she named each drink. Some of the cocktail names were lewd and she enjoyed saying them.

A man came in the door of the bar in a red-and-white checked Levi's shirt and blue jeans. He wore a big metal belt buckle with the silhouette of a cowboy riding a bronco. He wasn't wearing the buckskin jacket with the fringes he'd mentioned on the phone.

The guy sat down on the stool next to Patterson without glancing at him or speaking. He ordered a rye and Coke. He asked for something to nibble on.

The bartender put down a bowl with Nuts'n Bolts between the two men and Patterson pushed it an inch or two away.

He had run five miles that morning and lifted weights at a

gym on the outskirts of town. He'd skipped rope. He was trying the Hollywood diet. Half a grapefruit, first thing. He'd read grapefruit was a miracle food. Red meat, no carbohydrates. You weren't supposed to exercise. He was exercising.

You're late, Patterson said. In a previous generation, sweat had currency, Patterson thought. It was a show of honesty, sweat on your brow. Patterson's father had been a farmer. But within a generation sweat had become a stain.

It stained his underarms and the backs of his white cotton shirts. It could bead up on his forehead in a meeting. His cheeks would shine under office light. It dripped down his temples very slowly and it was all he could do not to touch it, not to draw attention.

His doctor had asked was there a family history.

There had been his father clutching the edge of the table with a one-sided wince, lowering himself to the floor, down on one knee, then both knees, and finally out flat on his back, an arm flung out on the linoleum, when Patterson was eight. This was history.

I had to run an errand for my wife, the guy beside Patterson said. He took a billfold out of his breast pocket and flicked it open, holding out a Sears picture of two infants wrapped in flannel blankets, a background of an English fox hunt in progress.

These here are my boys, the man said.

Patterson put his glass down on the paper napkin and turned it one way, then the other. He lifted the glass but the napkin stuck to the bottom. The glass was sweating.

Where's Slaney? Patterson said. The guy flicked the billfold closed and put it back in his pocket.

I picked him up. We were together a good three hours. I had him.

He's gone, Patterson said.

I stopped to get gas, the man said. A few snacks. I come out and he's gone. The only thing I can figure, there was a station wagon on the lot when I went into the store and I guess he got a ride with the lady. Housewife, it looked like. All I can tell you. He was willing enough to have me take him to Montreal, drop him off where we said. But I come out and he's gone.

He say where he was headed? Patterson asked.

He said Alberta. Patterson dropped his hand in the little glass bowl. Miniature pretzels and bits of cereal spilled up over the rim onto the bar and his fist was full. He knocked the flat of his hand against his mouth and started crunching. The crumbs caked his bottom lip.

We talked about Montreal, the guy said. He's definitely on his way there.

There had been lateral moves, over the last five years, in Patterson's career. The moves had signalled a kind of quietude on the part of the higher-ups.

He could be moved sideways, they must have said. O'Neill must have said.

Patterson was in his mid-forties and he should have been an inspector by now. He had been considered and it had come to nothing.

A band was setting up in the corner of the bar. They'd turned on a smoke machine and a thick fog was wending its way through the legs of the tables, turning blue, yellow, green, with the switching spotlights. The woman in the shiny pant-suit had made her way to the edge of the stage. She became a hazy smear of red in the drifting smoke.

One of the musicians crossed in front of the strobe light to a mike stand, a mechanized hyper-blink of swinging arms and flopping hair. He spoke with solemnity: One, two, one, two, test, test, and the feedback squawked and spat.

Patterson had every reason to believe he had been overlooked but then O'Neill had called him into the office. O'Neill had slapped down box after box of files onto his desk.

They had a job for him. Very high profile. You pull this off, Patterson, and the promotion is a sure thing. Sweat gathered at Patterson's hairline, the back of his neck. He'd rubbed his palms against his pant legs.

The Newfoundlanders, O'Neill had said.

Dead
Man

New Brunswick

Slaney hit the bell on the reception desk and the *ding* rang
out in the empty lobby. It was after midnight. The sound of
a radio on low volume broadcasting a big orchestra of violins and thundering drums came from a room in the back.
Slaney waited and then hit the bell several times with the flat
of his hand.

There was the loud *thunk* of the elevator behind him and a
deep rumbling. It clanked and shuddered and the panel above
it lit up. There was a folding cage-like door over the threshold
but the elevator was empty.

Slaney hit the little bell again and he heard a woman's rough
voice yelling for him to hold his horses.

A minute later the woman bustled out from the backroom,
patting her hair into place.

She was not more than five feet, with several soft mounds
of fat beneath her bosom, and her skin was soap white.
She stopped abruptly and held her hand out before her. She
wrapped a fist around her index finger and drew it near her

waist. The woman's nails were long and bright red and the index fingernail had cracked off and hung on by a filament of skin.

Damn it, she said. Now I have to start growing it all over again. That'll take me a good solid month.

She was wearing a limp black satin skirt that seemed to have been stained permanently by road salt and a sleeveless blouse of rustling taffeta. A faint moustache had been bleached and the skin above her eyes was hairless and inflamed, though she'd drawn on angled eyebrows that made her look sly and affronted. Her black crocheted shawl was smeared over her with static electricity.

What can I do for you, she said.

I was looking for a place to get in out of the cold for a couple of nights, Slaney said.

Oh, me too, she said.

Doesn't have to be fancy, Slaney said. I'm short on cash at the moment. I'd be willing to do some work for it. I'd sleep standing up in a broom closet if I had to.

Wayne will be along in a minute, she said, lifting a hand to her shoulder and waving vaguely in the direction of the room with the radio. The orchestra halted in its tracks and a two-fingered piano tinkling began. The piano stopped abruptly too. Slaney and the woman stood in silence then, taking each other in.

Handsome bugger, aren't you, she said.

Thank you, Slaney said.

Anybody ever tell you that? she asked.

A girlfriend once, Slaney said.

Anybody ever say those eyelashes are a bloody waste on a man? I'm not going to come out over this counter after you, don't worry. I suppose you're not long out of diapers.

Slaney said he wasn't worried.

Let me touch something, she said.

Pardon? Slaney asked.

You got a handkerchief or piece of jewellery you keep on your person? I'd like to do a reading.

Are you a psychic? Slaney asked.

I am subject to visions, she said. Ever since I was a little girl. Sometimes I just touch a personal belonging and I get a whole life story.

Slaney worked his mother's engagement ring out of his pocket and passed it to her. The orchestra had started tinkling again and the violins swayed back and forth like they were deciding about committing for the long haul. They were noncommittal but the drums were building up. One drum boomed hard and deep.

A tall, stooped man in black gabardine pants with shiny knees came out of the backroom behind her. He was shrugging on a red uniform jacket with gold braid on the sleeves. A yellow nicotine streak sluiced through his white hair. His eyes were the Nordic blue of a welder's flame, and there was too much bone in the juts and crevices of his face. He had a forehead-led walk that caused him to look up under his eyebrows at Slaney. The look appeared incredulous but knowing. Slaney saw that part of the man's shirttail was sticking out his open fly.

I got this, Izzy, he said.

He's anxious to get settled, Wayne, she said. Out here hammering on that bell like there's no tomorrow.

How can I help you, young man? he said.

Give him a bed, Wayne, the woman said. He don't have any money.

I was thinking I could do some maintenance, Slaney said.

Just give him the room, Wayne, the woman said. She had his mother's ring in her fist and she was holding the fist to her forehead with her eyes squeezed shut. She spoke as if reading off a teleprompter printing on the inside of her eyelids.

The man turned to a large board behind him with fifty keys hanging on it and after a long moment he took one down.

How long you planning to hang around? he asked.

Long enough to catch my breath, Slaney said. I could mop up this lobby for a couple of nights after the day's activities.

Think you could tar a roof? I got a shed needs some tar.

I could do that, Slaney said.

You've got room 213, he said. You can stay in there until somebody else comes along. The shed is at the end of the field. I can show you where it leaks in the morning. How'd you hear about this place?

I just happened upon it, Slaney said. The elevator *dinged* and the doors shut again. There was an explosion of trumpets from the radio as the orchestra gathered power and every instrument was hammering and rang out and then stopped, allowing the solitary tinkle of a lone triangle.

You're soaking wet, the woman said. Take my shawl.

No thank you, ma'am. I'll be fine when I get up to my room.

Don't be so foolish, take the shawl, she said. She walked to the end of the desk and lifted a hinged wooden inset and came out under it and pulled the shawl off and it crackled with electricity and sucked itself onto him. She reached up on tiptoe to arrange the shawl on Slaney's shoulders.

We can't have you dripping all over the lobby, she said. She handed him back the ring.

Did you see anything? Slaney said. She stood back with her hands on her hips.

I saw a journey, she said. If I could dissuade you, I would. You could turn back, but you're not a man takes free advice.

There's a few things I have to mention, the man behind the desk said.

Wayne, you don't want this fellow tarring a roof, she said. Sure as shit he'll fall off and ruin the hotel's reputation. What are you putting him in a room with a thirteen in it for?

The man asked her not to start up. He reminded her it was late in the evening and everybody was tired.

There's other rooms, the woman said. She crossed her arms under her chest and tilted her chin up.

I wouldn't stay in room 213 if my life depended on it, she said. You know what goes on in there, Wayne. There's ghosts in that room every night.

The man shut his eyes and his lids flickered.

At night blood seeps into the room through the light fixture in the ceiling and pours down the walls until the whole room is red.

Maybe I ought to tar that roof, Slaney said.

It's 213 or nothing, the man said.

You got to have second sight to see that blood, the woman said. But it's there.

I'm grateful for the room, Slaney said.

Toss some salt, the woman said. A little dash of salt in a circle around the bed.

I'm going to ask you not to do that, the man said. I got a hard time keeping the place clean already without somebody throwing salt all over the carpet.

Slaney thought he'd stay a couple of nights, long enough

to give his picture a chance to fade out of the papers.

He thanked them both and headed for the elevators, the tassels of the shawl clinging to his knees.

Pulling Your Weight

Patterson shouldered his way through the crowd to the pay phone after Gulliver left the bar. He got O'Neill's secretary and she sounded sweet and abrupt. Marcie or Martha.

Superintendent O'Neill is waiting for your call, she said. There was a pause. He heard her draw in a deep breath.

I'm going to transfer you, Staff-Sergeant Patterson, she said. You hold on there.

There was a *kachunk* and a silence long enough for Patterson to think he had been disconnected.

The woman in the red pantsuit was collecting her things to go. She was swaying on her platform sandals; all the intelligence in her expression had drained away. She looked stupefied and wayward.

Then O'Neill was on the line.

We lost Slaney, Patterson said. He heard O'Neill taking a sip of his coffee. Slurping, basically, in Patterson's ear. It was an amplified susurration of scalding liquid.

You lost him, Patterson, O'Neill said. *You* lost him. He spoke in a measured, adenoidal drone. The false calm in his voice, Patterson knew, would be carrying through the frosted glass of his office door.

Patterson thought of his wife. He thought of Delores nudging the fridge door with her hip, the kiss of the rubber seal when it smacked shut.

Delores drank a ginger ale on the patio in the late afternoon with a fat biography or she read poetry. Sylvia Plath, or the other one she loved. Lowell or Larkin. She had been so happy when they gave Patterson the case.

Hurray for you, she'd said. She'd tossed her gardening hat in the air like Mary Tyler Moore and hugged him. The tip of the pruning shears, still in her hand, had jabbed him, puncturing the skin.

Slaney couldn't have gone far, Patterson said. We've got three cars out there.

I spoke for you, O'Neill said. People didn't think you were the guy, Patterson. I'm going to be honest. Your name came up: people didn't jump. There was a deflated feeling at the table. You're seen as too interior. A guy who keeps to himself. These were the comments. There were guys didn't think you were the man for this.

Integrity, yes. Absolutely. Integrity, nobody argues, Patterson. A good guy, nobody argues.

Thank you, sir, Patterson said.

They were thinking initiative, though, see? Drive. Ambition. That little bit extra, Patterson, that makes a man stand out. Puts him just that tiny bit ahead of the crowd. Somebody said your name and a few guys expressed doubt. You want to know the truth? Nobody was jumping up and down. I would say nonplussed.

But I spoke for you on this occasion, Patterson. I said this is the guy. We give him a chance, he'll come through.

We'll find him, sir, Patterson said. We're checking the hotels. He's on foot. It's all over the papers. He's young; he'll make a mistake.

O'Neill asked: What if Slaney walks away from all this?

He's not going to walk away, sir, Patterson said.

Did you liaise?

I have alerted the local detachment to the sensitive nature.

We need Slaney on the move. We don't want him stopping to contemplate.

We've got ghost cars out. We'll trail him, offer him a ride to Montreal, Patterson said. We figure, Montreal, he'll make contact with Hearn.

Don't make me regret I spoke up, Patterson.

Slaney's going back to Colombia, sir, there's no question. And we'll be on his tail.

If he walks away now, the whole thing goes down the toilet. We lose Hearn too. *You* lose Hearn.

He won't walk, sir, Patterson said.

An hour later Patterson stood in the narrow hall at the back of the men's clothing store, his arms hanging loosely by his sides. The hall had floor-to-ceiling mirrors on one wall and dressing rooms on the other side. The clerk stood behind him with a length of yellow measuring tape. He was studying Patterson's frame. Then the clerk stepped forward and looped the tape around Patterson's neck.

Harold Molloy, the jailhouse source, had said about a transport truck meeting David Slaney and he had said the appointed time, the approximate location. Molloy had been dead on. Gulliver had blown his cover. He might have scared the kid off for good.

I lost him, Patterson thought.

One of the dressing room doors swung open by itself. The mirror on the inside of the door reflected the mirrored wall opposite and a trillion Pattersons fanned out down the empty hall, all jerking hard when the door bounced on its hinges. Jerking and jittering, until the door slowly swung back and the infinite Pattersons, buff but dejected, folded back inside themselves and collapsed.

He was crashing from a sugar rush. A box of stale Danishes he'd devoured in the car. He had been light-headed from hunger and pulled into a grocery store.

Patterson would never be promoted. Slaney was gone. The shirt didn't fit.

I'll take it, he said.

The Bride

There were three girls in shiny formal dresses on the second-floor landing. Slaney heard their shoes making the steel stairwell above him boom and clatter and then he came upon them.

Their dresses, in the gloom, were as bright as sixty-watt light bulbs. They were smoothing their skirts, touching their feathered hair. The girl in the pink dress had wiggled out of a slingback pump and lifted her foot up with both hands almost as high as her waist to examine it. Her skirt had a cascade of noisy ruffles under the pink. She brushed something away from the toe of her stocking, hopping a little, and then she bent to hook the shoe strap back over her ankle.

They were giggling and straight-faced by turns; one girl had an arm draped around another girl's neck so she wouldn't collapse from laughter. Slaney had to angle sideways to push past them and their skirts were crushed against his jeans and they held their cigarettes up in the air, away from their dresses. It was a semi-sexual jostling and the stairwell was full of their baby-powder scent and cigarette smoke.

A lot of traffic in the stairwell, one of them said. A couple of cops just come through here in a big hurry.

Where'd they go? Slaney said.

Gone on up to the third floor, the girl in the pink dress said. And no sooner had she said it than the door above them screeched open. Slaney excused himself and pushed through the door to the hall and broke into a run and he saw a bride peeking out the door of the room adjacent to his own. Just a slice of white dress and the pouf of veil. She waved him over to her.

Did you see Paul? she asked. I don't want him to see the dress until I get up to the altar. Slaney said there was nobody around except some girls having a smoke in the stairwell.

Lot of good they are, she said. Here I am with my zipper stuck.

She kept her foot in the door to keep it from shutting behind her and she turned for Slaney to see how the dress hung open in the back.

Can you just give it a little pull, she said. It got stuck once before. It just needs a sharp tug.

Let me come in and have a look, he said. He pushed her gently back into the room and followed her in and the door shut behind him. Slaney took both sides of the dress and held them together with one hand and gave the zipper a tug with the other but it was still stuck. His hands were trembling.

I've put on weight since I bought the damn thing, the girl said. I can hardly breathe when it's done up. I just have to get through the ceremony and then I can ditch it.

He heard the elevator *ding* and the door to the stairwell

wheezed open at the same time and three or four men were running down the corridor. One of them said there was nothing on the third floor.

It's boiling hot in here, the bride said. The windows are painted shut. She turned and flounced over to a stool in front of a vanity table and sat down in front of the mirror and the voluminous skirt of the dress collapsed around her. The heat in the room was suffocating.

There was a rectangle of sunlight on the beige carpet and Slaney was standing in it. The cops were next door knocking at his room. They knocked and waited and knocked again. The elevator *dinged* and somebody said they had the manager with a skeleton key.

What's all the ruckus out there? the bride said. You'd think people would have the decency to simmer down.

She bent one arm back and her fingers fanned over the zipper where it parted in a V and she stopped reaching and rolled her shoulder twice. The dress didn't move with her. It had ribs or rods, something that made it stand up by itself.

You're not much help to me all the way over there, she said. Slaney stepped up behind her. She gave the tiny gold bulb dangling from a bottle of perfume on the table a couple of squeezes. The perfume misted into the sunlight and the silvery particles, smaller than dust, sank away.

That's something borrowed, she said. She told him she had an aunt who had loaned her the perfume and had made an off-colour remark at the wedding shower. She squeezed the gold bulb again.

Stinks to high heaven, she said. He could hear Wayne's voice now, the hotel manager.

I'm coming, he was saying. Give me a goddamn minute.

Slaney had tarred the roof of the shed in the early morning and had assured Wayne the leak was repaired. Wayne had held the rickety ladder for him. He'd called out from below to ask how it looked up there. He had a fear of heights, he said. He couldn't bring himself to go up on a roof.

He'd gone into the shed to work on a lawn mower that needed repair until Slaney was done and he held the ladder until Slaney was safely on the ground. Then they both carried it back into the shed.

Slaney had told Wayne he'd be heading out the next morning and thanked him for his hospitality.

You didn't get vertigo? Wayne said.

For me it's enclosed spaces, Slaney said. I'm fine in the wide open. I like it up there.

Wayne was outside Slaney's room now with the cops, taking his time, fumbling with the keys, making a lot of racket. He was telling the cops whoever had been in the room had checked out the day before.

The heat of the bride's hotel room was muddling Slaney. A bewilderment of heat and heady scent and the weird material she was wearing that must be made of some reconstituted petroleum product. It had a shine that seeped and crept like a living thing over the ultra-white folds and wrinkles.

She was looking up at him in the mirror. She had an ordinary face, her eyes protruded, and she was rosy-cheeked and had a dimple in her chin. He thought plain and then he thought beautiful. She was looking his way but she wasn't thinking about him.

I don't know where everybody is, the bride said. She had turned from the mirror to look Slaney over again. She twisted a little travelling alarm clock so it faced her.

I got a full hour of freedom left, she said. Then she folded the clock under the lid of the little black case to which it was attached and clicked it shut. Slaney heard the men enter his room. He'd packed his mother's blue suitcase and pushed it under the bed.

The bride had a cigarette going in a brown glass ashtray the size of a Frisbee. She picked up the cigarette and tapped it three times and put it down again without smoking it.

Slaney could hear somebody running a bath in the room on the other side of the bride's room. The water ran and ran, splashing and tumbling, and he heard the heel of a foot scrudge across the tub and then the water was turned off. The bride tilted her chin down to her chest and told Slaney to try again with the zipper.

Hurry up, she told him. Let's get this over with. Slaney stepped forward and gingerly lifted away layer after layer of veil until he found her naked back. Her spine. She arched away from his fingers.

Cold hands, she said. She was talking about the idea of being married and starting a family young so that you wouldn't be old when the kids grew up and moved out. How you could still have a life after they left. She knew she was young, she said, but you might as well start early and get it over with. She said she was a firm believer in if life put something in front of you it's important to deal with it. She tossed her head up suddenly and eyed him in the mirror.

You know what I'm saying. You're the kind of guy deals with things, am I right?

There was a knock on her door then and she called out she was getting dressed and to give her a minute.

The cops had left Slaney's room and come to hers, and they

moved at her command to the next door with the guy in the bath. Slaney heard the pipes shudder as the man turned the water off and sloshed out of the tub to get the door. There was talk but he couldn't make it out.

The bride lowered her head again and Slaney swayed the veils out of the way. There was a dark brown freckle on her white back and he moved his thumb over the freckle without thinking. After a moment he said he agreed. He said it was important to deal with things as they came up. He said it was a pity.

What, she said.

That you can't see what's coming, he said. She snorted.

Look at me, she said. Just look.

What?

Do you think I saw this coming? she said. She mentioned a flower girl, her little niece on the groom's side, who was spoiled rotten and had done her best to ruin all the fun at the rehearsal. She would have enjoyed slapping the child as hard as she could, if the kid were hers, she said. But then she said that she would never end up with a kid like that.

A bit of fabric was threaded through the head of the zipper on the right side. Slaney would have to pry the fabric free. He worked at it but his hands were shaking, knowing the cops would be back at the bride's door in a minute. The metal teeth beneath the fabric were bunching against one another; one of the slots in the head of the zipper was jammed with two crooked teeth.

She told him then that her father felt she was a disgrace.

I'm afraid I'm going to tear it, he said.

Is it not moving at all? she asked.

It's still stuck, he said.

Don't break it, she said. A broken zipper is all I need.

Why won't the bloody thing move? he asked. He flicked a loose curl over one of her shoulders. He thought of the stairs and he thought about the elevator. If the cops went into the room with the guy in the bath he might make it to the elevator.

He forced the zipper and it gave. It slipped soundlessly to the top. He brought the tiny metal hook and eye together. There was a flimsy loop of ribbon hanging out, under her arm.

You've got a thing, he said.

Could you just, she said. That's not supposed to show.

It doesn't seem to belong, he said. To the general look.

That's a loop, she said, for you to hang the thing up in the back of the closet where you leave it for the rest of your life until maybe your own poor daughter grows up and makes the mistake of looking sideways at a man during the wrong time of the month.

He stepped back. She was tucking the loop of ribbon into the top of the dress. She had raised one arm and she was poking the ribbon under with her finger and there was a faint shadow where she had shaved under her arm. Tiny black dots, like a sprinkle of pepper. Her underarm looked naked and grey-white next to the impossible white of the dress and it was secret-looking.

Slaney saw she was sexy. Then came the knock on her door again. The bride swished around in the chair. She appeared to be astonished, for the first time since Slaney had forced himself into the room. He ducked into her bathroom. He was behind the door but he had caught her eyes in the mirror. He didn't ask anything of her with his eyes. He waited for her to decide. She would have to do what she thought was right. The knock came harder and sharper and she left the mirror.

He heard her dress swishing across the room and she opened the door.

Officers, she said.

Good evening, ma'am, one of the cops said.

I hope so, she said. I'm about to get married.

We were wondering if you've seen any suspicious activity, the officer said. Anyone looking like they might be on the run.

Are you talking about the groom? she said.

We're looking for a young fellow, six-foot-two, blue eyes, black hair, slender of build, some would say handsome-looking guy.

I was looking for one of them too, she said. But you settle for what you get. I got to be at the altar in an hour, gentlemen, else the one I got might try to get away.

Sorry to bother you, ma'am, one of the cops said. She shut the door and leaned her forehead against it. Slaney came out of the bathroom.

You're set there now, he said. The zipper.

It's too bad we can't open a few windows, she said. There'd be such a lovely breeze. The room is so damn hot.

It is hot, Slaney said.

Or is it me?

You're hot, Slaney said. There was a loud slosh of water from the room on the other side of the wall. Whoever was over there had got back in the bath. The two of them were almost whispering. He was struggling not to kiss her, he realized. He thought a chaste kiss, and then he thought forget chaste. But he also knew she wasn't looking for a kiss.

Do you think it will rain? she asked.

They are calling for it, he said.

I know that, she said.

I should probably go, he said.

Paul is being honourable, the bride said. Doing the honourable thing. I guess you don't even know Paul. I thought you were a cousin.

I'm hitchhiking across the country, Slaney said.

You sort of look like them, she said. I thought for sure you were one of the cousins. Removed or something.

I'm heading out in the morning, Slaney said.

You're leaving? she said. He guessed her to be about eighteen.

Have you got something old? Slaney asked. Something old, something new, something borrowed, something blue.

I'm old, she said. I'm something old. I'm old and I'm blue. I'm something, anyway.

She arched an eyebrow at him. It flew up and the other one stayed still. He thought she would never get any older. She had probably been born with all the wisdom she had now and it was a sizable amount.

Maybe there is a moment in everyone's life when something altering occurs, and maybe you don't get any older after that. The bride would probably be eighteen forever.

And whatever happened to him on this trip would be his reckoning. Prison had introduced him to the notion of a consequence for every action, and he understood that freedom was the opposite of all that. He was pretty sure the bride had come across the same revelation.

Can I give you a present for your wedding? Slaney asked. He reached up behind his neck with both hands and undid a chain and then he held his fist over her open hand and the chain with a religious medal dropped out the bottom of his fist. The water was draining out of the bath in the next room, gurgling and being sucked down, and it was a hollow noise.

St. Christopher, he said. My mother made me wear it.

Hopeless causes? she asked.

Travel, he said.

You need that, she said. I'm not going anywhere.

I'd like you to have it, he said. He realized it was true. She had gone back to plain-looking.

I'm pretty well ready, then, she said. She was putting on the chain. She pulled the medal out from her neck and looked at it, and then she dropped it inside the dress and pressed her hand over the spot where it hung.

There, she said. She asked if he was the fellow who had been in the papers. And he said he was.

She wished him luck in a very formal way that touched him.

That night it rained hard. He watched the guests coming back from the wedding, cars crawling into the circular driveway, grinding to a stop in front of hotel entrance. The women poking their umbrellas out the doors of the cars, the wind popping the umbrellas inside out.

The Papers

The next morning Slaney could hear the bride and groom through the wall. The rhythm of their conversation had a stilted formality. They sounded forlorn and stoic. Slaney realized he didn't ever want to sound that way to somebody on the other side of a hotel wall.

On the golf course, across from his window, a man was about to take a swing. He raised the club and brought it down fast, jerking to a stop before it touched the golf ball, a white, white egg on the grass at his feet.

Slaney pulled the phone onto his lap. He lifted the receiver and pressed it to his chest. His mother had been ashamed the first time he was caught.

Such expectations, David, she'd said then. I trusted you.

He put the receiver back in the cradle. Slaney wanted to talk to her but they had probably tapped her phone.

He had to get the hell out of the Maritimes. They were closing in.

His mother never wore jewellery, except her wedding band and the engagement ring, a replacement for the original that had been lost in the hospital when she'd had a hysterectomy.

They all thought the ring had been stolen from her bedside table after the operation. Slaney's father got an identical one at Birks in the Avalon Mall because she'd been inconsolable.

Slaney's mother could not be felled by a lie. Her trust was a magnetic force field. She used it like a weapon; she shot a beam of trust into the dark from the centre of her forehead and it blinded whatever glanced that way.

Slaney was tossing the ring and catching it in his fist; he wanted to hear her voice. He thought of the phone in her house in St. John's, on the hall table next to all the framed school photos. His sisters, year after year, with their sausage curls, white shirts, navy tunics. The boys in striped ties. They had a look, his brothers and sisters. Missing front teeth, mussed hair. The tamped-down grins busting out despite the desired expression: deadpan boredom. A thousand watts of joy and badness.

Someone had drawn a ballpoint-pen moustache on Slaney's grade three picture and put it back in the frame. Lonny had a shiner in grade nine.

The phone would ring and his mother would bustle out from the kitchen, a dish towel on her shoulder. The apron with the embroidered butterfly. Her hand fluttering up to her throat.

Slaney wanted to tell her he was free. But freedom required a constant watch. His vision was twenty-twenty, he wanted to tell her.

The world was saturated with colour and it was making his eyeballs itch. The sky was something. Even if they caught him he'd had that night on a fire escape with the sky. He wanted her to trust him. He'd never be trustworthy without her trust.

Such expectations, David.

The papers, four years ago, had nearly destroyed her.

Slaney had recognized the dates and facts that appeared in the newspapers back then, when they'd been caught, but the story about him didn't fit. There were glimpses of the adventure and the guts it took, the long days of wind and sun on the water, the tokes and rough seas, the devastation when they were brought into port.

The biggest bust in Canadian history, the papers had said. Some of the bales were hefted into the courtroom on the shoulders of the clerks. There was a front-page picture of that.

There were flashes of what had happened, sparks of what was true.

The newspapers definitely had a shadow of the story.

But it wasn't Slaney.

It wasn't Hearn, either.

My ring, Jim, his mother had wept when she woke from the hysterectomy. Her engagement ring. She was overwhelmed with pain and disbelief.

Slaney's mother could not believe a person would steal someone's engagement ring.

She had failed whoever had taken the ring.

I left it lying around.

Some poor fellow was tempted.

Slaney and his father had gone straight to Birks. All the glass cabinets lit up. The rings in blue velvet boxes with cream linings and lids that snapped down. His father bought one and they pretended he'd found it under the hospital bed.

How foolish was I, Slaney's mother said then. Thinking somebody would steal the ring off your finger. She was ashamed about her loss of faith. It made her blush.

But the ring had been in the lining of the blue suitcase all along. She had been wrong to stop believing.

The golfer raised the club again, the iron turning into a flaring needle of sunlight in his hands. He sent the white ball sailing through the sky.

And Slaney thought of Hearn with his pickled eggs. They had walked home together, the two of them, every day after school, stopping at O'Brien's store on the way.

Hearn would buy a pickled egg from the jar on the counter near the cash register.

Every afternoon Mrs. O'Brien parted the bead curtain that hung between the store and the rest of her house with her hands pressed together like a swimmer about to do the breaststroke. She scudded forward in her black orthopedic shoes, spreading her arms wide open, and the strings of blue glass beads swung and clacked behind her.

When Mrs. O'Brien saw Hearn and Slaney she'd take out the two-pronged fork with the long handle she kept under the register and place it on the counter.

She'd pull the oversized jar of pickled eggs to her chest and grip the lid with her chafed, shiny, eczema-crackled hands and try to unscrew it.

Hearn had known that her pride depended on them letting her give it a shot.

The store was filthy and dim. People said rats and they said that Mrs. O'Brien was richer than Dan Ryan. Money in the mattress, the pages of the books, crammed into socks.

But the lid, rusty and stuck, was too much for her and she'd set the jar down on the counter and push it toward Hearn.

The picture in the *Evening Telegram* on the first day of their trial: Slaney and Hearn, and behind them their lawyers, walking along Duckworth Street toward the courthouse.

The long curly hair out over the necks of the boys' wide collars, the suits hanging off them because the suits had come out of their fathers' closets. They'd had a particular gait, Slaney and Hearn. They were sure they'd be back on the streets later that afternoon.

The gait said surety. They were folk heroes in the making. They were the new thing, as it had manifested in St. John's in 1974, where they had stood trial for importing two tons of pot. They'd been searched for weapons on the courthouse steps, the first time in the history of the St. John's courthouse anyone had been patted down before a trial. Hearn had revelled in it, his arms raised, as if addressing a crowd.

Now, now, he'd said to the cop patting his leg, don't get fresh.

Come on, fellas, it's only pot.

Michael Tucker, Hearn's lawyer, is caught in mid-step in the photograph. One foot off the ground, hands digging in the pockets of his suit. Tucker was a good lawyer and Hearn's father had liquidated his business, got a second mortgage on his home. Put up everything he had for Hearn's bail.

Hearn got out and took off. His father lost the business and the house that had been in their family for three generations.

A couple of months later, Hearn's father, driving his sister's big two-tone Cadillac, lost control. His arm went funny. His fingers like wood. He had to lift his arm into his lap with his other hand. And the deadening spread throughout his body in a matter of minutes.

They told Hearn on the phone when he finally made contact and they used the word *massive*.

They say massive and they mean a chunk of the brain gives out without warning. A massive stroke had left Hearn's father unable to move. A clot or misfiring of synapse, a vein opens, a mystery, but everybody said Hearn was the cause. His father lost in a prison of his own body while Hearn crossed the country free as bird.

Hearn had destroyed his father and he couldn't come home to visit.

Joseph Callahan had been Slaney's lawyer. He's in the picture too, strolling along behind Slaney, black-rimmed glasses, swinging a leather briefcase. They are purposeful men, the four of them, about to enter the courthouse on a sunny day.

Two boys smuggling pot, what a lark! Hey man, everything's copasetic. Chill out. Deadly.

And their confident, liberal young lawyers. The suit jackets flapping back, the long strides.

You're seen as a risk for bail, Callahan had said. Slaney was sure it was because Hearn had taken off.

Nothing whatsoever to do with Hearn, Callahan said. The law doesn't work that way.

They had been aware of the cameras on the courthouse steps but had not been beholden to them.

Somebody said dashing.

A court case was just something to win.

Hearn unscrewing the lid of the pickle jar and laying it on the counter.

You loosened it up for me, Mrs. O'Brien.

The old lady dipping the fork into the jar and the eggs tiptoeing and plunging in the murky brine until she stabbed one and the silver bubbles wobbling up with a sulphurous waft of vinegar and dill.

The golfer outside Slaney's hotel window had been strolling across the green and he stopped in front of the final hole, the club resting on his shoulder. He looked out over the emerald expanse. Took in the clear weather. He was just an inch away from the end. Then he brought the club down and hunched over it, as still as stone.

They'd thought a million dollars back in 1974. The ambition revved in their chests. They had motorcycle engines for hearts.

Then they said shag it, a million and a half. They got stoned and keeled over, giggling like girls, and Hearn held up a finger for silence. And then he said, Fuck it, two million.

O'Brien's store had been demolished and the field behind it that had been Gardner's cow farm — where Slaney and Hearn had ridden on their dirt bikes across gold and brown and rust-red acres of furrowed land divided by low stone walls and, now and then, traces of a foundation, a threshold and a hearth, a piece of cracked china or an old blue medicine bottle — had been sold for subdivisions.

The boys driving their dirt bikes for as long as they could

and then they'd stop and pick magic mushrooms and once they'd eaten up to a hundred each and they'd both died of heart failure.

Their hearts stopping. And stopping. And stopped. They were buried and wept for their own deaths and disappeared into a black hole that was not a void (the golf club moves half an inch, *ding*, the ball sinks) but full of pressurized experience.

Life coming at them through a fire hose; jackhammering them with Technicolor everything and they both understood that the paisley pattern on Hearn's shirt, each gorgeous swirl vibrating a neon crimson, was a link in an infinite chain that telescoped through wormholes of time and they realized that time is simultaneously in motion and inert and the engine of it all seemed to be Hearn's heart pulsing, calm and sure, under the paisley and they spoke about the wonder of it, and became morose and weeping because the swirling pattern was teeming with life, each paisley curl a sperm charging through the universe, hell-bent on the eggs out there, the big bang, and Hearn and Slaney were a part of everything and not *apart* from it, as they had supposed, and they were left, at dawn, when they woke, empty shells, newly innocent and spilled out.

The egg was stabbed with the two-pronged fork and drawn up through the cloudy yellowish fluid, nudging the other eggs and breaking the surface, and Mrs. O'Brien held it up, dripping, over a paper napkin. It glowed white in the weak winter light from the store's window.

Rebellion

Slaney left the hotel and got a ride right away with a girl driving home from her class at a community college. It was already dark and she brought him back to her house for supper.

The girl lived in a bungalow with a cracking concrete foundation not far from Quebec. The front door was high up on the house and there were no stairs leading to it. The house had an apron of crushed gravel around it and somebody had started to lay a lawn and had given up halfway through. There were rolls of yellowed sod in a pyramid at the end of the driveway. What had been laid down was covered in dandelion clocks. There were three newer houses on the opposite side of the road, each freshly painted, with dark green lawns and For Sale signs.

She took him around the back and they went up a set of stairs and took their shoes off in a small porch and left them on a rubber mat that said *Home Sweet Home*.

The girl's grandfather was sitting at the kitchen table, smoothing out the clear plastic cloth with wide sweeps, catching the crumbs in his cupped hand.

I was waiting for you, he said.

I told you I had a night class, the girl said.

I wondered to myself, Where in the world could she be at this late hour?

Persuasive Speaking and Managerial Communication, I told you that, she said.

I looked at the clock and I said to myself, She's usually here by now.

I'm sorry, Pops, she said. The old man stood up with great effort, pressing his fist hard against the table, and he started across the kitchen. There was an extra swivel in his gait, an almost lewd skewing of bone and pain and he was bent forward. One hip rode up too high and hitched on the way down. Or the left knee gave out at the last minute. The old man had a faith in the knee that he lost and regained with each step.

He turned to Slaney when he reached the counter and looked him over. He seemed to take a measure of his worth.

Who's this? the old man said.

This is Dave, the girl said. He's come in for a visit and a little bite. Slaney saw the old guy had a facial tic, his eyes blinked three times, hard blinks, every minute or so.

I never heard tell of a Dave, the old man said.

You're hearing tell of him now, the girl said. I just met him myself. This is my Pops. Pops, this is Dave.

Nice to meet you, sir, Slaney said.

I was in Korea, the old man said. I saw an arm on the ground. Just the arm. Not attached to nothing. Just lying there in the leaves.

Pops is decorated, the girl said. He got a few medals in there he could show you sometime.

We were marching, he said. I just saw this arm. It was lying on the dirt. Wet leaves stuck on it. That was one thing I saw. I saw a lot of things. You've done some travelling, have you?

Yes sir, Slaney said.

You got the look of someone with miles behind him, the old man said. He opened the cupboard beneath the sink and reached in with his fist and let the crumbs fall into the garbage and he brushed his hand against his jeans. He was so thin it seemed the new jeans were holding him upright. He wore a tucked-in black shirt buttoned to the neck and Slaney saw cufflinks. The old man was nothing but bones.

The girl got a tin of soup from the cupboard and she fitted the tin into the electric can opener and pressed the lever down and the can turned in small jerks. The whir of the can opener brought two miniature poodles running down the hall.

The girl lifted a chrome lever and detached the tin, poked one end of the lid down, and daintily lifted out the end that stood up. She held the lid between a finger and thumb and her pinkie curled up. Then she crouched down with the lid coated with tomato soup and held it near her ankle.

Little guys, she said. Little fellas.

I said to the dogs, Where is she, the grandfather said.

I'm here now, Pops, the girl said. I'm right here.

I was in watching the news, the grandfather said. Before you got home. There's a fugitive from the law on the loose. A young fellow named David Slaney.

The poodles knocked each other out of the way and slid on the linoleum in their hurry and piled into each other and licked the lid clean. The girl had a cooing voice when she spoke to the dogs, urging them to enjoy it. Slaney was transfixed by the girl's ladylike pinkie and the dogs' pink tongues and he was also thinking about how to get the hell out of there.

I heard it on the radio, she said. Just some guy smuggling pot is all. No big deal.

Well, there you go, the old man said.

There you go, the girl said. She was still speaking to the dogs, a little singsong voice. There you go. Isn't it nice to have a visitor? We don't get visitors very often, do we?

The dogs were shaved so close their skin showed through the film of fur and there were pompoms on the ends of their tails and on top of their heads and they whimpered, a building whine that crescendoed in a series of yaps.

It was nice to meet you both, Slaney said. But I should get going. I don't want to take advantage of your hospitality.

Slaney and the girl had talked about themselves on the drive home in the roomy Buick. They were accounting for who they were in small increments. It was clear they would be sleeping together from the minute he got in the car. Now he saw that nothing is ever as clear as it might seem.

They were the same age, twenty-five, and the girl was doing accounting, she told Slaney, and had a line on a job in the financial department of the local supermarket. The management was just waiting for her to present her certificate. She had mentioned the grandfather and it was implicit in these small statements that the girl planned to take care of the grandfather for the rest of the old man's life, but there would need to be, in return, the chance for her to be wild in other ways.

They say I'll rise up, the girl had said. Slaney thought she meant a rebellion. But she was talking about supermarket management and Slaney saw the girl's selfless side. The grandfather would hang on, Slaney thought. But it wasn't a bad situation. She was capable of loving the dogs and the old grandfather in a way that afforded her intense pleasure — he could see this now, in the kitchen, when she lifted the black poodle and touched her chin against the fluffy crown of its head.

Slaney had told her, in the car, that he'd just had a birthday and that he had plans to travel. Seeing the world was important to him, he'd said, because you could see yourself from the outside.

The heat makes you behave like another person, he'd told her. He said he saw himself as something that could change.

The radio had been on when he got in the car and they'd talked over the music and then there was the news and he heard about himself breaking out of prison and they gave a physical description.

The girl had switched off the radio and the car was very silent. Then the girl brought up going to Toronto sometime and how she'd like to live in a skyscraper. She said she liked the look of them, but she'd only seen them in pictures. She'd never been inside one. She liked the idea of a big wall of glass and a nice view way up high.

He's a nice boy, isn't he, the girl said to the poodles. She was flapping the ears of the black poodle as she spoke, leaning against the sink. She made it look as if the poodle had an opinion and was answering yes or no with his ears.

We like him a lot, don't we? We really do, yes we do, yes we do. Oh we really, really like this boy.

People begin to lose their minds, the grandfather said.

What's that, Pops? the girl said. She put the dog down and stood with her hand on her hip surveying the room as if she'd forgotten where she was or what she had to do. Then she tipped the tin of soup into a saucepan and turned the stove on high.

When they get to be my age, the old man said. The girl looked instantly fierce.

That won't happen to you, she said. We don't have any of that in our family.

It begins by you forget somebody's name, the old man said. You forget a birthday. You can't find things. You lose words.

We lose lots of things, the girl said. But we don't lose our minds.

The smell of Campbell's tomato soup filled up the whole kitchen. The girl reached up on tiptoe for a box of soda crackers. Her blouse rode up and Slaney saw the dimples in the small of her back above her jeans and he ran his hands down his thighs. The soup was boiling and spitting. He could smell it starting to burn. He wondered how long it would be before his jailbreak got to be old news. He had a brief insight: what the hell did he think he was doing? But it passed. He couldn't keep the insight in the front of his forehead where it probably belonged.

After the old man was asleep the girl got out a bottle of scotch and two Mason jars for glasses. She slid open a tiny window above the sink and the cool air rushed in. She took an ice tray from the freezer and twisted it and the cubes hopped up and she dropped some in each jar. The fridge emitted an insistent buzzing. They talked and talked. She pushed two fingers deep into the sugar bowl and swished around, spilling sugar over the side. She pulled out a little bag of dope and dropped it on the table and put her two fingers in her mouth and licked off the sugar. Then she rolled a joint and they smoked it and she gave him the rest of the dope as a birthday present.

After a while she got a package of pressed chicken from the fridge and they each took out a slice and rolled it up. The meat was salty and white and blotched with an opalescent sheen.

They drank a good part of a forty-ouncer without getting drunk and at the same time they were very drunk. She asked him about the escape and he told her. He told her about Colombia and the pleasure of sailing, how much he loved being on the water, and he talked about Hearn. They'd gone down there together the last time and that had been a mistake. This time Hearn would manage things at home, make sure they landed the cargo without any difficulty.

He said that Hearn had been his friend all his life practically and he loved him. He said he had never told anybody that before, not even Hearn.

Slaney started to tell her about Jennifer but she held up her hand for him to stop and turned her head to the side and shut her eyes as if she were walking into a strong wind and so he didn't say any more on that subject.

He told her, instead, about the pot they'd brought back and how he ended up in jail. And she nodded as if she could see it. As if she had been along for the ride.

I never hurt a soul, he said.

I can believe that, she said. He wanted to tell her all about the new trip. He didn't see how he could have sex with her if he didn't trust her. And he found, all at once, that he trusted her completely. Either he trusted her, or he had come to the understanding that he might be able to have sex with her whether he trusted her or not. He thought it was worth a try.

They were cold sober and loaded out of their minds and before he could tell her anything she brought out a game of checkers. Every syllable they said to each other was clipped and careful. They were each enunciating with the precision of a speaker new to the language.

There was the final *click-click-click* as she jumped him, wiping him off the board, and then the room was knocked sideways. They were ossified. The girl was all over him.

She was kissing him on his face and eyelids and hair and every kiss lasted. She opened his shirt and circled her tongue over his nipples, first one, then the other, and the light was still on.

They were lit up, Slaney thought. Her mouth was cold from the ice she had chewed. It felt like her tongue had been dipped in fluorescent light. He had that impression. He heard her hand slap the wall behind him and then the heavy *click* of the light switch and it was black in the kitchen and his eyes adjusted and he could see the shapes of the counter and stove and fridge in the moonlight. White enamel shapes, soft-edged, drawing themselves out of the dark.

She was wearing a checked shirt with pearl snaps and he tugged it apart with one go. He couldn't get the bra undone fast enough so he lowered the straps and pulled it down to her waist and her elbows were pinned to her sides by the sleeves of the blouse and by whatever way the bra straps were tangled. She had to work her elbows out of it, and she looked like a bird breaking out of an egg, shaking out a wing. He kissed her breasts and sucked her nipples and she climbed off him and stood swaying, trying to take him in. She closed her eyes, as if she could scrutinize him better if she were blind, and touched her fingers to her forehead.

The girl was deciding about him. The bra and shirt hung around her waist and she had beautiful breasts and he felt like he couldn't believe his luck.

She held out a finger and he hooked her finger with his and she tugged him up out of the chair and down the dark hallway. They tried very hard not to bang into the walls, but the walls were banging into them.

She swept a pile of laundry off the bed and sat down on the edge and he had her jeans undone but she tried to wriggle out of them without taking off her platform sandals and her foot was stuck and she struggled and kicked and he got down on his knees between her legs and tugged them off and then he was on her, kissing and licking. She had her hands wrapped around his head, holding him there.

She made sounds like a bird call, a loon or a pigeon, shivered and throaty.

Though he was very drunk there was a blundering elegance to every move he made with her, and he took his time and when he closed his eyes the room turned like a carousel and he held her by the hips so he would not fall out of the room and down into forever.

He woke to bright sunlight with the girl at the foot of the bed in a supermarket uniform of brown and white polyester. She wanted him to leave through the bedroom window, she told him. What she didn't want was the next-door neighbour flapping her gums. She said she'd meet him after work at Mel's snack bar near the beach and drive him to the highway.

You can hide out in the woods until then, she said.

Slaney was sitting at a picnic table on the edge of the crowded parking lot belonging to a snack bar and convenience store, in the early evening, when the girl showed up. He'd bought himself a pair of sunglasses and a baseball cap and put them on and felt conspicuous in them and took them off again. He knew he should be on the move but he figured it was safer to wait for the girl and get a ride as far as he could with her.

Every few minutes a woman would stick her head out of the snack bar window and bawl a name and someone would get out of one of the cars and pick up his order. Finally, Slaney saw the Buick pull onto the dirt lot, waves of roiling dust curling up behind it.

The girl was still wearing a hairnet and she had on a brown polyester apron that looped around her neck and tied at the waist.

He'd ordered them a large fish and chips to share and the woman stuck her head out the snack bar window and she yelled for him and he got up and paid her and brought the plate back to the table.

The girl said she wasn't hungry and didn't want any but she was picking out a french fry and dipping it in ketchup even as she said it.

She talked on in one long, breathy rush as if she didn't want him to leave and she could keep him there if she didn't stop talking.

Sometimes she pointed a french fry at him, stabbing the air to make a point.

She told him that her parents had died in a Ski-Doo accident. They had gone through the ice and when they were pulled out of the water they were frozen together, her mother's arms around her father's waist.

You saw that? Slaney asked.

I heard, she said. People drunk said the story while I was in earshot. I was eleven. People don't care what they say in front of a youngster. As she spoke she reached up with both hands and removed pins from the net in her hair.

She said her grandfather was all she had in the world besides the two dogs. Eventually, when her Pops died, she would move to Toronto and make a lot of money.

You better believe I will, she said. She took off the hairnet and set it on the picnic table and it glistened like a spiderweb and she shook her hair free.

She was starting off in a supermarket chain, but there were skills she was picking up that could apply elsewhere.

Management is management, she said. Basically you tell other people what to do. I'm good at it.

She took up his cup of soda and rattled the ice around and sucked on the straw and made a loud noise.

Then the woman in the snack bar called out for him and he went up for the chocolate sundae.

A crow dropped down from the branches and cocked its head. It eyed a maraschino cherry somebody had tossed on the ground. The bird was blinking, stern and quick. The glazed cherry was an unnatural red. The bird snatched it up and flew into the trees.

They drove for a while and held hands in her car before he got out and they said goodbye. The girl's blue eyes went a brilliant aquamarine and there was a limpid film over them and her crying had little hiccups in it.

Powder Blue

There's just the two of us, the woman serving at the snack bar window told Patterson. She said her name was Luanne Johnson.

Eleanor's in the back all the time and didn't see anything.

I can hear what's going on, though, Eleanor called out from the back. Luanne closed her eyes for a moment while Eleanor's piping voice swept through her.

She thinks she can hear, Luanne said. She can't hear a bloody thing.

I can hear, Eleanor called back.

So it's the two of you, Patterson said.

Just us two. We had quite a rush this afternoon, didn't we, Eleanor? I'm just telling the officer we were busy. She can't hear over the deep fryers.

It was very busy, Eleanor said.

You're sure it was the man in the paper? Patterson asked. He held the folded newspaper up so she could see Slaney's picture.

He's the one. He was over at that picnic table with a young lady. Had an order of fish and chips and a sundae. Gave me his name, Dave, so I could call out when the food was ready.

So you took his order, Patterson said.

And I called out over the lot when it was ready, she said.

What about his appearance? Patterson said. The woman said that he had been wearing a powder blue shirt and a pair of jeans.

A child came up beside Patterson and asked for a custard cone. The boy was wrapped in a sand-caked towel and his lips were blue. He was shivering and Patterson could hear his teeth.

The woman took a cone down from a dispenser attached to the wall and flicked a handle on the custard machine but kept on talking over the noise with her head turned to the side. The machine shuddered and growled. A thick column of ice cream spewed out and the woman lifted the handle and the machine clanked and she turned with the cone. She gave it to the boy through the window and took his change.

He was a good-looking young fellow, she said. Dark hair, and the eyes on him, blue like the shirt. The shirt brought out the colour. I would say handsome, definitely. He looked like that picture in the paper you got there. Few freckles.

What would you say was his height, Patterson asked.

He was tall. He rested his elbow on this window ledge here giving his order, and he had to hunch over, crick his neck to the side. He had a sense of humour.

What did he say funny?

Oh, I don't remember exactly, she said. And she smoothed her hair with both hands.

He gave me a compliment about this funny old paper hat I have on.

He was bent over talking to you at this window, Patterson said.

He took his order over to the table, they sat in the shade, a young lady was with him, like I said, drove a maroon Buick, and after a time he came back up and got his sundae, which he asked for two spoons.

How long ago?

You just missed him.

Did you happen to see which way they were going? Patterson asked.

They were at that picnic table, next thing they were gone. I'd say — what, Eleanor? Twenty minutes? Half hour? It looked like they might be heading up toward Quebec.

Thank you for your help, ma'am.

That's all I can tell you, Officer.

Patterson thanked her again and used the pay phone in the convenience store to call in the Buick. Then they sent out the three ghost cars and Patterson went back to his hotel to wait.

The late show that night was *How to Marry a Millionaire*. Patterson laughed when Marilyn Monroe took off her glasses at her vanity table and walked right into the wall and bounced back and without delay tried again for the door.

He had a shower and came out into the bedroom with a white towel wrapped around his waist. He ran his fingers over the muscles in his arms and chest. He'd lost another pound.

The phone startled him when it rang. Sergeant Farrell, with the New Brunswick detachment, said they'd located Slaney. One of the ghost cars had picked him up hitchhiking and offered him a ride to Montreal.

Patterson hung up and settled into bed and switched off the light. In the dark, he spoke a single word out loud to the room. Gotcha.

Montreal

Slaney arrived in Montreal and wanted to be in the noise of a pub, warm and amber-lit, full of glass glint and after-work racket.

He wanted a phone. He wanted to eat something soaked in old, coagulated gravy, something they had added to all week. He'd tried a couple of places already but he was having a hard time finding something with enough substance that you might try to call it soup.

He ducked down a slippery set of concrete steps smelling of drainpipe and pigeon shit into a place with a gold and black sign swinging over the door that said YE OLDE CELTIC PUB.

The waitresses were in denim miniskirts and tie-dyed T-shirts, starbursts of fuchsia and lemon and turquoise. Trays of beer balanced on one hand, level with their chins.

Slaney picked up the padded leather menu. He tapped the corner of the menu on the bar, gave his order, and made his way to the back where there was a pay phone.

Carved in the wooden brace over the phone with a ball-point pen was the promise of a good time if Slaney, or anyone else, were to call Charmaine. He dropped some coins and dialled the number that had been in his mother's suitcase. He listened to it ring. A guy named Dick answered.

Hearn's expecting your call, Dick said. He told Slaney about the sailboat and said it was just a matter of Slaney flying to Mexico to meet up with the captain.

They're thinking six days to Colombia from Mexico if the winds are good, Dick said.

Hearn told you all this? Slaney said.

I wasn't talking to Hearn himself, Dick said. There's a chain.

A grapevine, Slaney said.

Only a few people got Hearn's number, Dick said.

You got his number? Slaney said.

I'm going to give it to you right now.

You must be pretty high up in the chain.

Pretty high, Dick said. There's fifteen of us.

Mexico, Slaney said.

The hull's been refitted for the cargo, Dick said. Faux wood panelling. All Slaney had to do was get his arse to Vancouver.

There's going to be a party, Dick said. Hearn is dying to see you, man.

Forgive me, Dick, but have we met?

Dirty Dick, he said.

I can't put a face, Slaney said.

Richard Downey, Dick said. They used to call me Dirt.

The hockey tape, Slaney said.

I had hockey tape on my glasses.

You had tape across the bridge.

Somebody shoved me.

Stepped on your glasses.

Ground them into the dirt.

And the shoes.

So what?

The platform heels.

Your mother wears army boots, man.

Dirty Dick, Slaney said.

I've been keeping up with you in the papers, Dick said.

Dirt, I remember you, Slaney said.

I don't go by that anymore.

How you been? Slaney said.

It's Richard.

Okay. Richard. How the hell are you? Get your glasses fixed?

The papers got you figured in Montreal, Dick said. Hope you're not in Montreal, man.

Slaney wrote Hearn's number on the back of his hand with a pen dangling from a string near the phone and he thanked Dick and hung up.

A waitress with orange hair pushed her bum against the swing door. She had a tub full of dishes. After a moment she came back out and put down a paper placemat and a napkin and fork and knife before a guy in a suit. There was a pencil behind her ear. Slaney put some more money in the phone and he dialled Hearn's new number and he let it ring. Then Hearn picked up.

How's it going, man, Hearn said.

It's cool, Slaney said.

So, we're cool, Hearn asked. It's cool to hear from you, man. Hear your voice.

Montreal, man, Slaney said.

Listen, Hearn said. Tell me about it. Slaney was pretty sure Hearn was cooking something. He could hear a frying pan, something spitting.

They'd always had a way of not talking that was, in every

respect, exactly like talking. They already knew what the other would say. Talking was after the fact.

What's the French for soup? Slaney said. I'm trying to get myself a proper drop of soup.

The waitress behind the bar took an ice cream spoon out of a bowl of cloudy water and flicked it clean. She leaned so far into the freezer one foot lifted off the floor and her white polyester slip was visible under her skirt. The lid bumped down on her back. Cold light and steam poured upward from the freezer.

Consommé, Hearn said.

I said consommé, Slaney said. But it was just water. I'm here now in an English place trying to get a drop of soup.

Good to hear your voice, man.

You got someone there? Slaney said.

My old lady.

Your new old lady?

The new one, yes.

Where's your old old lady?

This is the real thing, Hearn said.

I thought the other thing was real.

She was real, all right. The waitress emerged from the freezer and the lid thumped down behind her. She had pale skin and a sprinkle of freckles on her cheeks. Her eyes were a blue so dark they seemed unfocused. Her hair caught the light and looked electrified.

The new one is different, Hearn said.

Different, that's deadly.

I'm different when I'm with her.

You're both different.

Never mind, man. I try to tell you something.

Go ahead.

Never mind.

No, go ahead.

I'm trying to express something.

I'm all ears.

I try, every once in a while, to say something to you.

Get deep, I hear you.

Never mind. Slaney? Never mind.

Philosophize. I'm here for you, man.

Slaney?

Go ahead.

Everything is not a big ha-ha, Hearn said. The waitress held the ice cream scoop above a piece of pie and pulled the trigger with her thumb. A ball of vanilla ice cream dropped onto the top of the pie and slid sideways.

Lay it on me, Slaney said.

Never mind.

What does she look like? This was the question Hearn had been wanting him to ask.

Built? My son, Hearn said.

Built is she, Slaney said.

Believe it.

Stacked?

Personality too.

You respect her mind, Slaney said.

But, you know.

Built, Slaney said.

Personality too.

Tits? Slaney asked.

Come on, man.

Just wondering.

Yes, tits, Hearn said. These tits. Do you remember Maeve Brown? Like Maeve's. Only somehow better than Maeve's. Her nipples are like Maeve's.

I never saw Maeve's nipples.

Yes you did. Maeve Brown's nipples. You must have.

When would I have seen Maeve Brown's nipples?

Everybody's seen them. Weren't you at that party?

I've been incarcerated.

I know that.

Maybe that party happened while I was in jail.

I know you were incarcerated, Slaney. I know that.

Better than Maeve's?

I'm sorry, Slane. I'm sorry, man. I'm sorry.

Better than Maeve's?

She's nice. That's all I'm saying.

And your other old lady?

She's gone.

I liked her.

She was okay.

There was something about her.

You go out with her, then.

 What was her name? Michelle?

Maureen.

There was something about Maureen.

Can you be serious here? The waitress put the pie down in front of the man and she gave the plate a little twist so the best angle of the pie faced the customer.

This one is from down home.

From the bay, Slaney said.

You should hear the accent on her, Hearn said.

The bowels of the bay.

I can't understand her half the time.

I'm sorry about your father, Slaney said. There was a roar in Hearn's kitchen from the deep fryer. Hearn had a basket of chips. Slaney could hear Hearn shaking them out of the wire basket.

He was a good man, Slaney said. Nobody knew that would happen. A stroke. How could anybody know?

Made himself from nothing, Hearn said. And what did I do?

You couldn't see a stroke coming, Slaney said.

I never got a chance to say goodbye.

I know.

I would have liked to see him.

I know.

Say something. Explain my actions.

I hear he communicates, Slaney said.

Squeezes your hand yes or no. That's all.

You hear from Jennifer? Slaney asked.

I have to tell you, Slane, Hearn said. She's married. She got married.

My God, Slaney said. The force of it. Slaney felt faint is what he felt. He slammed a shoulder against the wall and waited for the darkness in the periphery of his vision to clear. He looked for a chair but there was no chair. He needed to go home, to reverse everything. His equilibrium was askew. A surge of pain in the wrong places, limbs he didn't have, his organs, his tendons. He didn't know what he was feeling, queasy and unequal. He was unequal to this news, unable to believe it.

She got married a month ago, Hearn said.

Slaney pressed his hand down over his eyes and tried to get the sway out of the bar. It was all swaying and he tried to make it be still. Jennifer hadn't answered his letters but he couldn't believe that she was in love with someone else. If she had married somebody it was a kind of lie. A deceit that would cost her everything she was. She hadn't believed he'd come get her.

Dirty Dick heard she married a guy Decker from home, Hearn said. Went to Gonzaga, few years older than us.

Slaney was thinking Jennifer must have been coerced or brainwashed or bewitched. He needed to tell her to stop her foolishness. She was stubborn and spoiled rotten but they could have worked around all that. She had suffered a lapse of faith; they could have fixed it. But a marriage? She had married somebody. A marriage would be hard to undo.

He couldn't summon what he needed to roar against it. He wanted to throw back his head and howl as loud as he could. Put his fist through the wall of the bar, out to the parking lot, and beyond, into someone's face. Whoever the guy was, the husband, he wanted to grab him by the throat. He wanted to put his nose right up against the other guy's nose and just say a few things.

Or sit him down and gently explain. Tell the guy: Listen here. If he could illustrate for the guy the intensity of what he felt, what he and Jennifer had been through, how deep that love was — the guy would step aside. The guy would say: She's all yours, buddy.

What bullshit it was that a marriage had taken place. This guy had no idea. But Slaney couldn't draw up what was required to reverse everything.

Somebody, perhaps the girl Hearn had there, had turned on a radio. Slaney could hear the weather. The weather was going to be the same.

Where is she? Slaney said.

She's in Ottawa. The guy got something out there, a steady job.

I see, Slaney said.

Maybe she wants a safe place for her kid. She probably doesn't want to be caught up with all of this.

Who is he?

He's just a guy, some guy.

What's his name?

I don't know his name, Frank Decker, or Fred. He's a civil servant. Ticks boxes all day. He'd been asking for years, according to Dick, and she finally said to him yes. Dick got all this from his sister. His sister knew Jennifer growing up, kept in touch.

The customer at the corner of the bar hooked his finger in the knot of his tie and wrenched it left and right, stretching his chin up. For a second he bared his teeth. The man picked up his fork and stared down at the pie. Then he put the fork down. He made a fist with one hand and wrapped his other hand around the fist and he put his forehead to his hands. He was saying grace.

Slaney gave himself a shake.

I'm looking around, he said.

Where are you? Hearn asked.

Tried to find a place spoke English, Slaney said. Get a drop of soup.

This time it's going to be different.

Better be.

I've got everything covered, Slaney.

I have to tell you, Hearn, Slaney said.

Christ, Hearn said.

It's bad in there.

Christ almighty.

It was very bad.

We're doing it right this time. I have the name of a man for you. A guy you have to see, pick up some backing and get the hell over here. We're going to have a party for you, Slaney. A coming-out party.

I think I see my lunch, Slaney said. There's a bowl of soup there, going begging.

My father made himself.

Yes he did, Slaney said. He made himself. When you think of where he came from.

I ruined him, Hearn said. Slaney didn't say anything.

I ruined him. I ruined him.

I'm sorry, Slaney said.

You're sorry, Hearn said. Slaney could hear him opening cupboards. He was looking for the salt. Slaney heard the clunk of a glass bottle on a counter. It was the ketchup or Hearn had opened a beer.

I'm sorry, man, Hearn said. I'm sorry for the way it went down. I'm sorry you went to jail.

There was a paper placemat, already set, at the bar beside the man with the pie. The waitress had turned to the bright window behind the bar that opened onto the kitchen and there was the steaming bowl sitting on the shelf. Slaney's soup.

The girl lifted the bowl down from the shelf, holding it with both hands, careful not to slop. She looked over the whole bar until she saw Slaney at the back on the pay phone. Her blue, too close-together eyes. She tilted up her chin a bit toward him and he nodded to her.

I got a room for you to stay in Montreal, Hearn said. And he gave Slaney the address. There's a key for you with the janitor. You got your own bathroom and a phone.

You're going to pay a visit to this guy named Lefevre. Lay

low, Slane. In a couple of days, I'll call you with the details. You go see Lefevre and he gives you the backing. Then you get the hell out of there. They haven't forgot about us in Montreal.

I heard, Slaney said.

People are still hurting up there from the last trip. You get the cash from Lefevre and you take a train. We'll be waiting here for you, Slane.

Listen, man, Slaney said. I'll be there. I'm on my way. Slaney hung up and leaned against the wall and pressed his fists into his eye sockets and twisted the knuckles into the corners of his eyes.

The sound of Hearn's voice. The Newfoundland accent. Jennifer was married. She was in Ottawa and she was married. He was full-on crying now. She'd married somebody.

He put the rest of his change in the phone and dialled and waited for maybe twenty rings. He lost track of how many rings and finally a man answered. The man's voice was sloughing phlegm, and he yelled hello. He was alarmed, woken from a long sleep, yelling hello, hello in a quavering voice.

Is Charmaine there, please?

Where are you calling from? the man said.

I'm on a pay phone.

Don't make me get out of this bed, the man said.

You're not Charmaine, I guess, Slaney said. It says here, For a good time.

Because if I come down there.

Call somebody named Charmaine and it gives the number, Slaney said. For a good time call Charmaine.

I'm going to tear that pay phone off the wall and you're going to swallow it. You'll be talking through your ass.

Doll

The salesclerk in the toy department wore a white blouse with the sleeves rolled up and navy work pants. She was down on her knees with a pricing gun that spat out fluorescent orange tags when she pulled the trigger. She glanced up at Slaney and swung the gun around on her finger and pointed it at him from her hip like they were in a cowboy movie.

You tell me what you want and I'll help you find it, she said. We have everything here. She knew he was Anglo by the look of him and addressed him in English. She flattened everything she said like she was running it through a wringer washer. All the *th*'s were *d*'s and she was dropping *h*'s and she was emphatic. Her vowels had carbuncles and she resented having to spit them out and it was as sexy as anything Slaney had ever heard.

Yeah, bonjour, Slaney said. He said he was looking for a doll.

What kind of doll did you have in mind? the girl said. We got all kinds of dolls.

I want the biggest doll you got, Slaney said.

Plenty are big, she said. She had straight black hair parted in the middle that shone blue and hung around her white face. She wore giant silver hoops in her ears and bangles on both her arms. She was skinny, the bones of her hips two hard knobs and the hollows of her clavicles were deep and she had high cheekbones.

Have you got one of those dolls that can walk and talk? he said. And if it can do other things besides, I'd like that too.

It's hard to get one can do it all.

Slaney saw she was about his age and everything she said

was accompanied by a gentle sneer. He wasn't accustomed to irony coming from female salesclerks and he found it hard to get his footing. All he wanted was a doll.

We got one you can give a real bottle to and she pees. That one is supposed to nurture maternal feelings. I don't know if you want to encourage that kind of thing.

Slaney said he didn't know either. He said he was buying a present for a little girl, a six-year-old.

The best doll you got, he said.

Did you think of a fire truck? the clerk asked.

It's a little girl, Slaney said.

Or a Hot Wheels set?

Slaney said he had his heart set on a doll.

We have a fire truck you press a button the lights come on and sirens blare out all over the house.

I never thought fire truck, Slaney said.

How about a chemistry set? She could look at her own saliva on a little glass slide under the microscope. See all the things swimming around in her spit.

I just thought a doll, Slaney said. That's what I had pictured.

All right, then, the clerk said. Fine. You want to get her a doll, that's your business. Get her a doll.

Slaney followed the clerk down the aisle. They turned the corner together and there was a giant display of identical dolls running the length of the back wall of the department store. There must have been hundreds of them. Each doll was in a pink box with a cellophane window and a big pink bow over the outside.

Her name is Saucy Suzy, the clerk said. She got five or six things she says. You pull a string on the back of her neck.

What does she talk about? Slaney asked.

She has lots of interests, the salesclerk said. She counted the phrases off on her fingers.

Let's see, she says, Take me with you, and Let's play house, Change my dress, and Let's bake cookies. She says, Tell me a story, and Let's do acid and fuck like bunnies.

She's pretty provocative, Slaney said. The doll's hands stood out a little from her pleated skirt. The first two fingers on both hands were stuck together, but the other two fingers and the thumb fanned away from the rest. The hands gave the impression that the doll had suffered an electric shock.

Can I see her in action? Slaney said. The girl reached up and her bangles fell down her arms and she took the display doll down off a shelf and set her on the floor.

She pressed a button in the back of the doll, under her curls, and the eyes flicked open. The doll stared forward with bleak astonishment. There was a whirring and ticking of small parts. The doll tilted dangerously to one side. Her shocked fingers seemed to tremble. Each sausage curl quivered and she lifted her left foot. The step was part shove, part scuff. The foot dropped down and the doll tottered and the momentum lifted the other foot.

Jennifer had been in the courtroom four years ago and she kept her eyes on Slaney for most of the trial and she watched him shuffle away in chains. She hadn't known about the trip to Colombia until they were caught.

Slaney had gone through the door of the courtroom to the paddy wagon in shackles. His wrists were cuffed and a chain ran through the cuffs to the heavy bands around his ankles.

It had required a new shuffle to leave the court. It was a dance that had to be learned on the spot. That dance is a depravity they foist on you.

The salesclerk tossed the doll up onto her shoulder and walked Slaney to the cash register with it. She rang in his purchase and took his money and slammed the register drawer shut with her hip.

Jennifer, Juniper

Before the first trip, they'd had their big goodbye on the sidewalk outside Jennifer's Gower Street apartment, the Jamaican flag hanging in the upstairs window, sopping K-Mart flyers hanging out the mailbox, her tears wet on his neck while she held him.

Jennifer had thought Alberta, not Colombia. Slaney had said he was going to Alberta for work and as soon as he landed a job he'd send for her and Crystal. He'd have a nice house set up for them and he'd buy them everything they'd ever wanted, all the furniture and clothes and toys they could imagine. Jennifer wouldn't have to worry about money anymore.

Slaney had bent down by the stroller and pulled out Crystal's pacifier and kissed her and stuck it back in before she had a chance to scream for it. And Jennifer stood there on the sidewalk, one hand on the stroller, pulling it back and forth, waving with the other. She kept waving until the car had disappeared around the corner.

He'd loved to watch her eat cereal in the morning. A drop of milk clinging to the bottom of her spoon. Reading a paperback. The book in one hand and a film of milk coating the convex side of spoon, forming a single trembling drop, clinging and letting go, falling into the bowl. *Plink*. Turning a page. Or she'd put the book on the table and press the heel of her hand over the centre, trying to get it to stay open.

Crystal slept in his old army jacket, the silver stripes on the sleeves that glowed in the dark. Slaney smoothing the little girl's damp golden curls off her forehead while she slept.

Touching his nose to the child's soft neck and the smell of her. Dried breast milk, slightly soured and sweet, like cotton candy, and the clean Velour sleepers with the feet in them.

He'd sung the Donovan song to Jennifer, after they made love: Jennifer, Juniper. Whispering a bit of the song into her hair.

They'd go to Topsail Beach on his motorcycle, the child between them, riding under the trees near the railway bed, everything splotches of sun and shadow.

The noise Jennifer made in bed. She didn't care who heard, or she didn't know how loud she was.

She often said thank you after sex. She thanked him. He couldn't get used to that. He would say thank you right back. She always called out to God in the middle of it. She told Slaney she loved him over and over when they were fucking and he forgot to say it back. Sometimes she would sulk afterwards and it would take him a while to figure out what was wrong, then he'd say he loved her and she'd wrap her arms around his neck, nearly choking him.

Slaney had grown up with her. But she became new to him when she was sixteen.

He'd started seeing her around downtown and it confused him. The look she gave him when he came into Lar's Fruit Store that day in August after her baby was born.

Slaney had known Jennifer Baker since kindergarten. There were vast swathes of time when he hadn't thought of her at all.

But there were also the bright burning stars of her: she had played basketball (weaving through the thrash of girls, all elbows and knees, down the court, the sneakers squeaking to a halt, everyone turning at once, thundering down the court after her, and her leap, one knee up, arm raised over her head, the ball balanced on her fingertips, suspended in the air for a long, still moment, before tipping the ball through the hoop). She'd come to his door one Halloween and how earnest in her homemade Wonder Woman costume, a bodice of tinfoil and construction paper, matching wrist cuffs, a lasso spray-painted gold.

They'd both placed in the grade eight public speaking contest, he for the boys' school and she for the girls'. He'd argued that there was life on Mars and had the place in an uproar of laughter; she said it was wrong to dissect frogs and won without a single joke.

Neighbourhood baseball, and street hockey, water balloon fights, spotlight, spin the bottle, smoking pot behind Woolworth's and her uniform at the new A&W.

But she was like a stranger that day in August at Lar's Fruit Store. She had asked for a custard cone and she was blushing and she'd stumbled over her words. The first time he'd seen her since she'd had the baby. The ice cream had been soft and toppled off the cone even as she raised it to her mouth. She stood there holding the empty cone out with the ice cream on the floor at her feet.

Now my hand is all sticky, she said.

It's the heat, Slaney said. The woman behind the counter said she was going to get Jennifer another ice cream.

You just hold on there, the woman said. I can fix this situation. She wet a dishrag and handed it over the counter to

Slaney, who got down on the floor and tried to scoop up the mess. The woman said the weather was making everything melt. She said she was run off her feet.

Slaney said that if it were raining they'd be complaining about that. And the woman said he was right. If it wasn't one thing it was another. And she turned around with a new cone held up like a beacon.

Slaney had no idea what could have happened to Jennifer over the last couple of months. She seemed so changed. When he tried to imagine her giving birth he only saw white enamel bowls of blood-soaked towels, a nursery with row upon row of babies.

There you go, my love, the woman said. You enjoy that ice cream.

Thank you, Jennifer said. You didn't have to do that. Slaney handed the woman back the sopping dishrag.

I'll tell you what, the woman said. There won't be too many days like this. Mark my words.

Tomorrow is supposed to be beautiful too, Slaney said. He had looked straight into Jennifer's eyes when he said it.

We'll pay for it later, the woman said.

It's dripping, Slaney said. And Jennifer's tongue licked up the drip and she told Slaney to have some and she held out the cone and he put his hand over her hand to steady it and he licked it up the side.

She'd had a baby with somebody and she wasn't saying the father. After a while nobody would bring up *who's the father*. At least not in her presence. Even Slaney knew better than to ask.

I guess I'll see you around, David, Jennifer said. She said it like she was going somewhere but she just stood there in the middle of Lar's like she didn't know where she was going.

That was the summer they had all the beautiful weather. She was on welfare and set up in public housing on the west end of Gower Street and he slept over every night but left through the back door because they had to watch out for the welfare cops.

She was still breast-feeding when Crystal was two and her breasts would squirt little threads of milk all over him when they made love. Oh God. God. God. God. God.

Now she was married to somebody else.

Don't Call

Did you order a sundae in a snack bar back in New Brunswick? Hearn asked. The phone had rung near Slaney's head and he'd slapped around on the bedside table and knocked the receiver to the floor and pulled it up by the cord and said hello.

Somebody phoned the cops, Hearn said. It was in the papers. "Eyewitness Identifies Escaped Prisoner at Local Snack Bar."

I was with a girl, Slaney said.

You were identified.

Slaney hauled himself out of bed to the window. Across the street at ground level a man was dressing a window with silver stars and mannequins in diaphanous evening gowns.

Every time the window dresser adjusted the fold of a gown or a dummy's arm he stood back with his hands on his hips, taking in the effect.

Slaney's room was empty but for the sink with rust stains flaring up from the drain and the red wool blanket over the bare striped mattress. There was a closet with a lone wire hanger and the doll Slaney had purchased the day before stood in her pink box on the only wooden chair. One drowsy eyelid had fallen down.

You don't use your own name, Hearn said.

A girl picked me up hitchhiking. I went back to her place. What was it, three days ago.

We got to get you out of there, Hearn said. They're on you, man. Somebody saw you. Called it in. So there's been an adjustment to the plan. I'm going to tell you the plan and then I don't want to hear from you.

You're hurting my feelings, man.

Hearn said, Do me a favour.

I won't call you, Slaney said.

Don't call me.

I won't, Slaney said.

You are underestimating, Hearn said. How much they want to get us. Don't call. Don't use your name.

I won't.

You have to get a new name.

I'm on it.

They want to set an example.

I won't even think about you.

You think I'm kidding? I'm telling you.

I was ordering fish and chips from a snack bar, Slaney said. I gave the woman my name and she called it out all over the parking lot. I was with a girl.

Why would you say your name?

I said Dave is what I said, Slaney told him. There are a lot of Daves. Plenty of Daves.

Somebody put two and two.

I'll lie low, Slaney said.

Keep a low profile.

How are you?

How the hell are *you*, man?

I'm on my way.

You have to see the man, Hearn said. Lefevre is ready to see you.

Go there tonight, Hearn said. Around nine o'clock. And in the meantime.

I'll stay out of the limelight, Slaney said.

You go see Lefevre and he'll give you the backing. Then you get the hell out of Montreal. We got a cabin set up for you outside of town. You wait for a passport.

That's at least five, six weeks for a passport, Slaney said.

A place called Mansonville.

Five *weeks*?

You wait for the passport. You go to this cabin, Slane, and you stay in it. You've been spotted now, we need to be careful. You don't want to lead them here. You lie low, don't go out except to get supplies.

Five weeks, what? Practising tai chi? Jesus, Hearn.

The boat leaves from here, takes six weeks, more or less, to get to Mexico. There's a crew hired to sail her down with the owner. Beaver Noseworthy is going to sail her down, a few other guys. They'll fly home from Mexico.

They're looking for you in airports in the east now, Slaney. You get the passport, then you get the train out here. Five, six weeks, things have cooled down in the airports. We fly you to Mexico from here, you meet up with the boat, head on to Colombia, just you and the captain. You got to get the new passport.

There had been a lesson in New Brunswick, Slaney thought,

and it was that he had no name. He had left his name behind or he had passed through it.

You got it, Slane?

I got it.

Did you get any? Hearn said.

Pardon me? Slaney said.

The girl, the girl. At the snack bar with the sundae. Were you getting some?

I'll be seeing you, Hearn.

What did she look like?

Hearn, I'm not going to indulge.

Tits?

I'm hearing about feminism, Slaney said.

Don't mind that, Hearn said.

Some of them aren't shaving their underarms, Slaney said. They aren't shaving their legs.

But they have their own rubbers, Hearn said. They're sleeping with whomsoever they please.

I'm going to have to get a handle on it, Slaney said.

I Got Your Number

A young man stood in a display window with a giant silver star held out before him. Mannequins crowded around him, glancing in different directions; one had an arm raised, as if to flag a taxi.

They'd put the tap on the phone in Slaney's bedsit the day he arrived and they were waiting for Hearn to call. Once they'd located Hearn, Patterson would fly out to the coast and infiltrate the operation. He'd offer financing, get to know Hearn.

He turned on the car to give the wipers a flick. The rain hit the roof and the wind wrinkled the thick coat of water sluicing over the glass. Patterson gave the wipers a single sweep and the slurring world was put straight. He had hoped there'd be time to visit his brother on the way across the country. He wanted to sit with him in the sunny visitors' lounge, or to walk in the gardens holding his hand.

Patterson had met his brother for the first time when they were both eight. A second family had shown up for Patterson's father's funeral, more than three decades ago, in the small town of Portage la Prairie.

They'd come to the service, a boy and his mother, by bus and then cab and they arrived late. The door of the church screeching open in the middle of the ceremony, the sound of the rain coming in with them. They'd taken seats in the last pew, causing everyone to crane their necks around when the boy yelled out, an ungovernable, eerie noise like weather, followed by a hard slap on the wrist that interrupted the priest's homily. Everyone reached for the hymn books.

The church had filled with the rustling of pages so thin the print of both sides showed through them. The organ sent out a phlegmatic, vibrating wheeze. People began to sing, and above all the voices there was a new soprano.

A voice chilly and transparent, full of unapologetic power, precise in pitch.

Patterson's mother had known nothing about the woman, whose name was Clarice Connors, and who worked as a charwoman. She was fifteen years younger than Patterson's mother and she looked fast and drawn in a worn, wet coat with a fur collar, a hat with black netting over the brim.

What Patterson remembered most of Miss Connors on that

day was the red, red lipstick, wet and dark. The lipstick set the woman apart from his mother in every way.

Patterson's mother was earnest and finicky. She took offence easily and without outward sign. Her judgements were arrived at instantly, and once conceived, rarely altered.

Patterson had grown up in a house that was helplessly clean, where good taste was expressed in a showy lack of ornamentation. The silence in a room was guarded with a vigilance that caused them to cringe when their cutlery scraped the china. The rustle of a log burning in the wood stove made do for conversation.

The lipstick, Patterson knew, even at the age of eight, was fantastic. It meant that Clarice Connors did not care what other people thought of her.

He became aware that day, watching his mother under the trees with his father's mistress, that people were motivated by two distinct and opposing forces. There was the desire for truth and there was the need to conceal it. Of course he couldn't have put it into words when he was eight. But he came to know that if a truth were lying out in the open for anyone to trip over, there must be something at stake.

Alphonse was Clarice Connors's only child, and he was Patterson's age, almost to the day. The boy looked just like him except that everything soft in his half-brother was hard in Patterson.

Alphonse had Down's syndrome and lived, now, in a home on the outskirts of Guelph for which Patterson paid exorbitant fees. He had received notice three months ago that his account was in arrears and the management had requested Patterson schedule a meeting to discuss the matter.

The facility had earned a reputation for its progressive

treatment. The fees went up every year. Patterson had moved Alphonse into the facility when Clarice Connors died of lung cancer. The move had been traumatic. Patterson would not move him again, no matter what it cost. He needed that promotion.

The man in the display window leaned the giant star at the foot of a blond mannequin in an evening gown of filmy chartreuse. He flicked a light switch and the window flared with thousands of tiny white lights inside the stars that decorated the back wall.

Clarice Connors had been standing outside the church when it was time to leave for the graveyard.

Patterson's mother settled him into the back seat of their family car. She leaned over him and did up his seat belt.

Fingers in, she said. She pressed the door shut behind her. Patterson watched as she strode across the parking lot in her old Hush Puppies with the tarnished pennies in the leather slots. She had worn them for as long as Patterson could remember.

The two women stood on a dry patch of earth under the branches of a spreading oak and Patterson's mother was pointing at the ground in front of her. Stabbing at the ground with her finger, the way you might if you were telling a dog to come and sit at your feet. Her eyes remained downcast while she spoke because she could not force herself to look up.

Throughout Patterson's mother's speech Miss Connors had one hand wrapped around her elbow, and her other tilted out, palm up, with her cigarette, in a posture that seemed both casual and belonging to another era, perhaps one yet to come. She squinted her eyes in an effort to take in the rapid, soft-spoken stream of invective.

When Patterson's mother had stopped talking, the younger woman took a draw on her cigarette and let the smoke come out her nostrils and the corners of her mouth like a dragon waking from a long slumber. She flicked open a clasp on her purse so the mouth of it yawned wide. She took out a sheaf of papers and gave it to Patterson's mother. She had loved Patterson's father, Patterson later came to understand, with a passion so beyond his mother's emotional range that it would have been cruel to make reference to it.

Clarice Connors was not interested in discussing matters of the heart. She had a ratified will that proved to be more recent than the one Patterson's mother had in the back of her stocking drawer.

Clarice Connors dropped her cigarette to the ground and twisted her high-heeled shoe over it. She would not take their house, she said. She was looking out for her child.

Patterson heard her call to her son. The eight-year-old Alphonse was spinning in circles, beyond the protection of the tree branches, where the asphalt had already darkened with rain. His arms out like wings.

You'll make yourself sick, Miss Connors shouted. Patterson watched them with his nose pressed against the cold glass. The car must have looked empty before he moved, the shadows of the branches above the car concealing the interior. But when Patterson leaned forward, Alphonse noticed him. The strange boy's sole-eyed face was instantly full of love and naked humour. It was an unconditional offer of friendship.

Alphonse skipped toward the car, his thumbs in his ears, his fingers wiggling, his tongue lolling. A lopsided saunter that broke into a run when his mother said his name again, a full-on, charging escape. When he reached the car he slapped both his hands against Patterson's window. The suddenness of it made Patterson rear back and he had just a second or so to recover and slap his own hands over the boy's before Miss Connors wrenched him away by the shirt collar.

The man in the display window had slipped through a hidden panel at the back and he was gone.

Patterson's radio buzzed and crackled. They told him to call in to the detachment for a message.

He stepped out of the car into a stream of water that came up to his ankles. He ran with his jacket over his head to a pay phone on the corner. A glass box with red mullions and a folding door. He was standing in a puddle, a cigarette butt with a touch of lipstick floating near his shoe. He slotted in some change and phoned through to the detachment there in Montreal and asked for Staff-Sergeant Mercer.

He was told the call had come through. Hearn had phoned Slaney and they'd traced the number and got his address in Vancouver.

Chunk of Change

Slaney took the subway and then a bus to the suburb of Pointe-Saint-Charles, and then walked the suburban streets of Montreal for more than an hour before he found the two-storey strip mall with the dry cleaning outlet. He pressed a buzzer several times but nothing happened.

Everything was closed and just a few bare bulbs burned over the doors down the front of the building. There was an antique shop on one side of the dry cleaner's with the same ceramic washbasin and matching chamber pot that Slaney's family had when he was growing up. Slaney was able to see the price of the piss-pot by cranking his neck to the side and it made him swear out loud.

The place on the other side of the dry cleaner's sold sports equipment. Tennis rackets and water skis, a mannequin in a gold lamé bikini. Slaney was staring at the mannequin with his finger on the buzzer when the door of the dry cleaning outlet swung open.

Stop with the goddamn ringing, Lefevre said. You want to wake my wife? Lefevre had a hard round potbelly and sagging breasts and he was very short.

He brought Slaney through the shop floor. There were racks of white nurses' uniforms, evening gowns, tuxedos and army fatigues. The clear plastic sheaths over the clothing rippled in the breeze from the front door. The scent of chemicals and scorched cotton.

They took a cobwebbed staircase at the back, each wooden step so damp and rotted Slaney felt the give underfoot. Lefevre's weight caused him to wheeze and huff and lean for long moments against the rickety stair rail as they descended.

They passed through a maze of concrete walls weeping condensation, corridors that twisted under the stores.

Piles of junk encroached on them in places, spilling over, like in the illustrations of pirate caves in storybooks. Engine parts, cooking pots, broken furniture, and old calendars with faded porn stars; mannequins in fur coats, sequined show dresses, feather boas, and studded black leather get-ups that Slaney had never seen the like of before.

Finally Lefevre stopped before a door of heavy steel that appeared to lead into a walk-in safe. He took a ring of keys from his pocket. He unlocked the door and ushered Slaney inside and the door slammed shut behind them. They stood for several minutes in absolute darkness and Slaney remembered he was supposed to use his intuition and he felt certain he was about to get a knife through the ribs and he stepped sideways, about a foot, crashing into a coat rack that swayed and staggered until he caught it.

Lefevre thrashed his arms around and swore in French. Slaney heard a chain pulled taut and let go and the light bulb hanging in the middle of the cramped office came on and swung hard, making their shadows stretch across the ceiling and sink back into their shoes as if they were knocking each other down and bouncing up for more.

Lefevre forced his bulk between the desk corner and a filing cabinet until he was stuck. He tried to heft the mound of his gut, using both hands, over the corner of the desk and finally told Slaney to help him for the sake of Jesus Christ and for the sake of all the fucking saints in heaven. He asked Slaney why he was just standing there like a useless bastard. He asked other things in French that didn't seem to call for an answer.

Slaney grabbed the heavy desk and dragged it to the side and the man fell into a swivel chair behind it. The chair creaked under his weight and the casters sent it lurching sideways over the concrete floor.

Lefevre's face was as grey as newsprint and he was working hard to draw breath. He held one hand, girlishly, over his heart and pointed a finger toward the corner of the room with the other, unable to speak.

Slaney got the bottle of whisky and a glass off the filing cabinet. The glass had a picture of an airline stewardess on the side of it. Slaney poured some and glanced at Lefevre, who rolled his finger in a circle, so Slaney kept pouring until the whisky threatened to spill over the lip. As the whisky filled the glass the uniform of the airline stewardess became transparent and she was naked. Slaney put the drink down on the desk.

My doctor says I have emphysema, Lefevre said when he finally spoke. From which you don't come back.

He fished in his breast pocket with two fingers and found a white tablet and dropped it into the glass and it fizzed on the bottom and Lefevre drank it down and hammered his chest with his fist, his eyes bulging, a white foam creeping into the corners of his lips.

He drew his chin down, making three distinct folds of his jowls. His neck was spilling out of his tight collar and a slow snarl stole over his broad face until he managed an expulsion of swampy air. The glass touched down on the desk and the airline stewardess's uniform faded back.

I look at you, Lefevre wheezed, and I see myself. He squeezed his eyes shut and nodded emphatically. He had loosened the tie and was struggling with the button at his neck.

I see myself, Lefevre practically shouted. I see myself forty years ago. Have a drink.

I'm fine, Slaney said.

Please, Lefevre said. Help yourself. Slaney took down the other glass from the filing cabinet. There was a tiny spider stuck in the tacky, dust-furred film at the bottom of the glass. Slaney poured the whisky and he took a swallow.

I hear things, Lefevre said. He pulled open a drawer beside him and offered Slaney a cigar.

I don't trust hearsay, Slaney told him.

You should be moving around, the man said. He slipped one of the cigars under his nose, inhaling deeply. Slaney watched him and did the same.

Then Lefevre bit off the end and spit it on the floor.

Slaney bit off the end of the cigar he had and also spit.

You've been at the same location since you got here. This is what I'm hearing, Lefevre said.

I've only been here three days, Slaney said. But he was astonished that Lefevre knew where he was staying.

We're all involved now, Lefevre said. I'm involved, your friend Hearn, I believe he goes by the name Barlow? There are a few major investors in this enterprise.

He waved his cigar in a circle toward the ceiling to indicate all the people who knew about the job. The people Hearn had involved.

I'm wondering if this venture is compromised. I'm speaking aloud here.

Yes sir, Slaney said. He pushed his chair back an inch. He didn't like how thick the door to the room was. He thought soundproof. Slaney wished he knew more about who was involved. Where they were getting the rest of the financing.

I'm thinking your friend Hearn may have drawn undesired attention, Lefevre said. He opened the desk drawer again and took out a pistol.

You come out here on your own, Lefevre said. You don't know me. You walk into a meeting like this? Know what you're dealing with beforehand. Hearn has left you in a vulnerable position.

Lefevre let the gun glint in his open palm, as if testing the weight of it while he talked. It was a snub-nosed pistol with pearlized plates on the handle and it looked pudgy and coy in Lefevre's hand. He pointed it at Slaney and gestured for him to lean forward. The light bulb overhead had stopped swinging and Lefevre's shadow reached to the ceiling.

If my wife finds out about these cigars, he said. He pulled the trigger on the little gun and there was a crack and a flame burst out and he lit Slaney's cigar and he lit his own.

The smoke made Slaney light-headed and the perfume of it was earthy and floral and he thought of Colombia, an afternoon when he and Hearn got drunk in a bar and two girls joined them at their table and took fans from their straw purses and snapped them open in unison and the fans fluttered so fast they were soft blurs hovering in the dense heat.

Hearn had led one of the girls to the dance floor. They'd stood a couple of inches apart, straight and still. There was no music. Just the clink of glasses as the bartender tidied up and the sound of the surf. But Hearn and the girl were listening hard and then they were gliding all over the dance floor. Hearn twirled her and she spun out and curled back and her skirt flicked up. The girl left at the table with Slaney suddenly turned her fan on him and the cool breeze tickled him all over and blew his curls back off his face.

The same room since you got here, Lefevre said. How do I know this? Again, I am speaking aloud here. I am airing my concerns.

There was the old woman who lived across the hall from Slaney's bedsit on de la Montagne and she had given Slaney money from a beaded change purse, each of the three mornings since he'd arrived, to buy her a pack of cigarettes. Some of the beads hung on loose threads, this purse she had was threadbare, and her hands shook, pressing the coins, one at a time, into his hand. Slaney wondered if someone had questioned her.

You come here for advice, Lefevre said. And I see myself. We are the same. I'm telling you for free. I hear rumours. I speak as a friend. This is a friend speaking to you now. Why not? I am saying if I were you. This is talk I'm hearing.

Slaney said, I don't pay attention to talk.

Pay attention, Lefevre said.

People just want to hear themselves, Slaney said.

You listen, the man said, you learn.

Slaney took a moment. Thank you, sir, he said.

You play your cards, and you end up like me, the man said. He waved a hand again, to take in the office and the dry cleaning establishment upstairs, the street and the apartment with his wife above the outlet.

The old lady in the room next to Slaney's with at least four cats, there might have been more. The first morning she had opened the door a crack with the chain across and looked out at Slaney. She had been startled and afraid.

But then she beckoned to him from the doorway and he spoke to her about the heavy rain and asked how she'd slept and she listened, standing sideways, her ear to the door, like a priest hearing confession, though it turned out she didn't speak English, and then she closed the door and shuffled away and he'd waited.

She'd shuffled back, these slippers she had, they were a men's size ten, Slaney figured, and they were fur-lined and the cats were mewling and surging between her feet. He heard the chain unslide and she handed out the money and closed the door. Once Slaney heard some visitors. It sounded like a couple of men, low tones murmuring through the door.

Your partner has a mouth, Lefevre said. This is why I am saying keep moving. This I tell you because I look at your face, your eyes, and I see we are the same, you and me.

Slaney shifted in his chair. One of the legs was shorter than the others and it tipped under him.

I have word the cops know exactly where you are, Lefevre said. They will pick you up tomorrow. This makes investors nervous.

Nervous I can understand, Slaney said. He could smell dry cleaning chemicals, a bleaching taint of citrus, bitter fumes seeping through under the velvety stink of the cigars. His mouth was smackingly dry.

You don't make this kind of return on your money without nerves, Slaney said.

I like you, Lefevre said. My wife would like you. We tried for children, but sometimes this doesn't happen. The problem is not on my side. I can hear Monique now. He's just a boy, she'd say. If she met you, she'd say, Jean-Marie, he's just like you. She's very tiny, Monique, but don't cross her. Once she hit me in the face with a cast-iron frying pan. She would take a shine to you.

I'm sorry I won't get an opportunity to meet her, Slaney said.

Don't go back to that room, kid. Sleep on a bench somewhere. You think I'm joking. I'm not joking.

I didn't think you were joking, sir, Slaney said.

Let me ask you, he said. Can Hearn be trusted? The ash on his cigar grew as he spoke. His index finger hooked over the top of it, his thumb underneath. He was both wedged and slumped in the chair now. It was listing to the side. He put his wet purple lips over the end of the cigar and he squinted his eyes philosophically at Slaney while he inhaled. Each hairy black crumb of tobacco burned orange.

Because the rumour is, he can't be trusted.

The phone rang in the quiet of the office and Lefevre let it ring. It rang for a long time and he and Slaney observed a silence until it stopped.

Was that your wife? Slaney asked.

My wife is one of these people, she doesn't take no. You have a girl?

I had a girl, Slaney said. Lefevre opened the drawer again and took out a black vinyl banking sack.

Slaney unzipped the bag and saw thick stacks of twenties and fifties and stacks of one hundred dollar bills with elastic bands and he removed the piles of money and counted them. He put each bundle back in the sack neatly as he finished with it and when he was done he zipped the bag and patted the side of it.

What did you come up with? Lefevre asked.

There's twenty-five thousand dollars, Slaney said. Lefevre slammed his hands down on the table.

That's exactly right, he said. The slamming caused another coughing fit. Lefevre's eyes watered as he hacked. His mouth hung open and his tongue didn't look good. His shoulders curled in and he was humbled and Slaney thought heart attack.

The wet coughing turned soundless and dry and there was an ugly straining for breath. Slaney thought mouth to mouth. He wondered if Lefevre would die in the chair and whether he would be able to get the door open. Would he pull the man's carcass up over the staircase, or go upstairs and bang on every door yelling for a woman named Monique who might clock him with a frying pan?

He jumped out of the chair but Lefevre held up his hand to keep him away. Finally he managed to gasp in a hard, rattling stream of air.

They say with emphysema you just get worse and worse. There's no light they can offer you. It's all doom and gloom.

I don't give a good goddamn what they say. I'm healthy as a horse.

You look good, Slaney said.

It's the wife's cooking, Lefevre said. She's trying to poison me. She thinks I don't notice.

I should get going, Slaney said.

She brings home a brochure and wants me to consult a quack. This is a guy they heat rocks and lay them on your back under glass cups. I say to her, Monique, ease up on the arsenic.

It was a pleasure to meet you, sir, Slaney said.

That girl you were talking about.

She's gone, Slaney said.

Take her out on the town.

I wrote letters but I don't think she got them.

Take her out on the town.

I will, sir, thank you.

Spend a little money on her, Lefevre said.

If we ever see each other again.

Leave that bedsit tonight, son, Lefevre said. Don't even go back.

Thank you, sir.

They left the tiny basement office and went back through the corridors of junk and up the staircase and through the dry cleaning outlet.

Lefevre unlocked the plate-glass doors at the front of the building and made Slaney stand in the shadows while he stepped out onto the sidewalk to take a look up and down the parking lot. The old man's shoulders shook for a moment with another, smaller fit of coughing. Then he came back inside and grabbed Slaney by the shoulders and kissed both of his cheeks.

The next morning Slaney stopped at a department store and bought a pair of white evening gloves with five rhinestone buttons that went up to the elbow and had the girl in the store wrap them and she asked him to put his finger on the string while she tied the bow and the knot came down on his fingertip and she said, I've got you now.

Back in the room Slaney ordered a taxi and then brought his mother's suitcase and the doll in her pink box and the bag of money from Lefevre out into the hall. He heard the door lock behind him. All night he'd watched the passing headlights on the street below slide the shadows of the lace curtains across one wall. He was awake until dawn.

Lefevre had made him paranoid.

He knocked on the door across the hall before he left and the old woman opened it and he handed her the wrapped box with the gloves and told her it was a goodbye present. She held up a finger for him to wait and closed the door and slid the chain lock through the groove and let it dangle free. She invited him in and gave him a cup of tea and the stink of cat shit nearly knocked him out.

She told him to wait at the table and she was gone a while and she came back with two cigarettes, a ribbon wrapped around them, and a French translation of *Moby Dick*.

Truth and Knowledge

Slaney had walked in on his parents in the gloom of the living room at the end of the day, cabbage boiling in the kitchen, salt beef, potatoes; he was twelve years old and there were his parents with an encyclopedia salesman.

After school, after a game of baseball in the park, after he had lied about being safe.

He said he had touched the base and then he allowed himself to believe it. He made it up or remade it. I touched the base. My foot was on the base. I was safe.

Safe, he'd called out. He imagined his foot and then the smack of the ball. He reconfigured it. Changed the order between those events. And he had kicked up a cloud of dust sliding in. There was an argument, a bitter fight. Which he waited out.

Hearn had taken his side is what happened.

I saw it, Hearn said. Striding across the field, his body bolt-straight, stiff with the injustice. Hearn already a foot taller than everybody.

I saw it.

Hearn turning to take in all the kids on the field, they were boys and girls. The interminable, sluggish game mattered very much. The *pock* of the ball hitting the bat, the brief moment when it crossed the sun and was invisible and came back, black at first, visible again on its descent, and the slap in the glove, the yelling: everything mattered very much.

You all saw it, Hearn said. Slaney touched base.

What happened, Slaney supposed, was that Hearn convinced him. It was not so much that Slaney was lying, but that he'd succumbed to Hearn's version of events. He believed it.

Hearn with spit flying: You all saw it.

They had a piece of cardboard for third base. And his father and mother, when he got home, and the salesman who had a too-small jacket — a smarmy jacket and a red tie with slanted silver stripes.

The tie should have tipped off his parents but the guy was mentioning the merits of an education.

The jacket was constraining. The fabric torqued at his shoulders. His socks on the carpet.

And his eyes.

They had forgotten, his parents, to turn on the lights in the living room and the man's pale eyes lit up in the gloom. His toes in the navy socks were scrunched. He might have pounced on Slaney's father and torn out some organ with his bare hands. He looked ready to eat them. But the jacket was holding him back. The jacket had him by the arms and he couldn't move.

Where was everybody else on that afternoon? Slaney was pretty sure his sisters had been in their rooms, the ones still living at home, getting dressed for an evening downtown. Or they were in the kitchen cooking supper. Slaney was the youngest and his older brothers had already left for the mainland. Three of them had married and already had kids. He had a sister studying to be a nurse. But the house was weirdly quiet. They hardly ever used the living room.

They were like two children themselves, his parents, facing a scolding. They both wore funny looks; they were earnest and smarting. They looked as if they'd been told to be quiet. Whatever they had been told, Slaney was pretty sure it was new to them.

Here's my youngest son, his father said. Come in, David, and meet Mr. Corrigan. Slaney had been the subject of talk. The current of talk swished through, encircling. There was something bigger than usual in the room. His parents were appraising him. They were trying to decide if it could be true.

They had been told that something depended on him. Perhaps everything.

He would be the beneficiary of the encyclopedias; he would make things better. He was going to have a chance his brothers and sisters had missed out on, just because they'd arrived before him. That was why his parents had kept on having children, all thirteen of them. Because eventually something like this kind of opportunity would come along. Or they'd had Slaney and his brothers and sisters because they'd never questioned the idea of children. The rightness of it. But now they had been given to understand there was design and continuance in the decision.

Good afternoon, Mr. Corrigan said. He stood up and put his hand out. Slaney had never been made to shake a man's hand before. It was a rite, he saw now, and his parents had sprung it on him.

We've been talking about your future, Mr. Corrigan said. It seemed that Mr. Corrigan had made his parents a promise of some kind. Whatever he was offering, it seemed to be something they couldn't afford and couldn't go on without.

The Books of Knowledge. The salesman had unwedged a volume from the carton at his feet and let it fall open to a section of plastic overlays, the skeleton, the arteries, the organs, letting each clear plastic page float down, one after the other, to build a man from the inside out. The last page fell over the blood and guts, a quiet covering of beige skin. The man in the illustration was bald, his chin set, his head in profile, his arms held out on both sides.

Hearn holding out his arms to everyone in the baseball field, a natural orator, commanding, We all saw it. Didn't we? I saw it, and you saw it.

Jennifer Baker sauntered over to Slaney. The game was breaking up. The heat was too much and the tension. There wasn't a cloud, her hips, the terry cloth halter top.

You can trust me, Jennifer said. She was close enough to his face that he could smell the candy she was sucking, he could hear it clicking in her teeth when she moved it from one cheek to the other. A green barrel candy. Everything collapsed. The lie collapsed. Her face had a sheen of moisture, and a flush from the sun, or exertion, and her dark sweaty hair, and she was suddenly very close to him. He could feel her breath on his cheek and how conspiratorial.

How exclusive their discussion was. The attention was a kind of ravishment. She had been looking at the ground, all the way across the field. He saw her coming. And then she was so near. Her eyes.

She dug one end of the baseball bat into the ground and she was leaning on it. Her teeth and the mint scent from the barrel candy she held between her teeth for a moment, before drawing it back, the icy green of her breath, and her lips and her eyes; it broke him. So close to him and the word: *trust*. He had believed. Had she whispered? He thought she had.

The encyclopedia guy snapped the outstretched book closed. They would have to pay for the Books of Knowledge.

You can tell me, Jennifer said, I won't tell them. Just between us. So, did you make it to the base or not?

His mother stirred in the chair. The sound of her nylons, a shushing, as she shifted in the chair and it creaked.

No.

You didn't?

No. I didn't make it to the base.

Bill tagged you first?

Bill tagged me first.

Before you got to the base. Between us, okay? Just, I'm curious, he tagged you before you got to the base?

Yes.

Slaney's mother wanted the Books of Knowledge. His father flipped the light. A lamp on the side table. The guy's tie, the silver stripes of it, some kind of metallic fabric, leapt up.

He cheated, screamed Jennifer Baker. Maybe he fell in love with her then: the vehemence. The truth. He had been found out. What a relief. The lie fell away. Everybody stopped in the field and turned to look.

He cheated, he admitted it; he just admitted it. He told me himself.

Graveyard

Slaney took the last bus to a town called Hudson that he heard was mostly anglophone and it was a warm night so he slept under some trees on a park bench. In the morning he walked to the nearest graveyard with his suitcase and the doll under his arm. The bag of money hung by a strap over his shoulder. He saw the same grey angel, skin-pocked and sightless, on three different graves, a forefinger raised as if to get him to stay quiet.

A bright blue tarp hung over an open grave and a yellow backhoe tilted on a hill of fresh topsoil.

Slaney was looking for a man born in 1950 or so, somebody more or less his age. The trees were black against the lightening sky and there were gravestones as far as he could see.

After he had walked for a while Slaney could no longer see the street. He stopped at a grave with a bouquet of yellow plastic roses. The petals were sun-faded and the stems jammed into a milk bottle with the bottom smashed out of it.

Douglas Walker Knight had been the beloved son of Mary and James Knight. It was hoped he would find Solace in Heaven with the Lord. The white marble was without ornamentation except for a carved wreath and two hands holding a chalice. Douglas Walker Knight was born in 1951 and had died in 1973.

Slaney stood the doll up on the marble ledge of the grave and took a joint from the back pocket of his jeans. It was the last of the stash the girl in New Brunswick had given him for his birthday. He opened his jacket and felt for a book of matches.

He struck a match and the burnt phosphorous hurt some nerve in the back of his nose. He lit the joint, hunching one shoulder over it. He inhaled deeply and held the smoke down in his lungs and then sighed.

It was a different kind of heat away from the ocean. It was hot very early and kept getting hotter. He took a pen and notebook out of his shirt pocket and wrote down the name and the date of Douglas Walker Knight's birth. Then he flipped the notebook closed.

He glanced over the graveyard and thought about Doug Knight growing up in Hudson, Quebec. Slaney wondered how Knight had died.

Doug Knight, he said. He spoke out loud. He cleared his throat. Doug. Douglas. He said it in a conversational tone, then he said it a little softer than that. Hey, Doug. Doug, over here. Jesus, Doug.

Slaney felt all the meaning uncleave from the word. The sacrilege of what he was doing. He was messing with something

larger than himself. He tried to let the name be just a sound.
Then all the meaning busted back.

This was a dead man. A man his own age who had died
before he had a chance to do the things Slaney was going
to do.

A dark blot, a rodent of some kind, moved liquidly over the
ground in Slaney's peripheral vision. The small body slipped
soundlessly over root and stone, then it shot up a tree, disappearing in the branches. The rodent was an embodiment of
some underworld demon, wet and red-eyed.

It was a weasel or sewer rat, moving through the transub-
stantiating dawn.

Then Slaney saw a set of bright green footprints in the dewy
grey grass behind him and his heart leapt, thinking he had
been followed. It was the dope; it took a second to recognize
that the footprints were his own.

He was going to go by the name of another man; and he had
caught up with himself, passed through himself.

Already the sky was much brighter. There was clarity of
purpose from smoking weed and the other Doug Knight no
longer existed. Slaney was Doug Knight now.

A shiver ran through him.

Somebody walking over his grave, his mother would have
said.

Somebody had said they had no respect for the law. A judge
said, back in '74, that they had exhibited no remorse. The same
judge argued that if they were not punished he had every reason to believe they would do exactly the same thing again.

Hearn said, Yes, sir, we'd do it again, all but the getting
caught.

It was just business. Back in '74 they had been cutting out

the middleman and nothing in their past allowed for that kind of audacity.

They were stoned the whole time they were in Colombia, laughing in cafés and on the beaches; they slept outside, a small bonfire, the stars.

Once a knife to the throat, an unlit alley outside a bar with the maracas and drums, those flutes they have, a punch to the kidneys that knocked Slaney's soul up in his throat. The point of a rusty blade digging into the cartilage or whatever that is, his windpipe. Roughed up and bleeding. Face down in the gutter. But Slaney came to and patted himself all over, looking for wounds. He was unharmed.

Wahoo.

They'd been arrested when they got back to Newfoundland and the local papers had said *Adventure on the High Seas*. They were folk, it turned out. The university had just begun to offer courses in folklore and Newfoundlanders were their own subjects, their music and dances, the way they courted and the way they constructed their flakes for drying fish, and Slaney and Hearn were modern-day folk heroes.

Meanwhile, the real folk, the simple fishermen of Capelin Cove, had turned them in.

The law was a folktale that changed every time it was told.

Slaney and Hearn had been altar boys together and knew every Latin word of the mass. The priest did not face the congregation because of a certain disdain the church felt for the people in the pews. The boys knew the moment when Christ entered the wafer of bread. It was held up by the priest, both arms raised, and one of the boys rang the brass bells.

Their gowns, red and white, were made of polyester and the hems whispered around the cuffs of their jeans. Their faces were spit-cleaned by their mothers on the steps of the rectory.

They walked down the aisle with the giant candle at Easter, careful to keep the flame lit. The light from the flame seeped a third of the way down the thick, white cylinder of wax encrusted with golden swirls and made it glow from within.

Everything was from within back then, Slaney thought. Every thought was within and unspoken, every rule was within, and the meaning of everything hid inside a wooden chair or a crocheted doily.

The candle was the Holy Ghost.

The Holy Ghost was a kind of middleman. Everything itself and something else at the same time.

They'd gone to school dances to sell pot and sometimes they were beaten up. Sometimes they were short on cash and someone would be waiting with a two-by-four.

Then they enrolled at Memorial University and sold dope in the Chem café and in the tunnels and Slaney did history and Hearn was doing E. M. Forster and D. H. Lawrence and Greek tragedy. He was reading Descartes.

Take a piece of wax, Hearn said. How do we know it's a piece of wax?

Christ, Slaney said. Pass the joint.

It's got texture and it smells like wax and it's hard. But what happens when we hold it to the fire?

We?

It loses those properties.

That's ivory tower shit. We're reading Marx over in history. Class struggle and empire, colonialism, and you want to talk about how we know what we know. That's a slippery ball of wax, my friend. Pass the joint.

Before the trip, Hearn had been involved with a Newfoundland theatre troupe that did Shakespeare. Hearn had wanted to play Iago but they'd given the part to someone else.

They said I'm too good-looking for Iago.

They said that?

They got Gord Horan.

And you think Horan's not right for the part, Slaney said.

He fails to convince.

He's not the actor you are.

Slaney, please.

But you're too good-looking.

They mentioned my strong facial features.

Iago is poor-looking? Where does it say that?

Gord Horan's face is funny.

He always looked okay to me, Gord Horan?

His chin.

I always thought Horan looked okay.

A weak chin, Slaney.

You're tormented by your good looks.

Maybe Hamlet, they said.

Hamlet is hard on the ladies. Self-absorbed.

Hamlet is a prince, Slane. Goddamn prince.

A flock of birds lifted all at once and flew in a fast dark ball over the angel on the gravestone, some scattering behind in a trail. Then the ball came apart and spread wide, the mass turning inside out, spilling across the grey sky and a greasy sun.

Slaney's footprints in the grass had startled the shit out of him. It struck him as funny but he would not be able to explain the humour.

If he tried to explain, it would become unfunny. Things could go flat. He was very stoned now and the footprints looked canny and deliberate. He was following himself, just slightly out of sync with the present. There was a lag.

Or it was the ghost of the dead man he was about to become.

The birds drew together again and the dark ball dive-bombed the tree and the branches trembled and filled up with birds.

He tucked the doll under his arm and he picked up the blue suitcase and left the graveyard. Slaney rode the bus back into town and went to a photography studio to get a passport photo.

Slaney's passport would have the name Douglas Walker Knight. He had jotted down the address of a local medical clinic and scrawled one of the doctor's names as a guarantor. But it was Slaney's picture. It would be Slaney's shorn black hair, already starting to grow out of its prison regulation cut, and Slaney's blue eyes.

In the photograph his eyes were large and his mouth was full and the passport would state he was six feet and one hundred and fifty pounds. It would say he was twenty-seven years old.

Slaney found a phone booth and started in with the Knights in the Montreal phonebook that hung from a steel cable under the phone. There were a page and a half. He called all the James Knights and the J. Knights and finally a woman answered who said her name was Mary Knight.

Slaney said he was calling from Revenue Canada and there were a few things with her file he'd like to go over with her if she had a moment.

My husband does all that, she said.

Just a few questions, Slaney said. You are obligated by law to answer, Mrs. Knight.

Oh, yes, she said. I'm just not sure.

I'll ask a few security questions, he said. Slaney went through it quickly; could she provide her date of birth and her correct mailing address. Marital status. What was her maiden name? The names of her dependants.

He hadn't expected the catch in her voice. He hadn't thought it through. He suffered a slow-breaking understanding of the consequences. The catch, a small intake of breath; how she breathed out. Slaney felt like he'd punched her. Why hadn't he thought? He should not have called her. What had he done? He wanted to hang up but he couldn't hang up now. He had to let her go through it.

We had a son, she said. An only child. She said her son had passed away.

Slaney told her he was very sorry. Now that he looked at it, he said, her file seemed fine.

You couldn't hope to meet a finer young man, she said. Everybody loved him. He was good at sports, he had high marks, he was thinking about going into medicine. His girl-friend was lovely. I don't only say this because I'm his mother. Anybody who knew him thought the same thing. A car accident took him.

Anyway, she said. No dependants.

Slaney said somebody had queried but he could see they were all wrong to question her file. He said it was a random check. He told her he was sorry for bothering her.

That's okay, she said. I wasn't doing anything. You have a job to do.

Thank you, he said. And he said goodbye. He went to a café and ordered a steak and fries and filled in the forms while he waited for his order. Slaney mailed the forms and returned

to the city on the afternoon bus. He took a bed in a boarding house under the name of Knight and settled in for a week.

Four days later Douglas Knight's birth certificate arrived in
the mail at the boarding house.

He took the bus to a motor vehicle registration office and
showed them the birth certificate and got himself a copy of
Douglas Knight's driver's licence. These documents were sent
to the passport office and he took off for the cabin Hearn had
arranged in Mansonville.

Cyclops

Skills

After four weeks and five days at the Mansonville cabin Slaney's new passport was ready. He went to the office and picked it up, along with the driver's licence and the birth certificate he'd mailed in, and then headed to the train station and bought a ticket.

The formality of the photography studio and the blast of the flashbulb had rendered an unfamiliar look in his passport photo. It was an odd angle. Something, perhaps the false name, made Slaney feel like he was not himself.

The large white umbrella in the studio had been set up to bounce light and there was the need to be unsmiling. There was a look of bafflement.

Bafflement is a precursor to wisdom, was what the picture made him think. The picture looked like someone who would have to wise up. They were embarking on the next adventure. They were going to be rich. Look out, world. The guy in the photograph was him and was not him.

The picture said, Look out.

Or it said: Bon voyage.

Slaney was leafing through a newspaper in the Montreal train station and he came across the obituaries. He never read the obits, but her name popped. Rowena Spracklin.

The start he got. What a start. He could not connect the name to the idea of her being gone. He went cold all over. They'd had a session on his last day in prison. More than a month ago now.

He'd gone to their last session and he didn't say anything about the break. He didn't hint. Now he read she had a sister in the States and there was mention of her dog and he started at the beginning and he read the whole thing again. They mentioned about her job.

Slaney thought about the four years of work they had done together. She called it their work.

Break a man and reconstitute him. That was the work.

They had completed the breaking part of the procedure, as far as she was concerned. But he had news: he was not broken.

Slaney had wrapped a splinter of himself in a kryptonite handkerchief that she couldn't penetrate with her superhuman flames or X-ray vision. He'd dipped that part of himself in dragon's blood. Nobody could touch it.

She had close-clipped grey hair and her floral blouse was purple and mauve and yellow. She had a blouse that was striped. She had five different blouses. He had caught glimpses of a shiny bra, grey with washing, frayed. She wasn't fat, but solidly built, and her hands were large.

There was a tiny lucent skin tag on her cheek.

These little things registered with him without his realizing it.

Her eyes were dark brown and they turned hazel when she looked out the window. The light brought out flecks of amber.

You got a view, he said. The first time they met.

Nice view.

She told him to make himself comfortable and he sat down with his legs sprawled. He'd made a parody of being comfortable with the lady psychotherapist in the prison setting, sprawling all over her chair.

Then he sat up straight, one knee jiggling. The window was tinted the brown of a photographic negative and it made everything outside ashen and nostalgic. There was a duck pond, a giant white fire of sparks in a black field. You looked out her window and you thought the world had been bleached. A monochrome of bone and soot. The ducks moved together, a single black stain spreading over the white surface.

I'm not big on talking, he said. Beyond the duck pond, the chain-link fence with spirals of barbed wire at the top. She raised an eyebrow and waited.

Pot is good for you, he said.

She had a grin/grimace. Sometimes he couldn't tell if she was pleased or disappointed. It was a mask and he learned after a few months that she was often in pain.

Ms. Spracklin always looked as if what she said ran through her from somewhere else. She clutched the arm of her chair with a strong, liver-spotted hand and the talk was drawn out of the wooden armrest, up through her hand to her heart.

She had very personal queries and she eased the truth out of him. He came to know himself as the subject of her questions. Gradually, over the four years of his incarceration, he began to talk.

Slaney spoke about Jennifer and the little girl. He put both his hands over his face.

Take your time, Ms. Spracklin said. Slaney told her that

Jennifer hadn't answered his letters. He didn't know where she was.

Just take your time. But he didn't say anything else. And that particular session was over.

Ms. Spracklin was figuring out how he had gone wrong, she told him. They were paying lip service to the idea of a wrong path and what happens when you travel it. She spoke about metaphorical journeys. She thought of punishment as a gift.

You can't surprise me, Ms. Spracklin said. I've heard everything. Nothing you say will shock.

He didn't mention names and she didn't ask. There were things that were out of bounds.

How did you feel when he jumped bail? But she didn't expect an answer. She used the word *accomplice*.

Friend, he said.

Your friend?

My friend.

How did you feel knowing your friend was free and you were not?

Silence was her surgical tool and she was trying to excise the innermost thing.

He found he didn't want to bore her. She'd called him a natural storyteller. He loved to make her smile. If he could get her to laugh it made his day.

Listen, she said. There are forks in the road.

She was there to break him, but what if they had a few laughs along the way. They could both become stubborn and inert. Silence was the best tool for crushing him. Silence was the heavy equipment.

He forgot, sometimes, how dangerous she was. But he also understood the ways in which she could be trusted.

Ms. Spracklin would never betray a confidence; he was certain of that. Their conversations were locked up inside her, had not been committed to paper, though she took notes.

He had to be careful of what he said because she would be stuck with it long after he was gone. In that way she was tender. She wanted him gone.

Ten years from now, she said. She saw a path in the woods with birds flitting overhead.

I've lost the long-term view, he said. She licked her thumb and flicked through some papers and gathered them loosely and knocked the edge of the pile against the oak desk. A test that would discern what kind of work he should pursue when he was released.

It came up with dental hygienist. She was perplexed and then it made her giggle. A seizure of silent hiccuping laughter overcame her, a gulping for air. Tears came to the corners of her eyes. Finally she managed to wheeze out the words, *Dental hygienist.* Dental hygienist. He didn't see what was so fucking funny.

I'm sorry, she said. Phew. Oh my.

He folded the newspaper along the edge of her obit and tore it as gently as he could along each fold. She'd had a photograph on her desk of a yellow Labrador retriever and they'd talked about the dog. He remembered the skin tag on her cheek, her stockings.

He began to recognize when she was overcome with weakness. Whatever was wrong with her floated down over her face, a folding inward, and her concentration fled.

Do you have a first name? Slaney asked. This was after two years of sessions, once a week, an hour each. Do you have a first name?

He had not been broken.

The times when she would go absolutely silent he'd feel a great urge to fill the void.

He'd want to tell a story the way you'd gasp for breath if you were held underwater.

She said her name was Rowena. She put up her hand to stop him and shut her eyes against the onslaught of mockery she expected.

I will not put up with jokes about my name, she said. She blushed and it had been the only time she looked feminine. She was old enough to be his mother and that made her dangerous.

She asked his strengths and weaknesses, his skills.

Are you a good listener?

He didn't answer.

I'm listening, he said. He said he believed he could be a good lover with the right person. She sat back and folded her arms.

Don't bother, she said. You cannot shock me.

She was a former nun, he knew, because of her stockings. The stockings were waxy-looking, like sausage skin. He thought she suffered from chronic pain or insomnia. Something was killing her. He figured that out.

I always see the person, he said. This is what he told her. He didn't make judgements: ugly, fat, short, stupid, sick. He saw dignity, for lack of a better word.

He had to lean forward to explain this to Rowena Spracklin. He had decided, out of boredom, or some belief in a connection, a spark of human decency they both had, a spontaneous and breaching love that wasn't sexual or filial or romantic or anything he could put a name on, that he would tell her the truth about himself.

What happened then? she kept asking. She didn't care about feelings. They were transitory and unremarkable.

Action mattered to her. She was interested in his character and how it had been shaped through the things he had done.

He said that he knew how to look at people so they could be who they were, which basically meant he had a capacity for trust. He thought of trust, when he spoke to her, as a vestigial organ, near his liver, swollen, threatening to burst. Maybe it would poison him. But it was also his special skill. His strength.

Slaney had a way of holding his body, a gesture or look that said, Tell me.

And people told him.

Yes, he was a good listener.

There was a clot or some gathering of alien matter working through her veins toward her brain and the stockings slowed its travel.

What do you believe? she asked.

He wanted to tell her he had seen glimpses of dignity in everyone. He didn't believe in self-denial. He thought there was nothing redemptive about guilt. He thought incarceration was the wrong thing to do to a human being. It could only warp and deform. He believed in figuring out the limits and then going further than that.

She was good at her job but it was the wrong job. He thought she would have done well importing weed. He told her that. She had the same skills he had; they were matched.

The clot had worked its way through and it had killed her.

He folded the obituary and put it in the pocket of his shirt and stood at the edge of the train platform with his hand on the pocket.

She had developed a technology of now you are not the man you were before.

He hadn't looked down on her, though she was trying with all her might to smash him to bits. She was looking for the button that would blow him sky high, but she couldn't get at it.

He once told her he would do it again if he got the chance.

I'm shocked, she'd said.

I see the whole picture, he said. But what he meant was they had not broken him. They could forget about breaking him. He didn't judge people. That was what he had that they didn't have.

There's something I'd like to ask, she said. What makes you believe you wouldn't get caught again?

Her earnestness nearly broke him. She was so sincere it almost made him doubt. He would have told her he believed and that was all there was to it.

Believing is believing is believing is believing.

There's no reason to it. It just is, he would have told her that. But they had run out of time.

The Satellite

They had the eye of God. The world was wrapped with an eye. A glance lay over it now and forever.

Patterson looked at the giant screen in the front of the room and he saw nothing was impossible. They could follow movement all over the surface of the globe.

There was a smattering of applause as it dawned on the little audience, the thirty-eight RCMP officers and undercover agents and bureaucrats who'd gathered for the unveiling.

It turned out that the technology had always existed but lay in wait, wearing a camouflage of the not-yet-invented. That was what they were discovering in that high-rise office in Vancouver on July 2, 1978.

It had rained the night before and the asphalt was a black satin ribbon between the sidewalks below and the buildings were reflecting cloud and window flash when the sun came out. There were splotches of lime green and dark green and blue green covering the city.

It was the day that the yacht was scheduled to leave for Mexico.

Fine sailing weather, O'Neill said, standing at the window with his back to the room, hands on his hips.

It's just a sophisticated tracking device, Patterson told himself. But he couldn't help feeling proud. State-of-the-art technology; they were witnessing a leap.

A dish, an eye, a cyborg or Cyclops, and perhaps Patterson was the only man in the room old enough, besides O'Neill, to wonder about the hubris.

He'd gone to a party at Hearn's and drunk until five in the morning and smoked up with the boys. Hearn was going by the alias John Barlow. Even his girlfriend called him John.

Hearn had put on an evening in Patterson's honour. They'd tucked linen napkins into their shirt collars and there were a couple of hammers in the centre of the table.

Deep-fried cod tongues, lobster, scalloped potatoes. They smashed the shells and the lobsters squirted up at them and leaked.

There was talk about Saigon and Shakespeare, Jimmy Carter and Patty Hearst. Hearn was doing a Ph.D. in modern literature.

Joyce, Woolf, Lawrence, Elizabeth Bowen, Hemingway and Faulkner.

The girlfriend never took her big brown eyes off Hearn. She made Patterson so afraid for his own daughter he had to grip the edge of the table.

Two young guys from Newfoundland who were part of the crew for the Vancouver-to-Mexico leg of the journey. They were deckhands who would fly back.

The sailboat's owner — Cyril Carter, also from Newfoundland — sat at the head of the table and the young girl named Ada who had run off with him. She had long fair hair and her eyes were large and sooty with eyeliner and mascara. But the colour: one of her eyes was blue and the other green and the whites showed at the bottom of the iris. Carter had left his wife and children for the girl and he kept her hand locked under his arm most of the night. She looked like a teenager.

Carter drank steadily and became more prudent with each drink. His eyes became gleaming slits and he hardly moved except to nudge his glass forward with a finger when it was empty.

The girl was quick to fill it for him. She poured to the rim.

They'd brought out the instruments after midnight. They played Dylan and Cohen and Pentangle and Hearn's girl took the guitar from him and sang about times getting rough and hard and she looked up at her boyfriend and spoke the line: Why don't you lay me down in the long grass and let me do my stuff. Patterson had to look away.

Hearn took the guitar back and sang an Irish folk song about a love lost at sea.

They got maudlin and bellowed out the chorus, nasal and

off-key, like their lives depended on being honest when they sang. Hearn sitting on the straight-backed wooden chair: Let Me Fish Off Cape St. Mary's.

His foot going. He finished with tears in his eyes, though Patterson was pretty sure the kid hadn't fished off Cape St. Mary's or anywhere else except maybe off the side of a luxury yacht.

At dawn, when the sun was rising, the young girl, Ada, wandered over to the piano in the corner and lifted the lid.

She slid across the bench and touched the keys without making any sound at all. Then she began to tinkle out a little melody and her backbone became straighter and she was frozen and alert. A tangerine light was creeping across the varnished hardwood floor and up her back. It lit up her blond hair and burned across the white shoulders of her peasant blouse.

Patterson had never heard a piano played that way. She was violent with it, as if there was something inside the wood and strings that she had to rescue or exorcise.

It was not what Patterson thought of as music. He didn't know what it was. Her body jerked like she completed a circuit of high-voltage power; she was welded to it, couldn't lift her fingers away from the keys, the way a person being electrocuted can't let go of a live wire.

And when she stopped she was flushed and tigerish-looking.

Or maybe she was just stoned. Or he was just stoned. They had been smoking and drinking for hours. Maybe they had put something in his drink. He thought acid, maybe. He felt ravaged and elated. Whatever he experienced while she was playing, he doubted it as soon as it stopped.

Patterson thought she was going to expose him. That she knew everything. He half expected her to take off her clothes or set something on fire.

What the hell was that, Hearn said. His girlfriend got up from the table with a load of plates and let them clatter into the kitchen sink.

That was the piano, Hearn's girlfriend said.

Ada swung her legs over the piano stool and sauntered across the room with the filmy scarf she'd worn around her neck in her hand, trailing it on the backs of the furniture. She dropped the scarf over Carter's drunken face, a face set like marble, inert and puffy and desolate, and put her fingers on top of his bald pate.

Whatever had poured out of her fingers into the piano might pulse through the man's skull and fry him on the spot, Patterson thought.

She flexed her fingers in a kind of gentle massage, the chiffon scarf wrinkling up, swishing over Carter's nose and ears.

The girl told Carter it was time for bed. The sun had lost all of the orange flare by the time Patterson left the dinner party.

The next day he'd gone back with a terrific hangover and a briefcase. He handed Hearn twenty thousand dollars and Hearn gave him a tour of the boat, sixty feet, a big fishing rig in the back, mahogany and polish, a false floor under which they were going to store the cargo. The boat must have cost a fortune, even purchased, as it had been, in a foreclosure sale.

The satellite tracking system was installed that night by a couple of scuba divers, attached to the hull under Patterson's instruction.

But Patterson hadn't known the nature of the device they'd planted on the sailboat until now.

He knew, of course; it had been carefully explained. He'd read the dossier with its space-age jargon, the self-congratulatory bolstering. A military-led innovation, a dish in outer space that bounced signals, gave them a bead on anything that moved. But he hadn't understood the nature of it.

They could trace the boat as it travelled down the coast. They would know exactly where the boys were at least three times a day. They would know when they'd collected the cargo, when they were heading back, when they entered Canadian waters.

It was imperative they make it back to Canadian waters.

The boys would be arrested in Canada.

O'Neill stood at a podium waiting for the room to fall quiet. He was going to give a speech with the snow of the screen playing over him, an electrified tweed of hiss, a knit of static and spark, glitch and random flicker.

The technicians in the booth were connecting cables, hitting switches. A feed of light and dark spewed over O'Neill's face and hands.

He was thanking the scientist they had in from Ottawa to explain the technology, he was thanking the minister of defence, who wasn't present, of course, and he was thanking Patterson for his hard work and dedication.

He told how Patterson was the guiding force behind the operation. How it was Patterson's baby. There was applause and the guy next to Patterson clapped him on the shoulder.

O'Neill said that the RCMP in every province had been advised of the sting operation and they were behaving in accordance with the wishes of the Vancouver detachment. Mexico was on alert. Colombia was on alert. San Diego knew to keep an eye.

He made a joke about Patterson having to imbibe substances, both legal and illegal, while working undercover and how it must have been a hardship.

He said, Sometimes the job requires going the extra mile. Everyone chuckled.

We're lucky to have him, O'Neill said. He glanced up from his papers then and took off his glasses and tucked them inside his suit jacket. He looked out at the audience for a moment.

We're going to throw the book at these kids, he said. They won't know what hit them.

O'Neill sat down and they all watched the screen. The new technology gave them the exact co-ordinates. It gave them a picture.

It took the sport out of it, Patterson thought. There was a pornographic element, the way they could watch without a break in the flow of time.

They looked on in silence, now, and they felt the hair on their arms stand up, the way you're meant to feel in the presence of the supernatural.

Watching made them feel watched.

They knew they were next.

Everybody on earth was next. Perhaps they had always been watched. But now someone owned the eye.

They owned it.

This was the kind of eye: there was nothing to hide behind.

Patterson could not look away. He was glued. In the snow on the screen the yacht was a hard blur, a pulsing light on a grid. The yacht the boys would be taking to Colombia.

He had to admit a fondness. Hearn was well spoken and he had good manners. The kid thought the world of David Slaney; that much was clear.

Hearn believed one of them had to be on land waiting for the shipment. And it had to be Hearn because Slaney was too visible after the escape. Getting him out of the country would take off some of the heat. Hearn had worked hard, over the last four years, to establish his cover. He was serious about his studies; he seemed to be in love with his girl. Maybe he felt he owed Slaney the trip. The money would give David Slaney a fighting chance on the outside.

Hearn seemed to believe that working together, but from opposite ends of the trip, he and Slaney were invincible.

Is this unfolding? somebody said, pointing at the screen. The yacht was moving.

This is instantaneous, the scientist said. This is there's no delay. It's coming straight at you.

Somebody asked, It drops out of the heavens?

It's bounced, the scientist said. The pictures are coming from outer space.

But there's a delay, someone said. A woman. They had one woman on the team and she was at the back of the room. She was the one who said a delay. Because how could there be a picture without a delay, a picture bounced more than a thousand miles?

No delay, the scientist said.

It's moving, all right, somebody said. Patterson looked at his watch.

They're heading to Mexico, he said. Slaney's going to fly down and meet them six weeks from now, then it's on to Colombia.

Patterson didn't say about losing Slaney in Montreal. He didn't say the whole thing might blow up in their faces if Slaney didn't show. There had been no sign of him once he'd checked out of the room they'd bugged. Hearn wouldn't go on without him. Patterson was sure of that. Where was he this time?

We've got them, O'Neill said. He raised his fist in victory.

Bon voyage, somebody said.

You're the One That I Want

Slaney gave the porter his ticket, found his seat, and set the doll up in the empty one next to him. He nudged the pink box a little until the doll's eyelids dropped shut. Then he felt Montreal tug at itself, the *clack* of the rail ties, the slow, wrenching slide of smokestacks and concrete and sun-struck facades, a smooth emulsion streaming behind. He thought of her. Or she was just there. He was full of her. She was ultra-present, right there with him. Near him, or inside him.

Jennifer brayed like a donkey when something was funny. An honest to God donkey. She'd cross her legs to stop from peeing in her pants and beg him to shut up, holding one hand out. The laugh rocked her whole body and it was animal and mannish.

She'd felt ashamed about being on welfare. Her family had money. She had grown up with a charwoman but there was no trace of snobbery in her, except for the shame she felt cashing the welfare cheque.

She had a tab at the convenience store and she would go in and get smokes and bags of chips and wait, holding up the line, while the woman behind the counter wrote it all down. They conferred in quiet tones. They were like people in church when this transaction occurred, solemn and reverent about the vertiginous debt.

She smoked on the fire escape, sometimes, to watch the sun go down. If he had to pick a moment, it was her shoulders bent over a sewing machine with the smoke going in the ashtray.

Everything dropped away after she had cooked a meal and was having her evening smoke. She was five-foot-seven and bony and boyish. There was hardly anything to her. Her hair was long and thick and she coloured it a honey blond and her eyes were big and arresting. They narrowed and looked to the side when she had a problem to solve. When she was hurt or afraid she broke into a slow smile.

She made him butter her toast. Do things for me. That was the way she felt about him. Do things for me. She burnt everything she cooked. She had tried university and flunked out.

But she was full of patience for the child. The kid made her dopey with love. She had a way of being undiluted and present with Crystal; everything she was, she handed over to the kid.

Men fell in love with her and he watched her let them down easy. He watched as she gently, firmly destroyed several different men, and he was to remain unsuspecting about his own fate until she said: How do I put this.

She was funny. She did that thing of wrapping her arms around herself and turning her back on you, making kissing noises, and you could watch her hands groping at her own shoulder blades and waist with faux-passion. It was a raunchy parody and she'd glance back over her shoulder and ask if he were jealous.

She mimed a glass box, and the look on her face. She faked a fear of being trapped in the walls of glass that was pretty convincing.

Once he'd come home and she was in the oversized corduroy armchair with lumps of stuffing and exposed springs and she was crying over a book. The whole room was dark except for this light they had. A pole with five different lamps, each bubbled glass shade a different colour. Orange, blue, red, pink. He couldn't remember what book.

But he remembered her blinking him into existence. Looking up from the book and blinking her wet eyelashes, touching the corners of her eyes with the side of her hand and the blue light on her cheek, blinking until she was out of the sad book and present with him in the hole of an apartment they shared. And it occurred to him that he only really felt like someone, like a whole being, when she was calling him to account.

She was please and thank you and outrageously selfish, except for the child.

Could you put butter on that? Not even looking up from the book. Ordering him around.

She was the only person he knew who ate real butter.

Slaney got off the train in Ottawa. He went into the airy station, all glass and girders and pigeons, and he looked up Fred Decker in the phone book, the guy she'd married, and he found the address. He was going to ask her to wait for him until he got back from the trip.

Slaney caught her hand just before it struck his face. That was in the hall when she opened the front door.

Crystal said, Who is it, Mommy? She was all changed, Jennifer's little girl, she was so tall. The serious eyes and the pout. He squatted and held out the box with the doll. She hid her face, digging her forehead into her mother's thigh.

I'm a friend of your mother's, Slaney said.

Go ahead, honey, Jennifer said. Crystal had stepped out and taken the box in her hands and yelled suddenly, Guess what I got. Another one.

Jennifer let him in the apartment because of the neighbours.

I don't need them mentioning this up and down the whole building, she said. There were two children having a tea party in the living room with Crystal. They were trying to get the new doll out of the cardboard box.

Slaney and Jennifer stood in the middle of the room because sitting down didn't seem the right thing to do. She had her hand pressed to the side of her face. She was looking at the floor and she was rigid as a stone.

He told her he'd wanted to give her things, to build a life.

Don't pin this on me, she said. Don't you dare. He told her he was sorry.

Did you get my letters? he said.

Yes, I got them.

And you didn't answer?

Social Services came by, she said. They had questions, David, about was I a fit mother with a drug smuggler hanging around. They interviewed Crystal without my permission. Took her down to the department for the afternoon. Imagine what that was like.

She said she could have lost Crystal to foster care. Had he thought about that? Then she told him she wanted him to leave.

We could have been a family, she said.

He asked her to forgive him.

Are you kidding me, she said. Why did you come here? I'm married now, David. I have a husband. That means something. Not a guy who's going to take off on me. Not a guy who would abandon. A man, David. A good man who is honest with me.

Do you love him? Yes. Do you love him? Yes. Do you love him? Yes. Do you, Jennifer? Do you love him? I don't love him, no.

We are meant to be together, Jennifer, Slaney said. You know it. She spoke slowly then, almost stuttering. A quiet, deliberate tone that didn't belong to her.

If you walk away from this, David, I will pack a bag. We can leave. I mean it. Tell me you'll walk away from that racket and I'll go with you right now. No looking back. Crystal and I will take a few things and get the hell out of here. If you walk away from it. Do you hear me? Say the word. David, just say the word. We'll come with you right now. Start a new life together.

He took her hand away from her face and led her down the hall away from the children. He tried a door but it was a bedroom and he tried another and it was the bathroom and the last room was a laundry room and he took her in there and shut the door and lifted her up onto the washer which was going and they were on each other and he was inside her and the washer was rattling and rocking and it was not sexy it was fast and they were both crying right through it and it changed him the way no other sex had ever changed him and she said, Don't get caught. That's all. She was smoothing his hair out of his eyes.

Don't get caught, she whispered. Then she was tugging up her jeans and pulling her ponytail tight with a vicious tug and she was crying a little and wiping her eyes. He said he wouldn't get caught again and he was coming back for her. He didn't care about her husband. He only cared about her and Crystal and he'd be back.

She said, How do I put this, David. I really loved you. I did. But I don't want to see you again.

And he saw she meant it.

Audio, Girlfriend

Slaney was in love; Patterson could tell that. This was some kind of monumental love but it was already in ruins. Or maybe it wasn't in ruins. Patterson forgot himself as he listened. The big padded earphones. They'd bugged the apartment.

The girlfriend had married somebody.

Do you love him? Patterson hit pause and let that sink in. He rewound and listened to her say it again: I'm married. I got married. I married a guy. Four years you were gone.

You knew I was on my way, Slaney said.

You lied to me, Dave. She didn't curse or sound angry or cry.

Patterson hit pause. He thought of his own daughter. His own daughter had disappeared with a boy. They hadn't heard from her. He hit play. And he hit pause. He had to take the tape in small doses. Every second of the audio uncovered a mystery and a revelation.

Do you love him? Yes. Do you love him? Yes. You love him, do you? It's none of your business, David. Not anymore.

Do you love him? Yes.

The little girl was saying she wanted cookies. We're hungry. Mommy, we're hungry.

She's so big, he said. She grew. How do you like your doll?

I already got one just like it, the girl said.

You missed a lot, the girlfriend said.

The whole thing was unfolding with the children in the room. The little girl had a couple of friends over and he could hear them wrestle the new doll out of the cardboard box and they were excited and Slaney was saying she could walk.

And the girlfriend said, *You* could walk, David. And she

started to beg him to walk away and Patterson hit pause. And he hit play.

If you love me, David. You will walk away from this now. Patterson was rapt. She asked Slaney to consider what she'd been through. She talked about the lying, over and over. She said about waving goodbye.

There I was on the sidewalk, she said. I believed you. I thought you were going to send for us to come to Alberta. Christ, what a fool. I lay awake at night.

Why were you lying awake, Mrs. Decker? That was one of the little kids visiting the daughter.

Play with your doll, girls, she said. Don't pay any attention to us. This is just adult talk.

But you're married, Slaney said. You got married.

I'll pack a bag right now, she said. If you promise you won't go back there. We could leave here tonight.

Patterson hit pause. He could not listen. He put his hand over his eyes and rubbed his whole face vigorously. He growled. He started to pace but he was attached to the reel-to-reel by the earphones and they were yanked off his head and slid over the tiles.

Patterson sank back down in the chair. He retrieved the headphones. He'd been called in to the Vancouver office to listen to the tape. Patterson had been waiting for Slaney to resurface and Slaney had gone to visit the ex-girlfriend. Even Hearn didn't know, Patterson was sure. An unscheduled stop. Now Slaney was keeping things from Hearn. He must have known the dangers of stopping to see the girl. Maybe he was already gone. Maybe the girl had a hold.

He hit play.

She asked Slaney what he was going to do.

Come here, he said.

No, you tell me first, she said. You tell me what you are going to do. Will you walk away?

Jennifer, come here, Slaney said. Then they'd moved it to the laundry room and he couldn't hear over the noise. The washer and dryer were going.

That was the audio. Whatever else they said, Patterson couldn't hear it.

The kid was off course. And she was begging him to walk away. Hearn wouldn't go ahead without Slaney.

Patterson thought of the lobster dinner with Hearn. He'd been surprised to see the books all over the house. Literature. The artful throws on the sofas. The sheepskin rug in front of the fire, a sailboat in a glass bottle on the mantel. Hearn was charismatic and fiercely smart, but he wouldn't do it without David Slaney. Slaney was the raw courage and the will.

Patterson was alone in the office listening to the tape. He didn't have a window. The trip would fall apart if Slaney walked.

Caught

There's a kind of folk wisdom that has developed over the centuries and is passed down from father to son about how to get out of the fog but somehow it had not been passed down to Slaney or Hearn.

This is the story he told in prison after he'd been caught the first time.

They'd been swamped by fog a mile from shore. The boys had dug the caves and they would be waiting for them to help unload. The cargo was under tarps on deck. Dealers lined up all over the island.

Almost home, then the fog.

Drop a long rope and if it floats out straight behind the engine, you're going in a straight line, but if it curves you're going in circles. He would hear this advice much later in prison. How to find your way out of the fog.

As it was, a seagull flapped down on the rail. The gull was the same white as the fog but it was not dreamy like the fog. It was the opposite of a dream.

When Columbus approached Cuba he knew there was land because the water was full of coconuts. The seagull was Slaney's coconut. He thought they weren't more than half a mile offshore.

Slaney heard the trap skiff coming toward him before he saw it. He told Hearn to stay below deck.

The first thing Slaney saw was the dip and swerve of a fluorescent orange toque and then the prow of the skiff, white with green trim, and the engine clacked and chuckled and the boat pulled up alongside.

The pound of the trap skiff was full of fish. A cloud of blue smoke hung over their engine and the men were wearing sweaters and lumber jackets and rubber overalls.

I lost my bearings, Slaney said.

You're lost? the older man said. He sat on the wooden seat. The man's lips puckered tight around his mouth because he had no teeth. His nose hung low and shapeless and pitted. The nostrils full of grey hair and the same thick grey hair grew in his eyebrows, curling upward.

I got all turned around in the fog, Slaney said.

She's some thick, the old man said. I said to young John

here, you can't see a hand in front of you. Didn't I, John?

You can't see a bloody thing, the younger man said. He appeared to be the old man's grandson.

Slaney had time in prison to wonder why the old man had troubled himself to turn them in. He'd come to the conclusion that the man could not remember what it was like to be young.

You didn't know where you were, the old man said.

I thought I knew, Slaney said. He'd glanced behind him, tried to see something through the fog. He'd had a conviction, for perhaps five minutes, that the shore was behind him.

A fish in one of the buckets on the old man's boat wiggled violently. It bent itself double and bent back the other way and threw itself up in the air and landed on the gunwale. It lay there, startled and panting. All three men watched. The fish had flung itself up at least a couple of feet. It must have been dead and come back to life and it landed on the gunwale and was astonished and then it rolled over and fell into the water.

That one got away, the old man said. They could see it between the two boats, lying on its side on top of the lapping water. And then it wriggled and went under. Gone.

Jesus Christ, Slaney said. The younger man rubbed the back of his hand under his nose and stood looking down at the water where the fish had disappeared.

Then he hauled snot back up from his throat and nose and lungs and horked it over the side of the boat. He took off his orange toque and squeezed it in one fist and passed it from hand to hand and put it back on his head, settling the brim with his fingertips. He sat down and bowed his head and leaned forward to lay his hand on the side of the engine.

Every move the men made came back to Slaney in prison.

Some quiet, the older man said. He shook his head as if the quiet were regrettable.

The fish are gone cracked, the grandson said. He waved an arm over the buckets.

That's the fog, makes everything quiet, the old man said. Isn't it quiet? He had taken a cigarette from his breast pocket and he patted his chest and his hips with both his hands.

I'm lost, Slaney said. I admit it. He tossed the man a lighter. He had to throw it overhand and the lighter winked into the fog and clattered on the bottom of the wooden boat.

It was a silver lighter and the man picked it up and smoothed his thumb over the engraving and held it out in front of him to read it and then flicked the top back with his thumb and rolled the gauged wheel and the flame leapt up and did battle with the faint breeze. It was a transparent and weak flame, just a colourless crinkle of the air above the lighter, burning a clear hole through the dense fog that lasted only a few seconds.

The man lit his cigarette and tossed the lighter back and it went end over end between the boats in the fog and slapped into Slaney's upheld hand.

Follow us in, the old man said.

Give me a minute here, Slaney said. He went below and spoke to Hearn and he was in favour.

Follow him in, Hearn said. We don't have a choice.

The entire town had come out onto the wharf. There must have been three hundred people waiting. They stood in their overcoats and gaiters and the women had scarves on their heads tied under their chins and some had curlers under the scarves and there were two young girls came to the doorway of the fish and chips shop and they were wearing white aprons that seemed very white in the fog and the young children leaned into their mothers and some of them were coming down the hill in pairs and some of them were on bikes with banana seats and plastic streamers flying from the handlebars.

There were young girls in tight plaid bomber jackets and jeans, smoking cigarettes, and people had parked their cars on the shoulder of the road and left them idling and there were some men unloading their catches, paying no attention.

Slaney was upon them before he saw them because of the fog. The old guy was cute as a fox: all the Old Testament talk about being lost.

The crowd didn't seem to be saying much. They looked different from the crowd in town, shabbier and more robust. They were intent, as they might have been in church, and some of them had crossed their arms over their chests, or they leaned in to talk to a neighbour, not taking their eyes off Slaney.

When they'd docked, the cops swarmed the boat and Hearn came up with his hands behind his head, elbows out.

Slaney was pretty certain the cops hadn't said put your hands up but Hearn already saw the story of their capture as something worthy of telling and he wanted to look the part.

There was a stink of fish. The call of a gull. All of this came back while Slaney lay on his cot, hands behind his head, looking up at the mattress pressing through the slats of the bunk above him.

Name

Slaney headed back to the train station at dawn the next morning. The rain from the night before was steaming off the pavement. It was just a night; Hearn didn't need to know about Ottawa.

He walked past the parking lot of an abandoned strip mall with graffiti scrawled across the sodden plywood covering the storefront windows. A child's tricycle sat in a puddle under a street lamp.

Down a side street Slaney saw a man who looked like he was walking into a blizzard of snow. The front of his clothes and shoes and his face and even his eyelashes were pure white and it made his eyeballs look yellowish and blue-veined and watery and his lips wet and red, and his teeth were nicotine-stained. The man was standing behind a truck, smacking his arms against his sides, sending up little puffs of white dust. Another man in the back of the truck had been tossing him sacks of flour and one had broken when the guy caught it.

The train station was a fifteen-minute walk from the room Slaney had rented.

The man at the ticket booth asked for his identification. Slaney slid his passport under the glass and the man frowned at the picture and raised his droopy eyelids to look at Slaney and slid the passport back to him. Then he wrote out a ticket to Vancouver and slid that through too.

Slaney tried to call Hearn and the phone rang and rang. Hearn had probably gone to his classes. Slaney sat down to wait and got up at once and wandered out on the platform and paced a bit and sat down on a bench with the suitcase between his knees. The heat of the day was already building and some broken beer bottles between the rails glittered and shone.

He could not think of Jennifer. Her hands tightening her ponytail, the washer surging and rattling under them. She had held on tight to him, her legs crossed behind his back. They had hardly even undressed. His jeans around his knees, the change from his pocket spinning and bouncing on the floor. His mother's engagement ring had fallen out with the change. When Jennifer turned to open the door he lifted the lid of the washer a little and dropped the ring into the churning water. He wanted her to have it. He wanted her to remember him.

He thought about what he had done to her. He'd left her, is what happened. How do I put this, David. That's what she'd said. But she meant he had made the choice, and he hadn't chosen her. He hadn't taken her up on the offer. She meant: And now it really is over, there is no going back.

The trip was starting; it was really starting now. He was shocked by the desire he felt to meet up with Hearn, give him a couple of fake punches to the belly, *pow-pow*. Get stoned with him. Just be with him, carousing. Slaney wanted to carouse. He wanted to tell Hearn about his heart. His heart was hurting in his chest as if he'd run a great distance. They say a broken heart, but it felt more like a tear or puncture. It hurt when he breathed, or even when he was thinking about something else. The pain could well up out of nowhere and surprise him.

There was a couple making out farther down the platform. The girl had on a long crushed-velvet coat with fake fur trim and a red tube top and denim miniskirt. The coat was slipping off her shoulders and she was wearing white go-go boots and her leg was hooked over the guy's hip and his hand was disappearing under the hem of her little skirt.

An elderly black man with a briefcase sat down beside Slaney. He was reading a library book and the plastic cover made a crinkling noise every time he turned the page.

Slaney took the passport out and flicked through it again.

Good book? Slaney asked. The man grunted in the affirmative without looking up.

Slaney beat out a tune on the edge of the suitcase. The black man with the book licked the side of his thumb and turned the page and then he looked into Slaney's eyes and then very purposefully at Slaney's drumming hands and Slaney stopped drumming. The man returned to his book.

There was a security guard who appeared to be snoozing on a chair in the meagre shade of a potted tree.

Then the train horn, a shrill hoot in the distance, and a deep, earthy rumbling. The amber lights in the station flashed on and off and the long, silver-sided blaze of train poured like a viscous liquid into the platform, the deafening squeal of brakes and engine hiss-huff, a steady clang of oiled metal and grind and the hoo-hooing.

Slaney tried to pretend he was not the name he had taken on but he had committed an act of black magic in that graveyard. He thought of the guy covered in flour, looking like he'd walked through his own private snowstorm, a narrow slice of winter gale in all the still morning heat. The name haunted Slaney. He was being possessed by it, overtaken.

He boarded the train and found his seat and they were maybe an hour out of the station when a man passed down the aisle to the bathrooms, moving with the sway and rattle, and Slaney thought familiar. But he could not place him. The guy went back and forth three times, and he took each opportunity to look Slaney up and down, lingering on the last trip.

Slaney turned his face into the crack of the armrest pretending to be asleep and at the next stop he grabbed his suitcase and jumped off the train.

He saw the guy in the window searching for him, his

forehead a flat white spot where he rested it on the glass and the reflection of the rusted-out freight trains on the tracks opposite sliding all over him.

The guy saw him and waved frantically, gave him a thumbs-up.

Joe Murphy. He went to Gonzaga, a year behind Slaney. Geraldine Murphy's brother. Geraldine Murphy played tennis. Slaney had kissed her a few times when he was thirteen, a game of spin-the-bottle, then he blew all his paper route money on her, a little red transistor radio. She never spoke to him again. Murphys from the South Side.

Joe Murphy was a math whiz everybody said was destined for the priesthood. A little touch of home. It pierced him through and through. Slaney's stomach turned to water. He couldn't go back to the train station a second time — somebody would notice. He picked up the suitcase and started walking for the highway.

Alberta

There was the endless drive through Ontario, all glittering lakes and foliage and bland sunshine, and the sudden baked flatness of the prairies.

The truck that picked him up outside Winnipeg was carrying a thousand chickens. The driver had pulled over and when Slaney got in, the man was holding a pair of glasses out at arm's length, frowning at the lenses. Then he handed them to Slaney.

Slaney breathed on the lenses and rubbed them in his shirttail. They were bifocals. He could feel the ridge of thickened glass with his thumb. He held them up and saw the rows of harshly yellow canola on the opposite side of the road, crisp and straight in the top half of the lenses, and below the ridge, the same flowers were magnified so they became a wind-ruffled blur of colour. He passed the glasses back to the truck driver.

The driver put them on and his mouth was solemn and judging. He pressed the bridge of the glasses up his nose, and then he lifted his chin to glance out through the bottom half. He turned to examine Slaney.

The ridge of the bifocals fell exactly halfway across the man's eyes, magnifying the bottom half; the brown irises were vulnerable and watery. There was a bright crimson dot in the left iris, just below the pupil. The pouches beneath the man's eyes were veined with violet lines and pressed upon by the black frames; in the top hemisphere, above the ridge of thickened glass, the irises were sharp and calculating.

The two men looked at each other and then they became aware of looking at each other and both turned back to face the road, embarrassed.

The trucker stared forward then, as if memorizing what was out there, and he took off the glasses and put them back in the case and tossed the case out the open window.

Jesus things, the man said. They belonged to my mother.

There was a spill of 8-tracks at Slaney's feet and the man waved at them.

Slaney picked up one and it turned out to be Johnny Cash. The machine pulled the tape slowly inside itself and the metal flap flopped down and it pushed the tape halfway out and then drew it back in. There was a dragging whir and hiss and then Johnny Cash sang about a burning ring of fire.

For a time the trucker sang along with the tape. He sang about flames as though he had come through them and he had an authority when it came to the subject.

You got some set of pipes, Slaney said.

You like that? the man asked, grinding down the gears.

They drove for an hour and all at once the sky got dark and the trucker cleared his throat. He said: I believe we're in for some weather.

The darkness seemed to charge across the prairie toward them, deepening as it came.

The yellow of the canola drained away. The bottoms of clouds were charcoal and smoke gold and the rain lashed the grass.

Slaney was hungry and it was close in the cab with the pine-tree air freshener and this driver had on a cologne and Slaney wanted to crack the window.

There were, at first, only two splats, the size of quarters, on the giant windshield and they trembled like things with a consciousness, things trying to hold together against a terrible force of entropy, and then they ran sideways and a drumming began on the roof and the world.

The trucker said there was a bunk if Slaney wanted to sleep.

Why don't you crawl in back there, the trucker said. Get yourself some shut-eye.

You don't need the company? Slaney asked. To keep you awake?

I'm good until breakfast, the man said.

Slaney woke when the truck pulled into the parking lot of a diner.

The driver told him they were in Alberta. The sun was a red ball hovering over the lettering on the window that said BLACKFOOT CAFÉ.

They walked across the steaming lot and as they got closer Slaney could see the white blouse of the waitress passing through the reflection of the sun and the place was packed and noisy and warm when they got inside, smelling of bacon and burnt coffee.

The trucker found them a table and the waitress came over and asked what they wanted.

Bacon and eggs, the trucker said.

Will you have toast? she asked.

I want a stack yay-high, he said.

Coffee?

That coffee fresh? the trucker asked.

Fresh since yesterday, she said.

I'll have some of that, he said. The waitress turned over the driver's cup and it chinked against the saucer and she poured. She wore sneakers with white tennis socks, a cotton bobble on each heel, and her hair was grey and mashed down in a fine net.

The driver rubbed his hands together, picked up his butter knife, and for a brief second drew his top lip back from his gums, checking his teeth in the reflection of the blade.

The teeth dropped, all of a piece, and slid wetly away from his lips, hanging, detached and gleaming, out of his mouth. The driver, absent and alert, watched the collapse of his face in the knife blade, and there was a hiss of saliva and the bridge popped back as if nothing had happened. The waitress, digging her pad out of her apron pocket, had missed the trucker's false teeth.

She turned over Slaney's cup and asked him what he wanted to eat.

I'm not hungry, thank you, ma'am, Slaney said.

A growing boy, she said.

Just the coffee, thank you, Slaney said.

Call me Lorraine, the waitress said.

Bring him same as me, Lorraine, the trucker said.

Just coffee, Slaney said.

Same as me, Lorraine, the trucker said.

Over easy?

I sure hope something is easy around here, the trucker said. He was seized with a quaking spasm. One of his fists raised and jiggling near his chest, the other hand slapping the table three times.

Aren't you the saucy one, she said.

Don't be shy with the bacon, Lorraine.

A police car pulled up into the parking lot and the cop just sat inside it. Slaney looked for the back exits. There was a hallway with a sign over it that said NO ADMITTANCE. He wondered if there'd be a window or door back there.

After about five minutes another cop car pulled up alongside the first. Slaney watched as the cops got out of their cars, one of them leaning on his door. They both looked at the window of the diner and they spoke to each other at length.

When the cops came into the café the bell tinkled and the screen door hitched against the frame and jostled and then it clapped shut. They looked around the diner and then sat at the counter on the swivel stools and the waitress poured them each a coffee.

It's getting hot out there already, the cop said.

We're having a stretch of it, Lorraine said. She brought Slaney and the trucker fried eggs and bacon on thick white plates. Slaney cut the egg in half and folded it over and jabbed the fork into it. Then he took a triangle of toast and wiped it over the spilled yolk and folded that and ate it too.

The waitress came back with more coffee and the trucker told her about a hydraulic lift he had installed in front of his house going up the five steps to the porch.

Slaney kept his eye on the cops. He watched them and strained to hear what they were saying. They had walkie-talkies on their belts that hissed white noise. But they hardly spoke to each other. They were intent on the meals they'd ordered. Slaney could understand the first cop, but why had the second one shown up?

He looked out the window. There was a thin bank of trees, mostly skinny birch, the white trunks like bones, and the leaves so green they seemed lit up and the branches were trembling hard with the breeze. Beyond, fields in every direction. He realized he had slept most of the drive and had no idea where he was, except that he was somewhere in Alberta, which seemed as vast and flat as the rest of the prairie, without so much as a shadow to hide under.

This was for Mother's wheelchair, installed to the tune of several hundred dollars, the trucker was saying. It was installed only a couple of weeks and she had to be moved to an old age home. I couldn't take care of her no more.

I've heard of them lifts, the waitress said.

Both the cops had swivelled around and they were surveying the dining room and they swivelled back and continued with their food.

We never used it no more than a few occasions.

I'd say she enjoyed the ride, Lorraine answered.

Happy as a clam, he said.

You can tell what a man is made of by the way he treats his mother.

She's no more than a feather now, he said. Wheelchair and all. I could lift her up with one hand if she required it.

Gone away to nothing, Lorraine asked.

She's not all there, either, the trucker said.

I've got one like that at the house, the waitress said.

When Slaney was done he wiped his mouth with a paper napkin and scrunched it in his fist and dropped it onto the table and balanced on the two back legs of his chair, his hands linked behind his head. He nearly tipped over so he dropped back down.

Thank you, sir, he said.

You're welcome, son, the man said. The trucker worked his fork and knife under his second egg and in a delicate man-oeuvre he transferred the jiggling mass so that it hovered over Slaney's empty plate and then slithered off and landed with a plop. He put the two pieces of toast he could not finish on Slaney's plate and an extra piece of bacon.

You don't need to do that, sir, Slaney said.

All I got to show for a lifetime of hard work is that truck out there, the man said.

It's quite a rig, Slaney said.

I've got complaints, the man said. Heavy lifting. A man gets a certain age. No pension, no nothing. Eat your egg.

Thank you, sir.

I can't eat it. I got half a stomach gone to cancer.

I'm sorry to hear that.

Just eat.

Thank you.

Eat the egg, son.

Sir, do you think the chickens will survive the heat? Slaney asked.

Those chickens are frozen solid, the trucker said. My rig is a refrigerator freezer.

I thought you had a cargo of live chickens back there, Slaney said.

Those are chicken legs. I don't know where the rest of them is, the breasts and what-have-you. On somebody else's truck.

I thought they were alive out there.

Dead as doornails, far as I know. Slaney and the trucker looked out at the lot together and they both lifted their coffee cups at the same time and sipped and put them back down.

I'm going to freshen up, Slaney said.

Powder your nose, the trucker said. Go ahead.

Slaney headed to the bathroom where he washed in the sink and crossed the parking lot and climbed up into the truck and shut the door as quietly as he could and he hunched low. After a moment or two the driver sauntered across the parking lot and climbed up into the cab and slammed the door. Slaney saw the driver had a toothpick. It wagged up and then down.

Then Slaney jerked with fright: a fist rapping the glass.

Son, those police officers have some questions, the driver said. Slaney rolled down the window.

Good morning, the officer said. Where you from, son?

Down east, Slaney said. The cop looked down the highway toward the east. He hooked his fingers into his belt loops and stood there for a long moment. He watched the horizon as though Slaney had yet to show up, as if he were still down east, living his life, breaking the law, getting caught, busting out of jail, and he might appear any minute on the horizon, heading west, heading toward this very truck stop.

Slaney glanced around for the other officer. He was leaning

on the open door of the patrol car, still talking on the hand
radio.

Mind if I ask you what you do for a living, son?

I'm a university student, Slaney said.

What's your line of study?

I am hoping to become a dental hygienist.

Looking in people's mouths, the cop said. He took out a notebook and pen and flipped to an empty page. He clicked the pen
with his thumb and held it over the page and there was a pause.

It was a pen from Florida and the top half was clear glass
filled with water and a dolphin swam up and down the pen
against a background of a beach and blue sky. The cop moved
his lips. His lips formed a word or two, but nothing came out.
He gave up. Clicked the pen again.

I got a bad tooth myself, the cop said. I believe it's rotting
right out of my head. Sometimes I'd like to take a gun and
shoot myself in the mouth. Just blow the damn thing right
out of my face.

The cop moved his lower jaw from side to side and touched
his fingers to it.

I'm not qualified yet, said Slaney. It was as though the cop
had been rebuked. He seemed instantly angry.

I don't see how someone could find fulfillment looking in
people's mouths. Turn your stomach. You'd want to be pretty
hard up.

People are starting to take better care of their teeth, Slaney
said. He wanted to move his hands up and down his thighs
but he didn't do it. He let his hands rest lightly on his knees.
He kept them still.

There's flossing daily, he said. Fluoride. Sometimes just
removing the tooth.

Just yank it out, you're saying, the cop asked.

Get a professional, Slaney said.

And you're studying it?

I've done history courses so far, Slaney said. First you have to do general things. Before you can get into the school of dentistry.

Which you are going to do, the cop said.

Which I hope they'll accept me, Slaney said. The cop winced as though he were uneasy with what he had to say next.

What's your name, son? the cop asked.

Douglas Knight, Slaney said.

Do you have any identification on you, Doug, I could take a look-see?

Slaney took out the new passport and the cop turned the pages and he glanced at the picture and up at Slaney. Then he lifted his sunglasses and let them rest on his forehead. He brought the passport over to the other cop, who leafed through and then got in the car and spoke at length on the radio.

Slaney and the trucker waited in silence, looking forward. The trucker rolled down his window and tossed the toothpick. He put his hand on the gearshift and gave it a vicious shake as if he wanted to make sure they could move if they had to. The cop came back to Slaney's side and handed up the passport.

Doug, I have to be honest, the cop said. I don't like your personality. I don't believe you are a dental hygienist or that you will ever become one. I don't think you have it in you. It's a distasteful job. But it requires discipline. You look like the kind of guy doesn't get up in the morning. I don't think you're college material.

Slaney lifted his hip and fit the passport into his back pocket.

I don't like the look of you, the cop said. Slaney looked straight ahead.

Get a haircut, Doug, the cop said. And he strolled away.

Something funny happened there, son, the trucker said.

I know, Slaney said.

Why didn't they take you in? They made a phone call and they decided to let you go.

Moved by a whim, Slaney said. I don't know.

It wasn't a whim, the trucker said.

You had my back.

Something funny, the trucker said. I don't know what the hell you done, but they sure as hell wanted you for something and then they let you go.

The trucker was watching in his side mirror as the cops pulled away from the parking lot. He started up the truck and let it idle.

I don't have your back, the trucker said. Nobody has your back.

Party

Slaney could hear the party before he saw the house. He walked up a grassy lane and could feel the music thumping through the soles of his sneakers. He saw yellow ribbons of lit window through the black tree trunks and at the end of the path the stretching rectangles of light cast across the lawn.

The party had spilled into the garden and he could smell a barbecue and there were children running around playing spotlight, patio lanterns strung from the low branches and along the veranda railing. A Hula Hoop wheeled past him and hit a stone and fell into the tall grass at the end of the lawn. He wandered into the house and found Hearn in the kitchen.

Hearn opened his arms and Slaney walked into them. They stood there hugging without speaking a word. Music throbbed in the walls and there was the racket of conversation. The crowd so thick bodies stood close and people had to work a shoulder or elbow through to pass.

They just held each other. They stood locked in each other's grip. They were hanging on tight. Slaney could feel Hearn's heart. They stood like that for a long time and Slaney let the beat of Hearn's heart enter him. Then they stepped apart and tried to take each other in.

Hearn's freckles and a red bandana he had knotted around his throat. He was skinnier and more muscled and he'd let his fiery hair spring out in an afro. He looked high and a little haunted.

I'm sorry about your father, Slaney said. He had wanted to say that in person. Hearn put his hand to his forehead as if taking his own temperature.

I'm sorry you went to prison, Hearn said. He said it in a flat voice and his eyes gleamed with tears and everything that had gone on between them since they were kids seemed to be present in the room.

Hearn threw back his head and howled. An animal noise that came from somewhere deep. He stamped his foot three times to urge the whole weltering cry out of himself.

We're going to show them, he said. We're going to show those bastards.

Is there anything to eat here? Slaney asked.

Gutfounded, I suppose, Hearn said.

Eat the leg off the lamb of God, Slaney said.

Get this guy a plate of food, Hearn shouted.

Are you crying? Slaney asked. They had to raise their voices to be heard.

Yes, I'm crying, Hearn shouted. He grabbed Slaney in a headlock and dug his knuckles into his scalp.

Of course I'm crying, he growled.

Let go, Slaney said. He jabbed his elbow into Hearn's ribs and broke free of the grip.

It is so good to see you, Hearn said. He folded his arms across his chest and shook his head slowly, as if he couldn't believe his eyes. Then he got Slaney a beer out of the old claw-foot bathtub full of ice someone had dragged into the kitchen. He knocked the cap off with a *puck* and smoky frost curled up. Slaney put the beer on his head and a few people hooted. He drank most of it in one long swig. Slaney found he was crying too.

A girl handed him a paper plate with a leg of barbecued chicken and potato salad and a salad of tinned pineapple and creamed corn. She dug around in the drawer for cutlery but she could only come up with a miniature spoon, an enamel oval in the handle with a portrait of the Queen.

Come meet some of the boys, Hearn said. Slaney put down the paper plate and followed him to the basement. The party pounded through the ceiling. There were five men sitting around a table in the corner playing cards. The room smelled yeasty, full of mould and concrete. A washer and dryer were going in the corner. There was a padded leather wet-bar and a lava lamp at least five feet high and shaped like a missile. They had a bottle of scotch on the table and poker chips. A collage of centrefolds covered an entire wall. Each man stood as he was introduced and sat back down.

Everybody, this is Doug Knight, Hearn said. He's heading out of here tomorrow for sunny Puerto Vallarta, Mexico. Doug, this is Roy Brophy. Roy came in at the last minute with some serious financial support.

Patterson stood and shook Slaney's hand.

Roy is a contractor, Hearn said. And you know Geoff O'Driscoll.

Good to see you, man, Slaney said. He reached over the table and they high-fived. It was Frank Parsons. Going by the name of Geoff. Frank had gone through school with Hearn and Slaney.

Geoff is responsible for the cargo once it gets to shore. Geoff's distribution.

Good to see you out, man, Frank said.

Good to be out, Slaney said.

These three guys, Hearn said, Harold Jesperson, Don Burn, Stan Summers, I think you know Stan.

Stan was Phil White, grew up on Slaney's street. Played sax in the school band. Phil had seven sisters, two of the older ones were nuns in Monsefú. He was wearing a transparent green visor and a Doors T-shirt.

Long time no see, Phil said.

Your ticket to Mexico, Hearn said. He handed Slaney the plane ticket.

You land in Puerto Vallarta tomorrow. Go to the Hotel Luna and you'll meet up with Dan Stone. You sail from there the next day for Colombia. We're thinking six, seven days on the water. Load up and head back here. It's going to take six to eight weeks to get back, you got the current against you, nearly five thousand miles; you give it to her, we're talking six weeks. And we're waiting for you.

Phil White was walking a poker chip over his knuckles as Hearn spoke. It flicked end over end and disappeared in his fist.

Men, let's raise a toast, Hearn said. The men raised their glasses and clinked.

Godspeed, Hearn said. They drank down the drinks.

Now we party, Hearn said. We bring in the dawn.

Can I talk to you? Slaney said.

Sure.

Just a few words, Slaney said.

We'll see you at the party, man, Phil White said. The men folded up their cards and dropped them on the table and the washer in the corner began to spin out and rattled and jittered on the concrete floor.

You got a screw or something corroded, Phil White said.

Something's loose in that machine, Hearn said. I haven't had a chance. The old lady is after me to fix it.

See you upstairs, man, Phil said. And the boys filed up the stairs and back into the party.

Hearn pulled the door shut behind them.

Dan Stone? Slaney said.

It's Cyril Carter, Hearn said.

Jesus Christ, Slaney said. Hearn said Carter was their only option. A master mariner and he had the sailboat, custom designed, mahogany, brass fittings, two engines.

A real beaut, Hearn said. Carter also invested.

He spent six months in the Waterford, Slaney said. Jesus, Hearn.

Don't call me that, Hearn said. I'm Barlow. John Barlow.

The fucking Waterford, Slaney said.

Six years ago, Hearn said. He was discharged with a clean bill of health.

The man's unstable. He had a nervous breakdown.

He's been dry ever since, Hearn said. I'm telling you, it wasn't easy to raise interest. Carter was interested.

A nervous breakdown, Hearn, Slaney said.

Don't say Hearn. Hearn doesn't exist. I'm a different person. I sloughed off all the old cells of Hearn. He's been replaced, cell by fucking cell. That guy dried up and blew away. I'm John Barlow. You have to become someone else out here. You are Doug Knight. I am Barlow; you are Knight. Slaney and Hearn don't exist. We're reinvented.

We have history, man, Slaney said.

Forget it, Doug.

Carter is insane, *Barlow*. A guy's got to withstand pressure down there. Anything can happen. He's got to hold up.

He'll hold up.

He's a drunk, Slaney said.

He's a sailor. He knows the water. He knows the boat. Treats it like his baby. He's not going to let anything happen to that boat, believe me. You're with him six weeks. Tops. All he does is sail. He doesn't meet anyone. He doesn't talk to anyone. You do everything else.

Who's that guy Roy Brophy?

He came in last minute.

Who is he?

Worry about your part of it, okay?

Where did he come from?

Old money.

Nobody said some guy I never heard of comes in at the last minute. Nobody said Carter.

Carter has a hundred grand on the boat to purchase the cargo.

Fresh from the loony bin.

You have to trust me. You don't know what's been going on out here.

You got that bloody well right.

You want to have this out?

But Slaney didn't want to have anything out. He wanted to believe.

I have to ask. Okay? Be straight with me.

Absolutely, Hearn said.

The contact in Colombia, Slaney said.

Colonel Angelo Lopez, Hearn said. He's a good guy.

Does Lopez know about the last trip? Slaney asked. That we owe?

Not a chance, Hearn said.

Because if that's the scene, I'm out of here, Slaney said.

Things have changed down there, Doug, that's what I'm telling you. They've never heard of us down there.

I want to know what I'm walking into.

Those people we dealt with four years ago are long gone. New management. Those old guys moved on.

I don't know, man.

You want out, Slane? You want out? You can walk. One of the *Playboy* centrefolds looked down at Slaney over Hearn's shoulder. The lava lamp gurgled and a fierce scarlet blob waggled up through the murky glass missile and when it reached the top it broke into a hundred balls and sank and reformed. A platinum blonde behind Hearn was laid out on a poolside, touching herself with long pink fingernails. Her mouth was a soft O. Astonished and mock innocent.

Wish I felt better.

Come on, man. Let's get a drink.

In the middle of the evening there was an argument between them about Hearn's keys. There was music and girls and beer and they'd had a disagreement.

Hearn couldn't find his keys and he was certain Slaney must have taken them. They'd gone out together for more liquor and when they came back he'd lost the keys.

You came in, Slaney said.

I came in and I had the keys. They were yelling because of the music. Hearn was using the soused logic of: if I don't have them, you must have them. And also: I gave them to you, I have a distinct memory.

Some girl jammed herself between them to get to the fridge. She was pressed against Hearn, writhing through, and he raised his arms in the air like it was a stick-up and gave a lascivious smirk and she knocked Slaney out of the way with her hip.

Did they fall out in the porch?

They're not in the porch.

On the lawn maybe?

They're not on the lawn.

You came in.

And I handed you the keys.

And you put the keys down next to the bag of booze.

I had the keys and I said, Here, put them in your pocket.

You put the bag down.

I put the bag down and I said, Here.

Let me ask you something, what would I want with your keys?

They all drank well into the morning. There were mushrooms, acid, pot, beer, and hard liquor of every sort. Slaney did not partake of the acid.

You're abstaining? Hearn yelled.

Big day tomorrow, right, Slaney said. He had a beer stein full of an emerald drink.

Straight and narrow, I get your story, Hearn yelled. Slaney watched him put a tab of acid on his tongue. A teensy square of paper with a happy face printed on it. He darted his tongue in and out like a snake.

You have to drive me to the airport in a few hours, Slaney said. Hearn swallowed and screwed one eye shut and shivered all over.

What do you think of the place? Hearn asked him. My girl-friend did all the decor. Those lampshades. They're antiques.

Where is she? Slaney asked.

In there, talking to Brophy. Slaney saw the contractor stand-ing in the corner of the living room next to a potted banana tree and a girl in a rhinestone-studded halter top, a pair of bell-bottoms. She had her hand pressed flat against Brophy's chest, as if to keep him from getting away. She had a bottle of vodka by the neck and she waved it in the air.

What did I say, Hearn asked.

Knockers.

I said ass.

Ass, yes. But also knockers.

Go talk to her.

I will.

Listen to her, man; she's beautiful. Really smart.

I see that.

Got any smokes? Hearn said.

I don't smoke, Slaney said.

Me neither. Thought I'd try one.

Slaney thought of the two cigarettes tied up with ribbon

the old lady in Montreal had given him. One of her cats sitting on the kitchen table, licking a paw, fluffy tail in the sugar dish. The old lady had spoken to Slaney at length but he hadn't understood a word.

She had become passionate, knocking her chest with her fist. She put on the kettle and talked while it came to a boil and Slaney stood until she waved at a chair for him to sit down. She poured him tea but he'd only had a couple of sips before she took the cup from him and waved him out of the kitchen.

The tone of her diatribe had changed. She'd become enraged. Perhaps she had told him her whole life story and was angry about where she found herself at the end.

Slaney had a sense that she'd pronounced on men in general and their ineffectuality and him in particular.

He was pretty sure she'd asked the question: Who will get my smokes for me now? He recognized the castigating tone but had only an intuition about the content. She shut the door on him and he heard the chain slide across again.

He saw himself backing out of her apartment with the suitcase and the doll in the pink box, trying to say thank you. Trying to say someone else would surely come along and buy her smokes.

Jennifer was lost to him.

She was gone.

He'd lost her for good. He swirled the stein in small circles, slopping sticky mint drink onto the floor.

Hearn was mouthing off about acting to a group of girls who were nodding along with everything he had to say.

Everything is in the fingers, Hearn said. Use the fingers. He began pinching at the air in front of him, as if grabbing butterflies. He was tripping.

Don't push away, he said. Bring it in, bring it all in. Whatever
you have is inside. Keep it there. Don't emote. Hearn shut his
eyes and waved his hand as if to wipe the idea of emoting off
the face of the earth.

Do you see what I'm doing here, he asked. His eyes flew
open again. Do you see what my fingers are doing? He was
pinching and pinching.

I'm transforming, he said. I'm taking the character from
the air in bits and pieces. I am becoming the character. The
girls looked aroused and dumbstruck.

Slaney listened to Hearn and watched the dancing in the
living room through the kitchen door. He felt a warmth
spreading in his solar plexus: what he felt for Hearn was
love. Eternal and thin, a steel cord from which he might end
up dangling.

We are just skin, Hearn said. We act with our skin.

One of the girls gathered around Hearn was nodding in
agreement and she had things she wanted to say and she kept
opening her mouth to speak but Hearn would hold up a finger and she would clamp her mouth shut and just nod more
vigorously.

They'd set up a black light in the living room and everything white out there was purplish and inner-lit and there
were arms churning in the air and people grinding hips. It
was all bright white teeth and a girl in phosphorescent hot
pants doing the bump. Slaney wanted to dance with her.

Go for it, Hearn told him. Go get her, tiger.

Slaney raised his beer stein in the air before him and gestured in big circles to clear a path through the bodies. But
nobody moved out of his way.

The girl beside him was talking about vegetarianism and he

hung on the edge of the conversation. There was a story about a chimpanzee reaching out of its cage with a tree branch. Its shoulder wedged against the bars. Raking a peanut over the pavement with the branch.

Primitive tool use, somebody said.

Tell me that animal wasn't communicating, the girl demanded. There was also a girl with a Spanish accent that made everything she said sound like a dare. Pass me a drink: that was a saucy taunt. Where's the john: a provocation.

Another girl, near the sink, was dancing to some pulsing lull that had nothing to do with the music on the hi-fi, her beer bottle raised over her head, more swaying than dancing. Eyes closed.

Somebody put on Chilliwack.

And then her eyes flew open and she yelled, Eat nothing with a face.

What about plants? somebody asked. And somebody else asked: Do plants have a consciousness?

It was agreed, almost at once: nobody in the kitchen could get behind plants. It wasn't that kind of gathering. Plants did not have primitive tool use.

Slaney stuck his arm out straight with the emerald stein in his fist and plowed his way out of the kitchen. He was making his way through the dance floor to Hearn's girlfriend and Roy Brophy. A blue light from the stereo console lit up the knee of Brophy's jeans. Hearn's girl had backed Brophy into the leaves of a banana tree. He had taken a handkerchief from his back pocket and was wiping his face.

Hello, Roy, Slaney said. Having a chat, are you?

Shooting the shit, Roy said.

You're Barlow's girlfriend, Slaney said. Her eyes were brown and very big and he could see she was smart, like Hearn had told him.

What are you drinking, Doug? she asked.

Crème de menthe, he said. No matter what I pour into a glass, when the clock strikes two it turns into crème de menthe.

Like water into wine, she said.

Or peach schnapps.

Yeah, she said. Peach schnapps. I've had that happen at two in the morning.

Aftershave, Slaney said.

No, she said. And she slapped his arm and he saw she was more than a little drunk.

No, not really, he said. What were you and Roy here talking about?

Housing, she said. Development.

Roy, you're a developer?

Subdivisions, Roy said. Apartment buildings.

We were talking about illicit love, she said. We were talking about when things turn around on you. Also a two-in-the-morning phenomenon, come to think of it.

Two is long gone, said Slaney. He was looking at the grandfather clock.

We were saying about first love, weren't we, Roy.

You were saying, Brophy said.

Now, Roy, she said. Coy Roy. Roy fell in love with his father's mistress.

Patterson touched the handkerchief to his brow. He had not meant to say it. Her eyes. The unabashed interrogation: she'd asked him what mattered to him. She'd asked about love.

She'd said, How old are you, Mr. Brophy? He found he liked the attention. Her hand on his chest, pushing him into the big tree behind him.

Tell me a secret, she'd said. Clarice had kissed him. His father's mistress. Thirty years ago when he was sixteen.

Patterson had come into being then. A ravishment. The wind in the trees outside her house. It had been windy and he'd ridden there on his bike.

A bead of sweat hung off Patterson's eyelash and the room became five distinct rooms arrayed on a wheel that slowly turned, the girl under the black light in the white hot pants, glowing like the moon, she was at the centre of each replicated floating crowd. Hearn's girl kept him pinned with her hand, and her eyes became five sets of eyes and they floated around him too. And the sweat dropped and his vision focused again.

Patterson had ridden his bike over. Delivering the monthly cheque. Clarice Connors and his half-brother, Alphonse, in the house at the end of a long lane outside of town. She'd drawn his tongue into her mouth and afterwards in the bathroom he saw the red, red lipstick smeared all over his lips and chin: the wanton girlish abandon of it. The affair continued for almost a year. He had been devoured and changed and he'd learned things and just as suddenly as it had started, it was over.

Your father's mistress, Slaney said.

Not really, said Patterson.

Yes, Hearn's girlfriend said. Yes, Roy, you told me. He loved her. Didn't you, Roy? After his father passed away. Have I got that right? Didn't your father cheat on your mother with this woman? What do you think, Doug, is he for real?

I don't know, Slaney said. Your boyfriend seems to think so.

It seemed likely to Slaney that Hearn's girlfriend knew everything about the trip. He wondered how many people at the party knew. How many people had Hearn let in on it?

Later, Slaney found Hearn in a lineup for the bathroom. There were five people ahead of them and someone was making out in there. The girl at the front of the line was banging on the door with both fists.

Barlow, how are you, man, Slaney said.

He's a better man than I'll ever be, Hearn said.

Who? Slaney thought he meant Barlow.

My father, Hearn said. He had his head tilted back so he could watch the ceiling.

There's a hole in the goddamn roof, Hearn said. I can see the cosmos. And the cosmos can see me.

Did you go upstairs? Slaney asked him. You probably left the keys up there.

I went upstairs, but I gave you the keys first. Or you took them.

Is that what you think? Slaney asked. He waited for Hearn's awakening. Hearn stood there accusing, but the awakening was imminent. It would burst over him in fits of anguish and euphoria by turns due to the acid he had taken.

Hearn had jumped bail and gone to university and everybody called him John and it looked like he'd made friends. Theatre people and people from the literature department where Hearn was studying for a Ph.D. They were students and it seemed like a life Slaney would never be a part of.

Hearn had friends. Slaney felt jealous.

He didn't think of Jennifer so much as she became present to him again. Once, they had been making out in his father's car near the ocean and a butterfly flew in his window and out the passenger's window, a yellow butterfly, and she hadn't seen it because her eyes were closed. It paused on the steering wheel, opened and shut its wings. It lifted off, and up, down, up, down, out the other window and she had missed it.

Jennifer's baby had come and her family had turned their backs.

It was astonishing to Slaney. His family was not capable of turning away. Imagine the resolve: to strike out on your own and give over everything to another person, a baby.

There had been pressure to give the child up for adoption and Jennifer had decided against it. That was resolve. That was what she wore, like a garment, and what had made him crazy horny and insane with love: the resolute independence that lit her up.

Because he felt certain he would never love like that again. They weren't who they would become. They were too young.

They couldn't have said, I am this or that. They had been making it up as they'd gone. They'd made it up together. But they also knew who they were better than they would ever know again.

In the morning he woke on the floor in Hearn's living room and Hearn was making chicken sandwiches in the kitchen and he said they had to get to the airport. He tossed Slaney a sandwich wrapped in wax paper and a bottle of ginger ale.

Let's roll, he said. Hearn got in the car and patted himself all over.

The keys, he said. They were in the ignition.

A New
Velocity

Mexico

What was the word his mother would have said: not vamp. A word that sounded like something part rodent, part Venus: a mink or sex kitten. Minx? Not minx. Something bold and fast.

This is Ada, Carter said. She's coming with us.

Don't leave me alone with her, Slaney thought. She had taken one of Carter's smokes from his silver case and she was looking around the patio for a light.

The eyes on her. She had eyes that were two different colours. One was blue and the other was hazel. Black eyeliner. He tried to figure out which eye was the most beautiful, but they were both beautiful.

An old-fashioned word his mother used about a particular kind of girl.

Ada slouched in her chair so she could rest her head on Carter's shoulder. Shaggy blond hair, a red bikini under a loose peasant blouse embroidered with red poppies. The whole patio checking her out. Slaney saw three different men patting their pockets for a match.

He thought he might punch Hearn's lights out if he ever got

near him again. He wasn't going to Colombia with a chick on board. Forget it. Bad luck. She looked to be about twenty if she was a day.

We saw a giant squid on the way down, Ada said.

Some dolphins, Carter said.

But it's a boring stretch, isn't it, Cyril? We were doing maybe a hundred and twenty-five miles a day, going about ten knots.

It'll be longer on the way back, he said.

We might have died of boredom if it wasn't for the squid, Ada said. She ran her fingers through her hair, tugging at the tangles. The clouds of ink, she said. These long beautiful tendrils.

Very rare sighting, Carter said.

It's a sea monster is what it is, she said.

Some kind of smoky word his mother had for women younger than herself who were too glamorous for their own good. A partly ironic word that held a glint of admiration.

I'm a pretty fair sailor, aren't I, Cyril? Ada said.

Hearn hadn't told Slaney about the girl. Hearn hadn't said. They'd partied all night, and Hearn hadn't thought to mention. He'd driven Slaney to the airport in a convertible, stoned out of his mind, passing everything on the road, nearly killing them twice.

Hasta luego, Hearn said, dumping Slaney's blue suitcase and tearing away from the curb.

Carter had now taken the tassel from the silk drawstring on the neck of Ada's peasant blouse in his lips. She tugged it away and limply slapped his cheek with the saliva-soaked bit of fluff. He submitted to the mock beating.

You. (*slap*) Be. (*slap*) Good, she said. She mushed her hand all over his face and pushed it away from her and he swung it back right away, nuzzled her shoulder.

Carter was a slum landlord, amateur actor, father of four, loving husband, philanderer, and sailor. He produced the British farces and annual Shakespeare productions at the Arts and Culture Centre in St. John's. Lunatic.

He's a good laugh, Hearn had said.

Slaney had been in Carter's Jaguar once when they were going to pick up a stash and Carter had stopped to get the rent from a three-storey hole he owned on Bond Street. A garbage bag taped up to a broken window and an old fellow coming out to the curb with his welfare cheque.

Treats the boat like a baby, Hearn had said.

Cyril was in his mid-forties. He was a man who surrounded himself with people a couple of decades younger. People said sophisticated. They didn't mention bald.

A beaut of a boat, Hearn had said. Wait until you see her.

Cyril had a way: you didn't think bald. You didn't think short.

Ada excused herself. She said she was going to visit the ladies'.

Be right back, she said. She gripped Carter's hand and took her time letting go, the tips of their fingers touching, touching, and then she turned and walked away. The walk on her.

It's my boat, Carter said. I'm the captain. What I say goes.

I thought you were married, Slaney said. There was a celery stick in Carter's drink and he stirred and tapped it against the rim of the glass and laid it down on the table. I thought you dried out.

I'll tell you something, Cyril said. But he didn't go on. He didn't tell Slaney anything at all. He drank down the remains in the glass, raised a finger in the air as if testing the direction of the wind. A waiter in a bow tie replaced his empty glass with a full one.

Are you kidding me? Slaney asked.

She's coming with us, Carter said. It's my boat. I make the decisions. Besides, we need her to sail the damn thing. Two of us can't manage it alone. She's a fine sailor. She can sail circles around me.

I thought you were a family man, Slaney said. The wife, the kids.

I'm leaving my wife, he said. This is love. Ada and I are in love. You know it when you feel it. I feel it. You feel it, David, and you're helpless before it.

Call me Knight. Doug Knight.

Okay, Doug. You know it when you feel it.

The door of the plane sliding open yesterday and the heat billowing in. The heavy air, it had just rained and stopped raining in the same instant, and the warm tar smell and the rundown airport and Mexicans, shades of brown and reddish brown and olive and black, black hair.

The dogs at the luggage carousel. Two dogs had sniffed aggressively at Slaney's jeans. He was afraid for his balls. A wet nose prodding his balls, teeth gently grazing. Manic panting and slaver.

Try to pretend nothing out of the ordinary is happening when there's a dog's snout driven halfway up your arse. They could smell it on his clothes from the party the night before. Or they were smelling his fear.

Guards wandering through the air conditioning with rifles over their shoulders had stopped to look. But just as quickly as they had been on him the dogs leapt away. One was on the carousel sniffing the seam of a big black suitcase and it disappeared under the rubber flaps at the end of the carousel that led to the loading zone. The other dog had a child pressed against a pillar. A tiny girl with big eyes and her tummy sucked in, holding herself away from the dog's teeth.

He got a taxi to the hotel. They drove past four men on the side of the road lifting a squealing hog. A rope through the animal's mouth, looped around to tie its legs, and the noise out of it. Honking more than squealing, full of terror.

The green of the ocean under his window, the hot sand. He'd checked in and splashed water on his face. It was just one night. He'd meet Carter in the morning by the pool as Hearn had instructed and they'd head to the marina right away.

Nobody said a girl.

Hearn must have known and he kept his mouth shut.

Carter picked up the celery stick and cracked it in half and crunched down on it. Then his whole face changed. It was as though years fell away, or he had sobered up. Slaney turned to look behind him. It was the girl. Ada was coming back from the john. Maybe Slaney's mother didn't have a word for this kind of girl.

There she is, Carter said. He drew her chair closer to him, making the legs clatter across the marble. He touched the girl's cheek, moving a strand of hair, tucking it behind her ear. She kissed his nose. She took his hand in hers and caught one of his knuckles in her teeth and growled.

Methinks Himself would like another drink, she said. The truth was, she could have been his daughter. She was younger than Slaney.

There's my girl, Cyril said. There she is.

I am glad to meet you, Doug, she said. What an adventure. A couple of weeks ago I was working as a receptionist in my father's office. And now look at me. Cyril swept me off my feet.

I certainly tried, Carter said. You were the most beautiful girl in Toronto. I had to steal you away from all those other guys.

We met at a gala dinner and dance and he swirled me off my feet, she said.

Slaney didn't want the girl on the boat. Jesus Christ. He didn't want this beautiful stupid girl on the boat with him. He would take Carter aside and tell him to send her back on the plane. He didn't care where Carter sent her. She was not getting on the boat. Nobody said the word anymore. Sexed or vexed or kitten. Vixen.

Hoist the Sails

The sailing was perfect for the first two days. They saw dolphins and a whale and Carter caught fish off the side and Ada gutted and cooked them.

Carter uncorked a bottle of wine he'd been saving for the occasion.

I think you'll find this very pleasant, he said.

We're celebrating our engagement, Ada said.

I'd be very much surprised, Carter said, while pouring Slaney a glass, if this is not the best wine you've ever tasted in your life, young man.

Cyril is developing my palate, Ada said.

He'd only poured a splash and Slaney looked at it with disbelief.

You have to taste it, Carter said. Swish it around in your mouth. Slaney tasted and said it was good and Carter filled his glass and Slaney drank it down in three big gulps.

Bought this in France, Carter said, when my first son was born. Slaney saw that Ada didn't flinch at the mention of the child. She knew about Carter's wife and believed the woman would be better off without a husband who didn't love her.

She had convinced herself that the wife would be better off.

Or: there was nothing that could be done about the wife.

Or: she didn't think about the wife.

Ada was reading murder mysteries and Hemingway and she had a Fitzgerald and a really good Dashiell Hammett, she said, and when she was done she tossed them over the side. She didn't lift her face from the pages but she'd raise her wine-glass and wave it back and forth and Carter would hop up to pour for her. She'd read three Agatha Christies in two days.

Did you know she mysteriously disappeared for a while? she asked Carter.

Who did, darling?

She had a nervous breakdown, Ada said. She just dis-appeared. Ada closed the book and sat up straight, looking hard at the horizon as if she'd just figured something out.

The big reveal, she said. That's my favourite part.

Why are you reading those stupid things? Carter asked.

There was a moment when Ada was at the wheel and Slaney was behind her and he had to lean in and she was between his arms and she glanced back at him to ask a question and her expression was innocent and avid.

She talked about knots and longitude and the sextant with its mirrors and spyglass. Lining up the sun, the horizon, and a star. She was quick with the math of it. She did not acknowledge his chest brushing against her spine. She was doing the math in her head. Figuring the speed and miles they had to cover.

They hit rough water around the coast of Costa Rica and they had winds of twenty knots and once the waves were ten feet.

Slaney went up every fifteen minutes to check the rigging and he had Ada go and check it while he slept. But he hardly slept. A half-hour, here and there.

Carter was drunk for the two rough days, and Ada was exhilarated. Her hair stood out like a flag and she'd had a straw hat she'd tied down with a scarf but it flew off anyway, the brim flapping like a wounded bird.

They were going very fast, smacking down hard on the backs of the waves, and Slaney felt it too: the exhilaration. Lashings of warm rain against his bare chest. He could hardly keep his eyes open on deck, the rain was so hard. The sleepless joy.

He was out he was out he was out.

What he felt was freedom. It was more potent than he had ever imagined or remembered while he was in jail. Potent because it had been lost and regained.

They should have been going ten knots at most and there were times they were going twelve. The wind was thirty knots and it felt like it might tear them asunder. They loved it. It terrified them. All the wave-sparkle and crashing down. The knocking from side to side. Carter's empty whisky bottle rolled across on the floor and rolled back.

They squeezed past each other in the galley, Slaney and Ada, and the thrust of a wave flung her against him and she pushed him away, hard, with both hands flat on his chest.

But they'd looked in each other's eyes and he thought:

Well met.

Hail fellow, well met. That greeting they used in old-fashioned books about robbers and rebels, anarchic and quaint, the kind of thing Robin Hood might say to his Merry Men, or the Three Musketeers.

But it was more than that. Just a brief glance that went deep. Her hands on his chest because the waves had toppled her into him. They weren't well met at all. Another phrase, from a different kind of book: undoing.

She would be his undoing.

Whatever he saw in her eyes: it was modern and harsh and willing. It wasn't brotherly.

On the fifth day the water was calm. The coast was so green and close they thought they could smell the earth.

Let's go swimming, Doug, she said. Let's get in.

Maybe Carter had drunk everything on board. He was snoring his head off.

Kicking

There were thirteen of us, Slaney said. Would have been fifteen but two were crib deaths.

He was lying on a blanket he'd dragged up from the bunk. His eyes were closed and the sun was flaring orange on the inside of his eyelids. Seven days on the water. Carter was below deck frying the fish he'd caught that afternoon. They could smell the onions. Slaney heard the suntan lotion.

She had a suntan lotion that squirted and spat from a brown plastic bottle that was warm to the touch and the cream came out in a warm squiggle and oil seeped away from the cream on the palm of her hand. She smoothed it over her legs and she did her arms.

Want me to do your back? he said. He didn't open his eyes. He wanted to listen to her.

I'm lying on my back, she said. She was resting on her

elbows, he figured, looking out to sea. For a while they didn't say anything and then it felt like she was going to speak. He thought he could feel that. But she lay down flat and said nothing. She lifted her back a little and settled her shoulders.

He heard Carter banging around in the galley, frying up some lunch for them.

Slaney tingled all over, the water evaporating from his skin, leaving a salty residue. They'd been diving over the side, he and Ada, and pulling themselves up on the ladder; they'd splashed each other, little splashes with their fingers, treading water, or skimming the top of the water with the sides of their hands, sending up sheets of splash and was it ever warm.

What a day, Slaney had said. Then she reared back and went crazy with her feet, kicking up a storm. They hauled themselves up the ladder and she was first, and her ass and her legs, what a body, the water a transparent sheet that peeled away from her shoulders and dripped from the bikini bows at her hips.

They lay down trying to catch their breath and he was getting a burn.

She talked about her mother dying and the boarding school she grew up in. A school with lawns rolling in every direction and big trees and forget it. You weren't getting out of there except on the holidays.

The teachers were strict and big on music and she'd learned to sail on Lake Ontario during the summers but during winter the dormitories were cold.

You could see your breath, she said. She told him he could never imagine how lonely. Not when he had all those brothers and sisters elbow to elbow at the one table, he couldn't. Not when he had both his parents.

She said that music was the only thing in her life she could depend on. I'd love to play for you sometime.

I'd like that, he said.

She said her father. She loved her father but she didn't know him at all. He was old already when she was born. Been through the war and what that does. A doctor in the navy.

He's administration now, she said. He runs a hospital in Toronto. He's high up there, a very busy man. She rolled over on her side, her head resting on her hand.

Very, very busy, she said. Her parents had grown up in England and they had wanted to get out. Sick to death of Europe after the war. They'd decided Canada. They'd wanted a clean break. Her mother had died when Ada was seven, a flu with complications. Then she was off to boarding school.

At seven? Slaney said.

You should hear me on the piano, she said. He kept his eyes closed but he knew she was studying him.

Cyril was going to buy her a baby grand. She laughed. Already she was doubting Cyril.

He's full of ideas, Cyril is, she said. But Slaney could tell, she was still willing to believe. The way he danced with her at that gala, she told him. Her father had been getting an award.

They had a twelve-piece band, she said. And one of those machines that makes bubbles. You know those machines?

Slaney said it sounded very different than the dances he'd attended.

Like Lawrence bloody Welk, she said. Bubbles floating down all over the place. I'm kind of a big deal, she said. On the piano.

Good for you, he said.

What about you?

I play the fiddle, he said. Nobody makes a big deal.

She didn't have anything to say to that. They both lay there in the sun not speaking.

Then Slaney told her his name. He said his name wasn't really Douglas Knight. That was the name on the fake passport. He said it was the name of a guy about his age who had died in Montreal. He said he thought about the guy now and then and he wondered if he was somehow keeping the guy going like this, if he was living the guy's life, not his own at all.

That's just foolishness I'm talking now, he said.

What's your name? Ada said.

David Slaney, he said. That's my name.

Colombia

Carter had a collapsible spyglass with four brass cylinders, a rosewood sheath on the last. He gave it a flick with his wrist and each cylinder shot straight out, until the spyglass was nearly as long as his arm. He put it to his eye and turned the wheels near the eyepiece. His other eye screwed up tight and he was showing his teeth. After a moment Carter announced they had the wrong spot.

They were anchored in a cove with a white beach about fifteen miles from Cali in the Valle del Cauca, Colombia, according to the map. But Carter said the map must have been wrong.

Carter had sobered up. They were picking up the cargo and Carter wanted to be sober for the occasion. He had joined Slaney on deck and he'd put on a white shirt and a linen suit.

We're in the wrong bloody place, you fool, Carter said. There's nobody around.

But it had been Carter who was navigating. Slaney snatched the spyglass from him and pressed it to his eye.

He moved the telescope and the water streamed by in hazy jerks and he steadied his elbows on the rail and adjusted the brass wheel and each melting sparkle of sunlight became diamond-hard. He swerved the glass six inches to the left and the beach flew sideways like a scarf tugged by the wind and lurched to a stop.

He lifted it half an inch, very gently, and there were the camouflaged army tents in the shadows, under the palm trees, beyond the beach. He counted fifteen tents.

A man in army fatigues was sitting on a chair in front of a large tent with a rifle across his lap. Another man approached him, took a pack of cigarettes from his breast pocket, and tapped it and held out the pack. The man in the chair swatted his hand around his head at insects. Slaney heard the far-off buzz of a boat engine, growing insistent and menacing and loud.

Here they come, Carter said. Slaney lowered the spyglass and saw a speedboat racing toward them. It was a blur in the afternoon haze, a streak of aluminum, mirage-kinked in the heat, bouncing on the waves. Slaney and Carter stood on deck and watched them come. They told Ada to go below.

Do me a favour, Slaney said. She turned the last page of her book and flung it over the side and it skipped three times like a stone and floated away.

You want me to miss all the fun, she said.

Make yourself scarce, he said, as a favour to me.

Slaney felt tense and happy. Carter had gone down below and come back with the suitcase full of money. It was an ordinary brown leather bag and it had heft.

Ada stretched one arm up and yawned and flapped her towel and wrapped it around herself. She had been topless and coated in baby oil all day.

They give you a choice around here, lead or gold, Carter said. Did you know that, Slaney? It means a bribe or a bullet.

Tell her to go below, Slaney said.

Go below, Ada, Carter said. You heard the man.

The man, Ada said. Yes, I heard the man.

Several minutes later the speedboat was upon them and turned sharply just before it hit and the wave splashed against the yacht.

You're not coming, Carter, Slaney said.

I'm coming, Carter said. I'll do what I bloody well like.

Carter climbed down the ladder and stepped into the speedboat, the men reaching for his hands to steady him.

Slaney passed down the suitcase with the seventy-five grand into the boat and Carter gripped it between his knees. Slaney had taken a quarter of the hundred thou out of the suitcase so that he could barter. If Lopez wouldn't let the pot go for seventy-five, he'd come back and get the rest of the money. After Carter was settled, Slaney climbed down the ladder and stepped into the speedboat.

They were soldiers with gold watches and gold teeth and they had houses with big pools and five years ago they were peasants making a handful of dollars a month growing coffee. Or they were the ruling elite who had lost the family fortune and had to maintain a lifestyle. Slaney got all this from Hearn, but he could see it for himself, a different kind of confidence than when he'd been here before. He felt like the mood had shifted.

Now they were armed with machine guns and a few of

them had grenades and leather belts of bullets hanging over one shoulder and they had hunting knives and some of them had pistols on each hip like cowboys in the movies.

The men asked if it was cold in Canada.

Mucho frío, sí, Slaney shouted over the engine. Carter attempted to explain hypothermia and they all laughed.

One of them said, Horses, yes? Carter clearly had no idea what they meant. There was a burst of Spanish and one of them said, RCMP. Carter said yes, they had the RCMP.

They were all hearty about the RCMP and then there was silence.

One of them said, Toronto?

Newfoundland, Carter and Slaney said in unison. Then there was silence until they reached the beach.

Slaney had expected Carter to make a fuss about getting his shoes wet. But he took them off without a word and rolled up the linen pants and he carried the shoes in his hand above his head and Slaney realized he preferred Carter drunk. The men offered to carry the suitcase but Slaney carried it on his head.

A few huts and the sound of a radio and excited Spanish coming out in bursts of static. A dog came out to greet them and she had big black teats hanging to the sand. A sad German shepherd face but the legs were too short. It had the hunching gait of something starving and maddened by flies.

There was nothing but the huts and then a roar overhead made Slaney and Carter duck and the soldiers laughed at them. The plane was so low they felt the pull of it. It touched the tops of the palm trees and they swayed in its aftermath and coconuts thumped down into the sand. Probably armed guards or field workers flown in for a few weeks' work.

They had a landing strip. Five years ago they'd had nothing. Slaney tried to look unimpressed. Carter leaned in and asked if he thought Sanchez was really a colonel.

It's Lopez, Slaney said.

Lopez, Sanchez, said Carter.

There's a difference, Slaney said. Do you want to get us shot?

We should have brought a bottle, Carter said. He reached to straighten his tie but he wasn't wearing a tie. They approached the man Slaney had seen in the spyglass but he was standing at attention with the rifle across his chest, staring straight ahead at nothing. The soldier lifted the flap of the army tent and Slaney and Carter ducked inside. Shafts of sunlight came through the mosquito-net windows, making the room a swampy orange. It was cooler inside and smelled like candle-wax and wet canvas.

Colonel Lopez was standing before an impressive table. He waved a hand at it, inviting them to sit. There was a platter of papaya and guava and melon and bananas and some roasted chicken and a basket of bread. Tomato and cucumber slices arranged in a spiral, shredded cabbage and beets, fried plantains.

Langosta, the colonel said, and he lifted a silver dome off a platter and revealed four barbecued lobsters. A young girl, of perhaps fourteen, lit the candles. She had thick black braids and acne on her forehead and cheeks and she kept her eyes on the wick until it was lit. Then the girl sat in a chair in the corner with her hands on her knees, ready to jump if she was needed.

While they ate they discussed the price. Slaney started at fifty.

Lopez asked about their journey and offered them coffee and had the girl on the chair bring in a teapot and they were given espresso cups and saucers. She kept one hand on the loose-fitting lid as she poured and eyed the stream of coffee with a fixed surliness. Everyone was silent as she moved from chair to chair with the teapot.

You must understand how many people are employed on this end, Lopez said. He said he would accept no less than one hundred thousand dollars for the two tons of marijuana they were purchasing.

I will go no lower, he said. He asked them to consider the unpredictability of the growing season, the peasants who broke their backs working in the fields, and the need they had to feed their children. He mentioned the heat they worked in, the sweat. He talked about the economic disparity between their nations, the growing violence in his country for workers in the industry. He said that an offer of fifty thousand dollars for the product they were going away with was an insult. As he spoke his face became flushed and his voice became louder and more sonorous.

Then he raised a hand to halt the conversation altogether and he said, Flan.

The girl at the back jumped up so quickly from her chair that Slaney saw Carter flinch. Slaney had no idea what *flan* meant but the girl snapped open the tent flap and disappeared and returned with dessert.

Slaney said he appreciated the position Lopez was in, and the position of his workers. He spoke about the imperialism of the United States, particularly in Central America, and he mentioned each of the countries there and the dictatorships propped up by the West. But then he spoke about Newfoundland and the relative poverty on the island and how cold the water was and how hard it was to make a living from the sea as his forefathers had done. He spoke about the Commission of Government, and how his grandfather had had the right to vote stripped from him and the bad teeth of Newfoundlanders and rickets and scurvy and frostbite. He spoke about weather, ice, and snow and the great sealing disasters.

Then he and Lopez bartered by five thousand, up and down, and then by a thousand. And five hundred dollar lots.

They were at eighty thousand when Carter began to speak about the coffee.

It's so strong, he said. He asked if the beans had been grown in the area. He mentioned the first occasion he'd tasted coffee; a distant relative in London, England, had served it to him when he was a child of six.

He'd been sitting across from the mounted head of a rhinoceros, he said. Poor creature.

The head was bigger than I was, Carter said. All that bone and horn, the glassy eyes. Before that I'd only ever had tea with lots of milk. He talked about staring at the mounted rhino and how he'd expected the rest of it to crash through the wall at any moment. He thought it had just poked its head through the plaster to look around before charging them. He believed it must have had terribly long legs, on the other side, and that he would be stomped to death.

Carter had been rocking the side of his fork through his flan, shovelling big pieces in quickly, talking with his mouth full. Slaney realized the bartering was frightening him out of his wits and that he needed a drink. Then Slaney saw that Lopez had his napkin scrunched tight in his fist.

Seventy-five, Slaney said. Lopez agreed immediately.

A soldier came through the flap and took the briefcase and

returned when they had finished the flan. He spoke to Lopez in a whisper, cupping the man's ear with one hand. Then he straightened up and stepped back against the canvas wall.

Everything is tranquilo, Lopez said. I prefer it we settle business out in the open.

Slaney said he preferred things that way too.

I prefer we be honest with each other in all transactions.

Slaney agreed.

Honest and open, Lopez said.

Open discussion, absolutely, Slaney said.

I understand you lost a great deal on your last trip, Lopez said. This turns investors, no? He winced when he said this and shifted uncomfortably in his chair, removing a pistol that had been in a holster at his waist. He laid it on the table next to his plate.

You are young, Lopez said. Mistakes, you begin to learn. Now you know.

I think so, sir, Slaney said. He glanced at the flame of a candle in the centre of the table. It was wagging low and stretching, making itself thin. It was trying to squirm off the wick.

Hearn had lied to him. He had not told Slaney about Ada; he had said Carter had dried out. But this was of a different order of untruth. Now there was a loaded pistol on a linen napkin near Slaney's crystal bowl of cubed papaya. Hearn had said Lopez didn't know about the other trip. He had given his word Lopez wouldn't know.

It was not Hearn sitting under the canvas tent in the rising heat surrounded by armed men. Hearn was probably sitting in an English class where the most loaded thing was the use or abuse of the semicolon in a thesis on Virginia Woolf's stream of consciousness. Hearn had let him walk into a situation blind. There was a kerfuffle outside.

Shouts from the men. People running.

Lopez shouted back and he leapt up and was out through the flap with his pistol in his hand. Slaney and Carter followed behind him, ready to take off into the trees. They thought a raid. They thought: Make a run for it.

Fifteen men had arranged themselves in a line from one of the tents to the beach and they'd been tossing the bales of weed from one to the other, loading a large speedboat with the cargo they would transport to Carter's sailboat. The sun was still very hot and the water near shore was crimson-streaked and too bright after the cool darkness of the tent.

Five soldiers were running over the sand from the forest behind them to the water's edge with their guns held out before their chests and they halted together, lined up side by side, the guns raised and aimed, and they cocked the triggers and stared down the barrels like a firing squad.

Who have we here, Colonel Lopez asked. Ada was rising out of the surf. She was wearing the red bikini.

One of the men moving the weed had been hit in the chest by a bale while his head was turned to look at her.

Ada had swum the two miles to shore. She stood at the edge of the water and tilted her head sideways. She knocked one ear with the flat of her hand.

We are lucky the sharks didn't get you, Lopez said.

He shook hands with her.

Come inside and have something to eat, he suggested. We have just finished, but there is lots left over.

I'm starving, Ada said. She had gathered her long hair in her hands and was wringing the water out of the length of it.

Do you mind, darling? Ada called to Carter. I'll be in the

big tent back there, getting something to eat. I was feeling lonely back on the boat.

Slaney and Carter helped the men load the weed and they were fitting the bales into the hold for the better part of three hours.

When they were done they screwed the false panelling in place and Carter slapped the wall and smoothed his hand down the length of it. They both stood back with their hands on their hips and surveyed their work.

They found that the wall looked like a wall. But they could smell the jungle stink.

Feathers

They'd been invited to a beach party with the Colombians and headed back to shore in the speedboat.

A young man showed the three of them the path to the toilet, a deep pit with a seat built over it, a hole in the middle of the seat. The pit was covered in lye that glowed weirdly in the beam of the flashlight. The construction involved hanging over the open pit but the support beams looked sturdy.

Ingenious, Carter said. But Slaney wasn't sure.

Lopez had broken out bottles of homemade whisky and they'd all smoked up. A bonfire going on the beach.

More people arrived in the back of a truck, men and women who had been working in the fields and had returned to the camp for the evening.

The weed was of a very high quality, stinking like Christmas trees, sticky with resin. It was strong and enlightening. Provoking of revelation.

Some of the men had taken out instruments as the night wore on and they'd sung Colombian folk songs and Carter and Ada had danced, her forehead resting on his collarbone. Two sisters sang a Spanish ballad in harmony, and everyone joined in the chorus. They sang with their eyes closed, nodding their heads slowly, as if they agreed with the words of the song.

Slaney asked Ada if she wanted him to give her a brainer. They were sitting in old frayed lawn chairs and Ada slid off her tilted chair and crawled to him, the mock slink of a wild cat, a panther or lynx, until she was between Slaney's legs. She raised herself up to kneeling, with her hands on his thighs, and she opened her mouth an inch or so from his.

Slaney drew in a deep lungful of smoke from the joint and put his mouth as close to hers without touching as he could. Then he blew out a soft grey column of pummelling smoke. It streamed from his open lips to hers until her mouth was a smoky O. Ada sucked it in, dropping her head, and then let the smoke pour back out and he was ready with another lungful.

She fell over in the sand, her arms and her legs spreading open and shut as if she were making snow angels.

Look at the stars, Ada said. I wonder if anybody is out there. Maybe my mother is looking down from heaven. Hi, Mommy.

Slaney was offered a violin and he played it like a fiddle, jigs and reels, and then something slow and full of need that he made up as he went along. Ada had rolled over on her side now, her head in her hand, and she stared up at him.

All the need he'd felt in prison came out of the wooden instrument under his chin. All the longing, terse and barbed and broken, hung over the bonfire. The flames near the crackled black logs were blue and flicking. It seemed like the fire breathed up and sank down with the music. The ocean roared and shushed. Someone had bongo drums; someone had a tin whistle. There were a few stringed instruments made of gourds. A silver flute. Everybody playing together, improvising. Looking up into each other's eyes so they could all know where they were going with it. Slaney leading the way, sawing gently, tapping his foot, urging them on by nodding yes and yes.

If Slaney had a reason for going on this trip in the first place, maybe it was this: so he could be on a Colombian beach playing all his sadness out under the stars, stoned out of his mind. He was there for the sense of abandon he felt.

That's why, he said out loud when he stopped playing. Ada had stood up and brushed the sand away from her elbow and dropped into the empty chair next to him. She was wearing army fatigues someone had loaned her, the fabric faded from washing. She rubbed her shoulder back and forth against his shoulder. She was flushed and grinning.

What's why?

What, he asked.

You just said, That's why. What's why?

You're why, he said.

I'm why what?

You're why. You're why, he said. His flimsy lawn chair, with its chrome frame and woven nylon strips of plaid, collapsed under him then. He stood, with great effort, and the trees behind them lurched sideways and he bequeathed the unharmed violin to the man next to him and took the flashlight and headed off to find the lye pit.

The flashlight beam bounced and jiggled over rocks and tree roots and then the swaying beam found a girl with shiny

black hair tumbling down one shoulder. She was sitting on a
wooden chair, her knees apart, her boots planted firmly. She
was plucking a chicken and she had a kerosene lantern that lit
her like a painting by Rembrandt, golden and shadowed. The
denuded, incandescent and pimpled bird hung by the claws
from the girl's raised fist.

There was a tree stump and the axe stood up in it, the blade
sunk into the blond wood that was stained with blood. A
chicken's head lay in the dirt, and when the flashlight beam
strayed to it, the chicken's yellow eyeball with its black pupil
and red warty-looking eyelid stared at Slaney, unblinking.
The eye looked full of consternation and acceptance.

The woman spoke a few words to him and he told her: No
entiendo. But she kept talking.

White feathers filled the air. They seemed forever suspended in the beam of his light.

She was pointing toward the lye pit and kept talking and
plucking though he didn't understand a word of what she was
saying. But he knew the gist. He had a good idea she was talking about the bathroom. The crude toilet was an entrance to
hell. He must be very careful.

She was saying life is magnificent. Freedom was running in
his blood now, it was part of him. Nobody could take it away.
She was reminding him of the light on the water, how bedaz-
zling it had been on the way down and the crack of the sails
when the wind picked up and the horizon and the smell of
salt in the air and the fish they'd eaten the minute they pulled
it out of the water and how fish as fresh as that could affect
your dreams. She was saying Hearn had been right about one
thing: they were no longer who they had been before.

They had been changed.

She warned him that once he was back in Canada he must forget Hearn. They should go their separate ways. Hearn was weak and dangerous, she said. Hearn had lied about Lopez and the first trip. Lopez knew everything. How they had failed the first time. What they owed.

You owe so very much, the woman said. She asked him did he think about his mother. What this was doing to his mother.

The feathers stirring in the little beam of the flashlight.

Watch out for the girl, she said. But it was unclear if she meant he should protect Ada, as a guardian angel might, or be afraid of her.

Everything the woman said came out all at once, every thought overlapping, currents of converging thoughts and tidal pulls and he was following her drift. She was speaking Spanish very quickly and pointing toward the lye pit, but what she communicated came in a gush of interior voice that Slaney understood without effort.

Then a man came out of the woods behind the woman and stood like a sentinel with his rifle, his hand on her shoulder.

What are you looking for? the man asked. For a second Slaney believed he had broken through the language barrier once and for all. Because he understood. Then he realized the man had spoken in English.

Looking for the bathroom, Slaney said. He thanked them with everything he had in him. He hoped they understood his sincerity. He thanked them in English and Spanish and he turned and stumbled on through the woods to the pit.

The three of them ended up sleeping in the same small tent, Ada in the middle between Carter and Slaney. He'd hit the ground hard after he stumbled through the tent flap. The ground rose up to meet him and fell with the rhythm of the sea. Great swells lifted him and let him slide down.

Slaney could not remember getting into the tent but he woke in the middle of the night with an amorphous terror pounding through him.

Nothing stirred outside except the surf. The ocean roared up over the beach and drew back. Carter was snoring the clotted, wavering honk of the trumpeter swan.

In the beat while Carter inhaled lived the hope the noise would stop. But Carter kept snoring.

There was the terror and then Slaney felt himself falling, as though from a great height, falling backwards into forever, arms and legs flailing. Below him, his friends had stretched a white sheet that glowed in the dark as the dancers' white clothes and teeth had glowed under the black light at Hearn's party. They were waiting to catch him. But as he got closer he realized the white circle was an aerial view of the lye pit. He was heading straight for it.

The fall gathered velocity the closer he got to the ground and finally he thumped down hard and his heart burst out of his chest and he passed out until morning.

He woke with his arm wrapped tight around Ada's waist, her bum sunk into his hips, his cock hard against her. He got up and tore the tent flap open and a shaft of bright light struck him in the face.

Slaney walked down the beach until he was sure he was alone and took off all his clothes and ran into the surf.

He strode forward until he was up to his chest and he watched for the right wave, rolling in from the horizon. The wave rose higher and higher, sunlight blazing through the thick glassy wall of it, the crumbling white crest plowing toward him. When it reached him he threw out his arms and let it carry him into shore.

Animism

On the first two days sailing up from Colombia, along the Pacific coast, Carter maintained a profound level of drunkenness. The drinking gave him a level gaze and his face slackened and his speech became prim and elegant. The effort of becoming sober for the visit ashore with Lopez had withered him.

It had been a mistake for him to get that sober. Now he was saying he didn't believe the man's military credentials.

He said that the lobster, which he had gorged on, dipping each morsel in a bowl of drawn butter, had disagreed with him. He thought he had been poisoned.

Carter told them there was a religion of animism practised in the region where they'd partied. He'd read about it in *National Geographic*. A mix of witchcraft and Christianity that made use of hallucinogenic roots, ground to powder.

Some of these rituals involved the ancient art of voodoo, he said.

Carter believed they'd given him something altering on the night of the party. Slipped something in his whisky. He'd given up on the idea of drying out as soon as Lopez offered some wine after lunch.

Don't mind if I do, he'd said. Now he believed they'd been trying to kill him. A formality crept into his diction that frightened Slaney. Then he became very sick.

I have acute indigestion, he said. He was flushed and pale by turns, clammy and sour-smelling, vomiting every hour or so. Ada said his temperature had reached one hundred and four. He'd broken out in a rash and the touch of the bedsheets hurt his skin.

Ada screamed for Slaney and he found that Carter had fallen out of the bed. He was wearing a Stones T-shirt and nothing else. His grey pubic hair a shock.

He sees rats, Ada said. The three of them stared at the bedsheets.

They were all over me, Carter said. The T-shirt was soaked through and Slaney helped him take it off and then he was cold and shivering. He collapsed, banging his head against the wooden bed rail, opening a gash on his cheekbone.

But he kept drinking. Carter believed the alcohol would kill whatever bug he had. He called out for whisky and Ada gave it to him. He slept deeply and sometimes they couldn't shake him awake. Slaney and Ada had to sail the boat by themselves and nurse Carter. She was determined and waxen from lack of sleep.

He'd started muttering to himself. Sometimes he looked straight through them and spoke about a teapot with a crack. He asked them to bring him a particular teapot and grew agitated when he saw it wasn't the one he wanted. He called out to his wife through the night.

We've got to get him to a doctor, Ada said. I am frightened out of my wits. She had her fists in her hair near her temples and she slid her back down the wall until she was hunched in the corner.

Please, David, she said. A fever like that could kill him. That's how my mother died. It was so fast. Please.

We'll get caught, Slaney said. They were off the coast of Nicaragua. He could go in there and try to find a doctor, but they would get caught. She looked up at him from the floor, her eyes glassed over with tears, her nose pink at the tip. She was pitiable and commanding.

Or brain damage, she said.

Okay, I'll bring him in, Slaney said. I'll get him to a hospital or clinic or whatever they have. First thing in the morning.

Oh, David, she said, and she rested her forehead against her wrist and sobbed.

The dread that coursed through him straightened his posture. He stood upright and rigid. He must have looked like he had been called to attention.

Why are you with him? he asked.

That doesn't matter now, she said.

But the fever broke the next morning and Carter became docile and grateful. He drank broth, cupping the bowl with both hands, slopping it all over the sheets. He looked like a mendicant or he looked cursed, munching the soda crackers Ada handed him one by one.

He stayed in bed except to go to the toilet. He hardly spoke to them. After three days Carter was up again, on the deck. Two days later he had fully recovered. By then they were sailing past Mexico. One beautiful morning Slaney found them necking in the galley. Ada had a frying pan on the stove and a pat of butter slid across the black surface, sizzling.

Darling, it's beautiful on deck, Ada told Carter. Go up and get some sunshine, I'll call you down when the pancakes are done.

She picked up the chrome bowl with the batter and the whisk chimed against the sides. She had been restored. The haggard fortitude that she'd called on to keep Carter alive had disappeared. She was girlish again.

I feel kind of light-headed, Ada said. Slaney wedged himself into the bench at the table. Ada swivelled more butter over the hot frying pan and put it down on the gimballed stove and poured the batter in and the smell filled up the galley.

I had a flying dream last night, she said. Ever had one of those, David?

I slept the sleep of the dead, he said.

Watch this, Ada said. Are you watching? She jerked the frying pan and the pancake flew up and flipped in the air and she caught it.

Did you see that? Ada asked. She turned to him holding out the pan. Her face was lit up.

You're making me hungry, Slaney said. She tried to open the bottle of honey, hitting the metal lid with a butter knife, holding the jar between her knees.

Give it here, Slaney said.

No.

Pass it over. He got up to wrestle it away from her but she turned her back and they were roughhousing over the honey and he had her pinned against the counter, but she was curled around the jar with her back to him.

I can do it, she said, and she was laughing. They were both laughing. Then the lid gave and they were embarrassed. They both blushed and Slaney stepped back and she poured out the honey and twisted the jar. A line of it wiggled over her knuckles and she licked it.

I am grateful, she said. I know what getting a doctor would have meant.

They were looking at each other, and her strange eyes, blue

and hazel, and what the hell was she doing, she was only nineteen and she seemed without guile.

Slaney thought there was something true in her. He could not understand how she had come to be there with an old drunk. They were overtaken by stillness. The sea was still and there wasn't a breath of wind.

Carter yelled for Slaney to get up on deck and she had the open jar of honey and they were both self-conscious. Slaney sat down at the table and picked up his knife and fork. He held them upright in his fists.

There, she said. She put the plate in front of him.

Fluffy, Slaney said.

Timing is the thing, she said.

Slaney, Carter yelled. I need you up here. He sounded sober and amazed.

Caroline

Hello, Staff-Sergeant Patterson, O'Neill's secretary said. She stood up from the desk and left the telephone, lit up and ringing, to lead Patterson down the corridor to the screening room. He'd been following the sailboat's progress over the weeks and he'd heard about the hurricane on the news.

Superintendent O'Neill is grateful you could come in on such short notice.

That's my job, Patterson said.

And how's Mrs. Patterson? the secretary asked. She was trotting down the corridor and Patterson had to rush to keep up. His wife would be making crayon shavings with a cheese grater. The children put the shavings between sheets of wax paper and his wife ironed them, melting the crayon, and they cut out autumn leaves to decorate the classroom.

Mrs. Patterson is fine, thank you.

Still reading her poetry, I guess? she asked. The secretary spoke as if she and Patterson were in collusion about how to deal with his fey and capricious wife.

Patterson had driven Delores through the New England states last year to see the fall colours. She was fond of Emily Dickinson and they'd visited the poet's cottage.

Oh look, her inkwell, Delores had cried out, startling the other people crowded together in the little rooms on the tour.

The guide had said, Don't touch. Delores spun around and her hand flew to her cheek as if she'd been slapped.

No, no, I wouldn't, she blurted. But she held up the inkwell before her like a weapon.

He'd been married for just over twenty years and it was a solid and narrowly focused marriage. Delores taught kindergarten and had kept her figure doing calisthenics and he could trust her to cook meals he loved; or he had grown to love the meals she cooked. She had lots of girlfriends, a rich social life with which he had very little to do.

The poetry mattered to her and she wrote it and went off to meetings and came back tipsy and raw. He didn't know what went on there but when she returned from a meeting she was distracted and amorous, or obscurely hurt and closed off.

He loved that there were things he didn't know about her. He couldn't say what made her tick or why she stayed with him but he felt lucky to live in her orbit.

The soap and candles and chocolates she brought home when kindergarten was over for the year.

The ardent and unformed love the school children had for

her — he'd once witnessed a mobbing, each child hugging her waist, digging in against one another for a handful of his wife, and Delores on tiptoe with a box of Popsicles raised over her head.

Their son, Basil, was a cadet in the RCMP, and Patterson would not brag. He would not boast, but it was an effort. And their daughter had broken his heart.

The secretary knocked on a door at the end of the hall and listened and opened it.

Superintendent O'Neill, Staff-Sergeant Patterson has arrived, she said.

He'd been called into the office and there were men with white shirts and ties standing in the dark room and they were facing the screen.

Patterson, O'Neill said. The men all turned to look at him. Come in, Patterson.

O'Neill and Simmonds and Tony Belmont were there and they had called in a few guys Patterson hadn't met before and O'Neill introduced him. Patterson looked them in the eyes as he shook their hands. He repeated their names, Greenwood, Capardi, Bennett, and Hughes, but he felt the magnetic pull of the screen.

It was a juddering picture full of snow. Washes of emptiness. Grit. There was nothing to see.

We think they're gone, O'Neill said. They may be lost at sea. We've lost them. The screen turned to sand and reconfigured. The picture swished away and came back and the whole image vibrated like the pelt of a frightened animal.

What's wrong with the signal? Patterson asked.

They hit Hurricane Caroline and we've lost the picture, Greenwood said. They are right in the middle of that thing.

It's very doubtful a vessel of that size will get through it.

The device must have been damaged, Bennett said.

There's no signal, O'Neill said. There's been a lot of wreckage along the Pacific coast, they've got flooding, fires, twenty-four people injured, twelve deaths reported since September 4, the count is rising. Fishing boats crushed. Cattle. Crops destroyed. We've got calls out all over the coast. But they haven't turned up. We think they must have been hit by the storm early this morning.

One of the men crossed in front of the projector and his shirt turned blue and grainy. The light from the projector was full of cigarette smoke. The secretary who had shown Patterson in knocked and opened the door again and she said she had Señor Vasquez from the Mexican Bureau of Immigration on the line for Superintendent O'Neill.

Excuse me, boys, O'Neill said.

Our guys are talking to their guys where we can, but the lines are down, Capardi said. We're trying to see if they turn anything up. But I'd guess we're the least of their worries.

The white screen flashed whiter and went grey.

What was that? Simmonds asked.

The projector blew a bulb, Capardi said.

Patterson sat on one of the chairs they had arranged in a row in front of the screen and somebody asked him if he took sugar.

For the first time Patterson felt complicit. He broke a sweat all over.

Carter. Carter had made his choices.

But David Slaney was just a kid.

And the girl was even younger than Patterson's own daughter. He thought about Ada playing the piano. Patterson had tracked down her father. Sebastian Anderson. He was a widower, a doctor in Toronto. A former medical officer in the navy, held prisoner in a detention camp in Italy. A decorated man, a war hero, probably wrecked by his feckless, wild child.

If something had happened to the girl Patterson would have to contact her father. He thought about the call. He would have to admit he'd met her, heard her at the piano, knew she was talented and strange, and that he'd let her go off with that filthy old goat of a man. Let her get embroiled in illegal activity. He had not taken her aside as he hoped somebody might do, another father, for his own daughter.

Patterson could have put a stop to it. He thought of shaking Slaney's hand. The boy had been earnest and, Patterson thought, intelligent and desperate. Audacious. The raw will in his eyes. That would be destroyed by another round in prison.

How much of this had to do with Patterson's promotion? He let himself ponder that question. What if they died out there?

What are they, he asked Simmonds, three weeks from home? Yes, I take sugar.

Upside Down

The sky dropped her fingers into the warm sea and leisurely trailed them along. The hurricane seemed to be a long way off but they could see the sky trailing in the waves.

Carter was charged up. He'd developed the thrusting walk of a man looking for a fight. He saw the storm swish and sway and turn to look over her shoulder at him.

Come and get me, he whispered. He gripped the rail and was transfixed.

Everything dead still, the water smooth and flat. Slaney saw a large glassy patch on the surface near the starboard side, the footprint of a diving whale, and he saw the long black shadow of it, gliding far, far below the surface.

Lower the mainsail, Carter said. I'll get the rest. The whisper of the canvas *flumping*, the creak of the boom, the rigging skittering, and they looked up and saw the lines were tangled at the masthead.

I'll go, Slaney said. He strapped himself to the mast with two loops of rope and climbed the mast steps. He held tight with one arm while he worked up the lines that secured him, lifting them a foot or two up the pole with each step he took.

Then it was upon them. Such instant force and power, seemingly out of nowhere. They were lashed with it, coils of snapping rain and the wind. It seemed to come because Carter had asked for it.

The mast was dipping down near the surface and swinging back up and down again and Slaney was yelling but he didn't know what he was saying. A wall of plowing white surf bore down on the boat, high as a house.

Slaney lost his footing on the mast steps and clung with all his might, bicycling his feet until he found purchase and he reached out as far as he could, the tangled lines just inches from his fingers.

Get down, David, Carter called out.

We can't afford to lose the sail, Carter, Slaney said.

Get down, Carter called. And he called David's name over and over.

I almost got it, Slaney screamed back.

David, Carter said. And Slaney saw the wave billowing over the side and Carter was lifted off his feet and buried by white foam, and the boat disappeared in the avalanche and Slaney was on a pole with the sky swatting him and there was nothing below. Then the prow pointed out of the curdled foam and the boat peeled itself out of the water, the deck emerged, and Slaney saw that Carter lay on his back, rammed against the gunwale. He was still and Slaney thought he might have been knocked unconscious and called to him because another wave was coming as malevolent and full of white mist and crumbling concrete as the last, and Carter got to his hands and knees and shook his head as if he disagreed with the way it was going down and he was rammed hard against the gunwale again.

Then the mast tipped all the way down and a wave bared its white teeth at Slaney's backside, hanging now over the water, his arms and legs wrapped around the mast. The wave below him was licking its chops, snarling, snapping, and then Slaney was swallowed whole.

It was roaring below the surface, roil and gush, foaming spume, and he wondered how far down he was and if he would ever see the surface again and his lungs were ready to explode. He drew in water and it burned like fire.

Then he felt himself lifted skyward in a great rush and the mast broke free of the fist of the wave and was upright again and Slaney gasped and gasped and slid down and was back on the deck and he untied the ropes around his waist and he couldn't see Carter.

Maybe Carter had gone below. The crack rang out like a shot canon and the mainsail, soaking wet, was ripped to shreds. Wet ribbons of sail draped themselves over the deck and Slaney waited for the next wave to wash over and pass away and then he slid over the deck to the hatch and was down below.

Where is he? Ada screamed.

Isn't he down here with you? Slaney shouted, but he was already heading back up to the deck and he saw Carter half-way over the gunwale as if he were trying to make a break for it.

Slaney staggered over the deck and grabbed Carter by the back of his shirt and they rolled together like lovers over the tipping boat and as the boat righted itself they both made it back to the hatch and Carter yelled *You first* and Slaney went first because he didn't want to argue and it took Carter a long time to follow. Then he half fell down the hatch.

The drinking had a purpose, Slaney thought. The drinking had called forth Carter's best self. A lifetime of being loaded had made him composed and stoic in the face of the hurricane. Slaney watched as Carter drew in a deep breath through his nostrils and slowly let it out. They battened down the hatch and went to their cabins to wait it out.

During the night Ada bawled out Slaney's name. Or he thought she did.

Go to your bunk, Slaney shouted back. Maybe she didn't want him to be alone. Carter yelled too. It sounded like they were fighting. He thought one of them had thrown something at the other.

The storm hadn't built; there was no arrival. They say the eye, and now Slaney knew what they were saying.

The eye of the storm.

The eye gave them a good hard look, then the eye lost interest. A roving eye.

The sailboat rose up and seemed to teeter on the crest of what felt like a thirty-foot wave and then it crashed down. It was a motion that entered each of Slaney's cells and undid all the rhythms in his blood and his inner ear and he felt upside down when he was right side up.

His blood had been touched by the same fingers that had stirred up the sea out near the horizon. For a long time he had the feeling that if he could just drink a glass of water everything would be put right.

There was lots of time to think about how wrong it all was. How funny it felt. Carter saying, You first. Slaney lay in his cot and listened to the vessel groan. A litany of splintering complaint.

The storm went on for thirty-six hours. Slaney didn't sleep because he kept being jerked awake. Then he was struck by sleep. It came like a blow. It took a fitful dream to draw him back to the surface. Slaney dreamed his way back.

When he woke, his neck was stiff, or it was the only part of him that wasn't stiff and it felt funny by comparison. The storm was over.

Slaney had dreamt a forest in Norway. He'd never been to Norway nor thought anything about it. In the dream he'd walked by himself through a spare wood of birch, the snow creaked underfoot, and there was someone walking behind him.

Slaney crawled out of his room and found that Ada and Carter were already on deck.

There was a rainbow.

The sun was shearing through the clouds, tacky looking, a velvet painting with religious tones.

There's land over there, Ada said.

The sails are destroyed, Carter said.

They were near a shoreline. A long, white beach with a few demolished huts, destroyed fishing boats, hulls smashed out.

The palm trees were taking a nap, all lying down next to each other on the beach.

The first thing I'm going to do, Carter said. I'm going to call my kids. My oldest girl does ballet. There'll probably be a concert. They've started school now.

I did ballet, Ada said. They offered it at school. You could do sewing or you could do ballet. I did tennis and ballet, but then I just played piano.

I'd have gone for the sewing, Slaney said. Ada leaned over the railing and vomited. She wiped her mouth with the back of her hand.

Can you read music, Slaney? she asked. I've been wondering about that.

I didn't learn that way, Slaney said.

What have I done? Carter asked. What have I done? He was holding onto the rail, looking over the side. He was shaking his head. Ada and Slaney didn't speak.

I want to hold my wife, Carter said. Little Mary is probably at her ballet class right now.

We're messed up by this storm, Ada said. We thought we were dead. I did, anyway.

I don't know what time it is back home, Carter said. They might be having breakfast. The first thing I'm going to do when we get off this boat is find a phone.

I think I cracked a tooth, Slaney said. He spit into his hand and held it out to Carter.

Is that part of my tooth? Slaney asked. Carter reached out a finger and touched the bit of tooth covered in saliva and it stuck to the tip of his finger and he looked at it closely and flicked it away.

I don't know what that was, he said. That wasn't anything.

Whatever strength Carter had summoned to get them through was the last reserve. He looked old and fragile and diminished. He looked like he was going to have another nervous breakdown.

Look at that rainbow, Slaney said. They were still alive. He lowered himself to the deck because his legs were giving out. They were fucked without the sails. Hearn. He would have to phone Hearn. The authorities would come aboard the boat. It would take a couple of weeks, at least, to get the sails repaired. They would have to go ashore. They were caught. They were as good as caught.

There's vomit all over the cabin, Ada said. I can't go back down there yet. But I'm going to need my hairbrush.

All I need is a phone, Cyril said.

My hair is just full of tangles, Ada said. She was raking her fingers through her hair.

You can't call your family, Slaney said. There'll be plenty of time for your family later. You can call your wife after we've all said our goodbyes.

I'm not saying goodbye to anyone, Ada said. Cyril and I are in love.

Is There Something We Should Know

Slaney sat in a wooden chair across from the immigration officer's desk. The desk was full of papers and forms. There was a stack of white forms and a stack of pale yellow papers and there were sheets of carbon and the officer had taken Slaney's passport.

We weren't planning on a visit, Slaney said. The officer met

Slaney's eyes whenever he spoke. It was a calculating stare devoid of welcome.

He was broad with a clean blue uniform, the cuffs and collar frayed. The officer had a black moustache and thick curly hair and his eyebrows were heavy. His skin was light and there was a black mole high on his cheekbone. The mole gave an otherwise rugged face a feminine haughtiness.

Do you have any illegal cargo on board your vessel, Señor Knight? Any firearms or large sums of cash, illegal substances, marijuana or cocaine?

Slaney said they didn't have anything like that.

That's fine, the officer said. Forgive me for asking. It's procedure, of course. I have to ask.

The officer spread Slaney's passport open on the desk before him and let his hands fall, loosely linked, between his knees and he rocked slightly in his chair as he stared at it.

We're heading home, Slaney said. The officer picked up the passport and brought it to the window and held it to the glass, tilting his head to look at it in the natural light. He left the room with the passport and returned empty-handed.

We will wait, Mr. Knight, the officer said. The vessel must be searched before we can let you go. The passport verified. These procedures will happen in good time.

The officer began to attend to the paperwork before him. He wrote on each page that he took from the stack on his left and when he had come to the end of a form he held it out in one hand before him, snapping it straight, and read it through. He frowned while he read and when he was satisfied he placed the completed form in a pile on his right.

The man appeared to have great stores of patience for the forms and became so absorbed in the work that he seemed to forget that Slaney was sitting opposite him.

There was a pile of smaller forms, all blue, that had been pierced with a metal spike. These he removed from the spike by the handful and he read each one and crunched it into a ball and tossed it in the wastepaper basket in front of his desk.

He used a stamp he had sitting on a red ink pad, leafing through another stack of papers in one go, the stamping a hard, fast rhythm like a tribal drum or a heart about to give out. Three hours passed.

I wonder if I could talk to my friends, Slaney said.

Your friends are taken care of, Señor Knight, the officer said. Once we've cleared the sailboat you can be on your way.

There was a knock on the door and a man in overalls came in with a ladder and set it up behind the immigration officer's desk and the men shook hands, speaking in fast Spanish. Both men put their hands on their hips and stood looking up at an air-conditioning unit embedded in the wall. The repairman climbed the ladder and took down the unit bearing the weight on his shoulders and neck and the immigration officer reached up for it, one hand against the repairman's leg for support.

It was a heavy unit and the two men struggled under the weight of it and Slaney jumped up and took a corner and together the three men moved the unit onto an empty shelf and they stood for a moment looking down into the guts of it, cylinders and coiled wire furred with lint and dust and the Mexicans spoke in Spanish.

The immigration officer noticed that Slaney was out of the chair and told him to sit back down without thanking him for his help. He returned to his desk and after a moment the repairman left the office. Two more hours passed without incident.

At one point the officer put his feet up on the desk and made a phone call and spoke for close to an hour. The conversation was leisurely and for a great deal of it the officer just listened. Slaney had the impression there was a woman on the other end. Part of the phone conversation cracked the man up. He laughed so hard he had to press the bridge of his nose between his finger and thumb to get a hold of himself. He was trembling with giggles and after he hung up he shook his head in disbelief, some story the woman had told him.

The door of the office opened and a woman came in wearing the same blue uniform as the first officer and she had a coffee and a snack for each of them. A taco with beef and guacamole.

Can I see my friends? Slaney asked. The woman told him she didn't speak English.

Señor Knight, the male officer said. I'm asking the questions here.

After another hour had passed, his taco untouched, the officer gathered up the papers on his desk and filed them in the filing cabinet, which he locked with a key that hung from one of the drawers. He put the key in his breast pocket. He lowered the blinds and left the room.

Slaney tried the door and found it unlocked. All of the offices in the corridor were occupied by people typing and speaking on the phone. There were guards with guns in holsters at their hips. Slaney closed the door quietly and gobbled down the officer's taco.

The officer returned and dropped Slaney's passport and a visa on the desk and he told Slaney he was free to go. You can remain in the country for three weeks to repair your boat, he said. I believe you have incurred some damages.

We certainly have, Slaney said.

Before you go, the man said. Is there anything you think we should know?

Not that I can think of, Slaney said.

Then you are free.

What about my friends? Slaney asked.

Your friends, the man said. Of course, they are free also. I believe they are waiting outside.

Get Down There

They were picked up by Immigration, O'Neill said. Little seaside town called Puerto Escondido.

Everybody safe? Patterson asked.

All accounted for, O'Neill said. Patterson had thought they were gone. He pushed his chair back from O'Neill's desk and stood. He looked out the window at the city below. Then he sat back down, the chair legs squeaking on the linoleum tiles.

He could see Slaney at the party and he thought of himself talking about Clarice Connors. The print of her dress, a sailor motif, anchors and rope and brass buttons. A nest of the oily white papers she used with her hair curlers. How they fell out of her curls, how they rustled on her little vanity table when the wind blew, toppling them end over end. A particular afternoon when the affair had first begun. He hadn't thought about Clarice in years. The gentle force she had been in his life.

He hadn't wanted anyone to get hurt on the sailboat. But

they were okay. They had survived. For days now he'd been haunted by the thought of Ada Anderson. She was just a child.

And he thought of Hearn's girlfriend waving the vodka bottle overhead, calling for change. She'd spoken about love and peace as if she were the one who had discovered them, half-baked rhetoric and euphemisms. But when she said forgiveness Patterson had fallen open like a lock with the right key.

He had been compelled to talk against his will. He'd watched for her reaction, horrified and hungry for it, hoping to catch some glimpse of his own daughter in her face. Why things had gone wrong; how to get her back.

He thought he'd let Hearn's girlfriend judge him and he might learn something. He had been stoned out of his trees. But he knew she suspected him. Her cool banter, the way she'd made him account for himself. So he'd made a bone of Clarice Connors, and he'd thrown the girl the bone.

Slaney had been polite to him. The boy gave the impression of a good upbringing. Patterson wanted to throw the kid back in jail, but he'd never wanted him to drown.

We've placed a few calls, O'Neill said. This operation is still a go. But we have to do it without the satellite now. Clearly it was destroyed by the storm. We need a little human contact. We need you to go down there, check out the situation.

Absolutely, sir, Patterson said.

The authorities picked all three of them up on the beach. Somebody went out there in a rowboat. Brought them to shore. We've asked our counterparts down there to stamp their passports, let them out. O'Neill had his hands in his pockets and he was jiggling his change, an erratic, nervous percussion.

But they can't go anywhere without repairs to the boat.

Patterson tugged at the cuffs of his shirt so about half

an inch of each sleeve was visible under the suit jacket. He smoothed his hands over the sides of his head. His hair was longer than he was used to for the purposes of the undercover work. It felt unruly.

Here's the thinking, O'Neill said. Patterson, I want you to make contact with Hearn. Tell him you've heard; say you have an inside source down in Mexico. Say you made inquiries after the hurricane. You were concerned about your investment, about the crew. Tell him not to give up yet.

You offer more financing. They get the sails repaired. Tell Hearn. Say they can bribe their way home.

We've got a guy down there in the military we can work with. The Mexican military is onside.

You fly down there saying you have the money available. Hearn knows you. All you've got to do is sell him on this contact. The fellow, Enrique Hernandez, whom you'll meet up with, inspects the sailboat, gives them the go-ahead in exchange for what appears to be a bribe.

We want you down there to make sure this thing goes smoothly. You talk to them, see what their thinking is, make sure they're on course. We don't have the surveillance now, but you can get a bead on them, if you go down in person. Ask some questions. Appear to be helping them out.

Tequila Sunrise

They'd gone into a crowded bar on top of a hill mostly undamaged by flooding. They could see the lower streets where the water had risen above the verandas and into the front door of an abandoned house. Walls had been torn off some of the buildings and they could see an exposed bedroom, wallpaper peeling in long strips, the mirror catching passing headlights as a few cars rolled by.

They sat near the entrance of the bar so Slaney could keep his eye on the road. There was a woman wiping the glasses with a red rag in the darkest corner of the bar. Slaney could see the rag prick the shadows as she snapped it between glasses.

Out on the cobblestones, a hen was testing the pool of light under the street lamp, touching it once and then again with its claw, jerking the inert lump of its blazingly white body forward by the neck, taking teensy steps. The hen froze in the centre of the light, full of trembling.

A motorcycle puttered through the strolling couples on the street. The driver had a black girl in a yellow dress sitting sideways between his outstretched arms.

The hen stopped thrusting its neck forward and assumed an outer-space stillness before it burst up like a thing shot, zigzagging into the restaurant, lifting off the ground with ungraceful leaps and crashes, veering toward a group of men who stood in a circle clinking their beer bottles, spilling froth.

A waiter brought over a bottle of tequila and three shot glasses and he poured for them and left the bottle on the table.

Carter lifted his glass immediately and held it close as if he expected someone to snatch it away from him.

Ada brought hers to her nose and sniffed. Slaney raised his glass to them and they did the same and they drank at the same time and touched the glasses back down on the table carefully and Slaney filled them again.

It sure goes down, Ada said. She laid her fist on her chest. Then she thumped her chest twice.

You're shivering, Slaney said. What did you tell the immigration officers?

I said it seemed like our last visit was a million years ago. They saw the stamp on my passport and asked what I was doing back here again. I said I was sorry for the devastation. I said it had seemed like such a pretty country a couple of weeks ago and now everything is different. I said I was here by accident.

There was a man with a white gym bag and a white shirt with a glittering appliqué Elvis on the front. The man unzipped the gym bag at the table next to them and there was a small commotion, people getting up to see, gathering around.

Slaney's eyes had adjusted to the dark and he saw, on the far wall, a giant turtle's head and its two claws mounted on a varnished plaque, the turtle floating in the murky shadows, covered in dust.

What happened in that office? Ada said. They kept us for hours and then they just let us go.

Carter showed all his teeth; it was the opposite of a smile. It was a naked wince Carter had no idea he was making.

What did you tell them, Carter? Slaney said. They'd lost Carter to some netherworld of spirits, or it was self-regard. He had decided to save his own skin. Slaney was sure of it.

Did you tell them about the dope? Slaney asked.

Of course not, Carter said.

Did they make you some kind of promise? Slaney asked. He poured Carter another drink.

Leave him alone, Ada said.

Your poor wife, Slaney said. Your kids. The bloody sailboat. They had moored the boat in a quiet cove away from the main beach, out of the surf.

David, stop it, Ada said.

What did they promise you, Carter? Slaney asked. You're going to have a rough time explaining Ada to your wife. You think they'll cut you a deal. They won't cut you a deal. It doesn't work that way down here. Did they say you could keep the sailboat? They won't let you keep her, Carter. We'll all rot together in a Mexican hole.

Why had Hearn trusted Carter? His height might have had something to do with it, Slaney thought. Not his height — his bearing. He was short and arrowlike. Everything he wore fit him properly. That might have been part of it. Or it was his voice. He was sonorous and slow-spoken when he needed to be. He had a deep voice that someone like Hearn might mistake for spiritual gravity.

Ada was tipping her tiny shot glass between her finger and thumb before drinking down the tequila in two swallows.

The guy with Elvis on his shirt turned out to be a magician. Slaney had thought it would be a gun in the white gym bag but it was a top hat and a white dove. It flew out from a red silk scarf and circled above their heads, perching in the rafters. They had come through the hurricane and here was a reward.

A magic show, Carter said, how perfectly quaint.

Are you drunk again? Slaney asked him.

There are men, Carter said, who build up a resistance, gradually, over years and years of drinking. Those men are visionaries.

And you're one of those men, Slaney said.

I am indeed, he said.

Cyril, it's going to be okay, Ada said. They let us go, didn't they? The hen had moved under a nearby table; they could see it now and then, through the legs of the crowd. It had lifted a claw and was standing on the other one, frozen mid-step, unable to move. Ada downed the third shot and she took up the menu. The crowd was clapping for the magician.

What a funny thing to happen, Ada said. Why did they let us walk?

I don't think it's funny, Slaney said. He could tell she was frightened. A woman came out from the bar and put a saucer with lime wedges on their table and she waited while they read the menus. She gazed out the entrance to the street. It had begun to rain again and there was a low, loud rumble of thunder. Several men were carrying a large sheet of corrugated tin down the road. It wobbled and boomed out a hollow metal twang.

Solo pollo, the waitress said. She gathered the menus and hugged them to her chest.

I think I'll try the chicken, Slaney said. The woman took a box of matches from her apron and struck one. She lit the candle on the table and Carter's shadow stretched from his chair legs to the wall behind him and up to the ceiling and rocked like a punching clown, though he hadn't moved. Ada picked up the bottle from the table and held the bottom of it near the flame and she said there was a worm.

Just rotting away in there, aren't you, little worm, she said.

The worm is lucky, Cyril said. Whoever drinks the worm, you're set for life. It contains everything.

I don't need luck, Ada said. I have you.

The waitress brought them rice and beans and chicken.

Slaney watched Ada eat. She crunched the bones and sucked the marrow. She was ravenous. He saw her glance toward the table the hen had run under. The hen was gone. She dropped the bone onto her plate and took up a napkin and patted her lips.

They had to get out, but Slaney wasn't leaving without the weed. He wasn't going back without it. He expected the military to roll through the doorway at any moment. He imagined Ada jittering and bouncing in her chair, arms flailing, as some Mexican soldier emptied a machine gun into her.

He would fall face down in his refried beans. Carter would be blown backwards, crashing onto the floor, chair and all. He could see it as surely as he could see Ada sucking on the bones, candlelight on her greasy chin. It came to him slowly but he was absolutely certain: there are worse things than dying.

Going back without the weed would be worse.

The sensible thing to do would be to get the hell out. Travel inland; keep going. Leave Ada with Carter and the yacht. He thought of Jennifer saying she would take him back.

But he wasn't going to do the sensible thing. They might know about the pot, but why hadn't they seized it? They had allowed the three of them to walk. It may be the authorities had a plan, but if they did, Slaney would wait them out. See what they had in mind. Slaney could be patient too.

The man with the Elvis shirt had a crowd now and he suddenly turned to Slaney's table and, leaning in, he cupped Ada's chin. He smoothed her hair behind her ear. She glanced up and her eyes were big. Believing. This must be what Carter had fallen in love with: a willingness to believe.

The magician showed the bar his empty hand and he rubbed it over her ear and pulled out a large gold coin.

Everyone in the bar laughing, applauding. Ada touched her burning ear.

They'd rented rooms in a hostel overlooking the water but they drank in the bar until light leaked up from the horizon a furious red. They could see the sailboat as they walked back to their rooms. The mast in silhouette, a needle swaying gently like a metronome. And the soldiers lounging on the deck, black against the orange and azure sky.

Dirty Laundry

He was walking by her bedroom door in the hostel, and he glanced in because she was raising her voice. She had a nasty edge. She was speaking to the maid.

Ada ripped down the top bedsheet. The maid was dark with high cheekbones and big eyes and a taut body. She wore a fitted black skirt and a white cotton blouse. She looked to be about their age.

Ada told her the sheets were dirty. The maid had her hands on her hips. The sun behind her punched through under her arms and between her legs. Carter was sprawled in a wicker chair, snoring. Every breath he drew caused the wicker to squeak.

These sheets aren't clean, Ada said. Her voice climbing notch after notch. He could hear the privileged childhood, her enunciation icy and clipped. An echo of a British accent she must have picked up from her parents, something he heard when she was tipsy or enraged.

What do you mean? the maid said. This might have been her only English sentence. Slaney thought it might be the only sentence anyone ever needed.

Look there, Ada said. She pointed and made a small circle with her finger over the sheet. And farther down another small circle. Slaney and the maid leaned in too. And then

Slaney could see it. Two stains. For a brief moment the three of them were frozen over the bed, leaning in, scrutinizing, and then they leaned back.

The maid tore the sheet off and bunched it in her arms and strode out of the room. Ada turned her back on Slaney and looked out the window at the water.

I'm not sleeping in someone else's filth, she said. So you can get that look off your face.

Cyril has a wife and three children, Slaney said. She didn't answer.

He's a dirty old man, Slaney said.

I'm not interested in you, she said.

What do you mean? he said.

Hello, Stranger

The next morning Slaney realized he was proud of coming through the storm alive. He felt he had been judged by it and punished accordingly and he had endured. He wanted Hearn to understand what had been overcome. It was time to place the call.

He sat on the wooden chair watching for the red blinking lights over the phone booths that indicated a call had been placed. He'd bought some peanuts and he tore the package with his teeth. A speck of plastic stuck to his bottom lip. He blew it away, a hard *pfft*.

Slaney tilted back his head, tipped the peanuts in.

He was overcome with the phantom thrust and fall of the sailboat battered by the hurricane. How it had shuddered against each blow. The rhythm of the storm was a violent sensation that visited him, swished in his blood and made the solid world sway.

The operator called his name: Douglas Knight. Numero ocho. It took him a moment to know they were talking about him. Douglas Knight. Numero ocho. Slaney was used to the name but he could forget about it. He jumped up and headed for booth eight with the blinking red light and inside the phone was ringing loud and shrill and he picked it up and he could not believe how much he wanted to hear the voice of somebody he knew.

Hearn's voice.

Listen, Hearn said. I'm sending a guy down there. I'm sending Roy Brophy. You met him at the party. The Mexicans know about the cargo but they can be bought off.

What do you know about Brophy? Slaney said. Where did he come from? You don't know shit about Brophy, do you.

Slaney wondered if a person comes close to death, or if a person's death is a fixed point that's always equidistant from the present, no matter what the present happens to be.

It leaps, that's what Slaney was thinking. Death leaps over the space between the future and the present. It was the heat in the waiting room.

Or the quaking pleasure of hearing Hearn's voice. He was suddenly scared shitless.

We nearly died out there, man, Slaney said. And now it feels like that again.

We're going to get you out, Hearn said. I'll be honest. Brophy's all we got.

There were turning points from which there could be no return, Slaney had learned. He wondered if he'd stumbled on one of those.

You didn't tell me about the girl, he said.

What girl, Hearn said.

Carter's girl, Slaney said. Ada.

What the hell are you talking about?

The girl, Hearn. The girl.

Get a hold of yourself, Slane. Doug. I mean Doug. You sound like a nervous wreck. You've got to be careful now.

I'm being careful, Slaney said. He thought of coming up from downtown St. John's, very drunk, with Jennifer one night, a particular night, dried leaves swirling around in the park. Leaves rising up from the frost-stiff ground, twisting up in columns of wind and scattering low again across the grass.

She'd had a bottle of Baileys in her purse. They weren't careful. There was no being careful involved in what he felt back then.

This was one of the things prison had done to him. He was full of care. Care worn.

Roy Brophy is going to meet you, Hearn said. He has a contact in the military down there. The military contacted Immigration. Brophy's already made them an offer. That's why they let you go. Brophy brings you the money, you give the money to the contact. You're free to go. We hire the locals to repair the boat.

Are you kidding? Slaney asked. This guy calls off the army? You're kidding, right? But he found himself believing it. Why not?

This is how things are handled down there, Hearn said.

You trust this guy, Slaney said.

I do, Hearn said. I believe him.

Lopez knew about the last trip, Hearn, Slaney said. He

knew all about it. Took a pistol out, laid it on the table while
we were having our lunch.

Get the boat ready to sail, hire some guys. Brophy will have
the money for fuel and supplies. You hand over a suitcase to
the authorities. That's all you have to do.

There's a girl here, Barlow, and she's very young and I'm
afraid she's going to get hurt, Slaney said.

I didn't know about the girl, Hearn said.

The Sails

Slaney saw three men on bicycles with dining room chairs.
They had removed the cushions and put their heads through
the wooden frames of the seats, the legs sticking up in the
air, so they could steer the bikes and pedal at the same time.
Moving furniture out of the flood waters.

Two men had walked past him with a giant square of sky
and cloud, a mirror they had scavenged unbroken from a
restaurant. There were men laying sacks of sand against
the bank of a rising river. Women sitting sideways on bikes
their husbands pedalled. And men, alone, riding bikes with
a flat of eggs held out on the palm of one hand. Here and
there, the stink of sewage. Broken pipes spewing up from
the ground.

Two days after the storm the town bakery had reopened,
despite the smashed plate-glass window, and in the evenings
women carried decorated cakes home from work.

Men had come in on the backs of flatbed trucks from villa-
ges farther inland to help with the reconstruction. Slaney had
hired five men to fix the sails.

In the morning he and Ada were alone at the communal breakfast table.

He asked her to pass the milk.

Of course, she said. Sugar also? She passed the sugar and turned her book over beside her plate and reached for the basket of bread.

I've been thinking, she said. She lifted her white sunglasses to the top of her head. David? You should get out. What are you doing?

I'm getting through it, he said. He meant he was moving through time. He was starting to believe something entirely different about time. In prison he had thought time was an illusion. But now he believed time was a natural force, like the hurricane, except he believed that it could be harnessed.

He made me feel like I was special, she said. Isn't that silly?

Carter was sleeping it off in the room over the kitchen. He slept most days until late afternoon.

We've got to keep going now, Slaney told her.

It was hard leaving my father, Ada said. She blinked very fast and the colour of her eyes changed. She was crying. Slaney didn't know how to compose himself.

I more or less ran away, she said. Cyril promised me a house after the trip. I didn't care about the house. I just wanted to be in love. My father was so proud of my music. He came to all my performances. I just couldn't keep playing, David. That was the thing. I started to hate it. And it was the only thing I loved. I didn't want to hate it.

She had no control over her mouth and it stretched slowly so her teeth and gums showed and the lump of wet bread and then she pulled her mouth shut. Her chin trembled. Her shoulders drooped and shook a bit. There was no other sound from her while this happened.

It was a mistake, she said.

I'm sorry, Slaney said. Then she giggled. She was laughing at her predicament.

The things you see in retrospect, she said. He's bald, for Christ's sake. You don't understand it, you couldn't.

You think I haven't been in love? Slaney said.

It is ridiculous to imagine you matter, she said. She waved at the room and the ocean beyond the room with the butter knife.

You matter, Slaney said. He thought it was true. She was only six years younger than he was, but it seemed like there were decades between them. He'd made mistakes too. He was living out the mistakes he'd made, doing it over, or trying to fix it, and look at him — he still mattered. He mattered very much.

It's impossible, she said. He figured she meant the hurricane and the money they stood to lose and Carter, almost catatonic for hours at a time. Carter demanding they let him go home to his wife. We'll have you back in a jiffy, Slaney kept telling him.

Just to love someone, Ada said.

I don't believe you ever loved him, Slaney said.

The whole thing is impossible, she said. She wiped her nose by flicking the bone of her wrist under it. Then she reached for the marmalade. It was just out of reach.

She brought the dish of marmalade across the table by sticking her knife into it. The little white bowl skittered across the table toward her under the knife tip. Slaney knew that he would never see this side of her again.

You're going to make it out of this, he said.

I'm getting a tan, she said. That's what I'm going to do.

She put the piece of bread down on the side plate and balanced the knife on the marmalade bowl and pressed the heels of her hands into her eyes. Then she pulled her fingers through her hair, patted it down. She threw back her shoulders. Slaney could see the print of her teeth in the piece of bread. He didn't try to touch her; he let her keep going.

You are probably in love with me, she said.

I'm not in love with you, Slaney said. Then Slaney told her. He didn't know what he was going to say before he said it. He told her about Jennifer and the kid, and how she was gone.

It had to do with the kid, he said. She wanted to feel secure. He said he had believed, for a while, that he was doing the trip for Jennifer. But that wasn't true at all.

He said how there were things you could make happen and he was good at that. It seemed that there was nothing he could not animate.

But there were things that just happened to you, he told Ada. Things you couldn't see coming. There were things that could knock you out. He'd already ended up in jail once and he might very well have fallen in love with Ada except he thought she was cold. He told her that.

If he had fallen in love with her it was something he would work his way out of as fast as he could, he said.

Cyril has a wife, he said. He's got youngsters. A family he's temporarily abandoned. But men don't leave their wives. They don't leave their kids. You're his Maserati. He's a lush. The two of you will probably be the end of me.

Probably, she said.

I am already in too deep, he said. Do you know that feeling?

Get out, she said. Why don't you get out?

Slaney had been forced to listen to them every night on the boat. There had been giggles and thumping and some cries that sounded authentic and he'd had to go up on deck and wait it out.

Did you ever get blamed for something you didn't do? Ada asked. She told him about a nun who taught her piano. The wooden ruler Sister Consilio used to count the beats as she paced behind Ada's back, listening to her bang out Mozart. The nun kept saying Ada wasn't trying hard enough.

I don't think I ever did, Slaney said.

After a while you decide you might as well do the things you're blamed for, she said.

I did them from the start, Slaney said. Otherwise there would have been a lot of catching up to do.

My father was a prisoner of war, she said. Being in the navy required a lot of him. They shot him in the leg, left him with a limp.

So he is brave, Slaney said. He'll be okay.

Whatever he gave, he didn't get it back, she said. Don't count on me, David. I'm warning you.

But I am counting on you, he said.

You can hollow yourself out, she said. Then it's too late. Do you believe that?

You think we're going to get caught, he said. She said she did think that. She was certain of it.

Then why don't you leave? Slaney said.

Because I'm going to make sure nothing happens to Cyril. He's helpless.

The hurricane threw us off, Slaney said. We can't let a little thing like a hurricane get in our way.

The Bull

Patterson was at the Plaza de Toros, in Acapulco, for the meeting with Hernandez. He had arrived early and the sun was high and the band of his hat cut into his forehead. The hat was white with a black ribbon at the crown and a very small red feather. He'd bought it off a revolving rack outside a shop that catered to tourists.

There'd been a rack of sharks' teeth beside the hats, the upper and lower jaws attached by a film of cartilage, and all the rows of teeth, pointing inward, very white and small. He'd tried on the hat and looked at himself in the tiny cracked mirror that hung from a piece of twine on a nail.

Hernandez would find him; he just had to wait. It was important to appear unhurried. He removed the hat and saw it was coated with dust. The dust gummed up and felt gritty and he saw that the hat was whiter than he had thought.

A speckled feather: he'd let the guy charge him a fortune because he'd needed to cover his head. There was a thing that happened to him in Mexico: he could be persuaded by a burst of colour. Everything was red and aqua blue and lime green and orange; you didn't see this in Canada, where it was all earth tones, dun and charcoal. There was nothing wrong with a feather. It was a nice touch. A person could get away with little touches of elegance in a hot climate.

The bull galloped into the arena and kicked and jack-knifed. It was maddened and desultory by turns. The shine and muscle awed Patterson and became ordinary and awed him again. The bull embodied unsustainable awe.

A cloud of dust was settling. His shirt stuck to his back and his pant legs tugged at him. The ribbing of his acrylic sock imprinted on his damp leg.

Hearn had called him: I need someone to talk to, man. He'd given Hearn a day. He had figured he'd give Hearn a day to call him before he tried to make contact himself. O'Neill hadn't wanted him to wait but screw O'Neill.

Come over, man, have a drink, Hearn said. Patterson was going to get the promotion. The promotion was a sure thing now.

He would visit Alphonse when he got back. He'd pay the bill in full. Sometimes he was afraid Alphonse would forget him between visits, but he never did. What if something happened to him while he was on the job? Who would explain Patterson's absence? His brother would feel abandoned.

He felt a drip of sweat move down his face, and another and another. Who would take care of Alphonse?

The matador looked like a china doll, prissy and brave. There was gold brocade crusted on the man's shoulders and chest and climbing up the legs of his stockings. The red cape flapped out and the bull charged through, kicking up dust. The matador twisted his hip to the side. He seemed to rise on his toes. Then he turned and ran like a cartoon stick-man.

The bull was full of pent-up violence and a sly heaviness.

And there, at last, was Hernandez. He made his way toward Patterson through the crowd. He was dressed in a screaming red shirt and white suit.

The Mexicans could do that, Patterson had observed. They could keep a bright linen suit crisp-looking in any kind of heat. Hernandez was not wearing a hat. A black ponytail hung down his back. He cut a figure.

Hernandez stopped and spoke to a young woman in a black dress. He wanted to show Patterson that he could be languid.

He wanted Patterson to understand that he would decide on the formalities. The woman stood and gestured toward her children. Three young boys stood up beside her. Hernandez took her hand while he spoke to her. Then he made his way to Patterson.

Señor Hernandez, buenos días, Patterson said. He shook the man's hand. Both men turned to the arena. They pretended to scrutinize the work of the matador.

You have to be tolerant, Hernandez said. He gestured toward the bull. Patterson was not interested in philosophizing about the bull. He found it a dull dance. There were lags. There was despondence. Currents could pulse through the crowd but there could be long moments when nothing happened.

Hernandez had worked his way up, as Patterson understood it. He had bought beach property for nothing at the right moment near Puerto Vallarta. Richard Burton and Ava Gardner had made a movie and Burton had bought Elizabeth Taylor a place and a cluster of hotels went up and Hernandez had invested.

He had a taxi stand with fifty vehicles; he owned three mid-sized vessels. He had been a drug runner and an informant. He was fit and unfathomable.

The cape caught on the animal's horn and a terror set up in the bull. There was nothing graceful now. It had been stabbed twice and its haunches shivered. It ran a few tight circles, shaking its great bone of a head. It was comical, the cape on the horn, causing a peripheral and stagnant terror. The bull had lost its animality, was all big brown girly eyes, coquettish and mannered.

Hippies, said Hernandez. Children. Something in the stalls had caught his eye. It was a redhead in a bandana and halter top.

The girl was lanky and pale and hunched, she was making her way over the knees of spectators toward the end of the row. She wore a long patchwork skirt. Patterson wasn't sure what Hernandez meant. He appeared disgruntled.

They are so free in your country, Hernandez said. Then the cape fell off and the bull trotted to the centre of the arena and stood still. It appeared that Patterson would have to accept a lecture on the desultory longing that had passed through a generation of North American kids. It was what he wanted to crush in Hearn and Slaney; his own daughter had fallen prey to it, he didn't need to be lectured.

The bull had given up or pretended to give up. It would not co-operate. It would not bother to make its own death worthwhile or full of sentiment.

Do you know Lorca? Hernandez asked.

Was he at the meeting with Intelligence last week? Patterson asked.

García Lorca, Hernandez said.

Patterson didn't answer. Delores read Lorca. He knew who Lorca was. This guy in his linen with his toned chest and gold chains. Hernandez crossed his arms and his shirt collar fell open and Patterson saw a cross. The man lifted his chin toward the redhead across the arena; she had squished herself between two Mexican men.

Playing with fire, Hernandez said. It's the pill.

Yes, said Patterson. This was something they could agree upon.

The pill is to blame, Hernandez said. Patterson had come across the flesh-coloured plastic dial, labelled with the days of the week, in his daughter's brassiere drawer. A rotating wheel with a window.

The wheel turned and allowed you to press the pill from behind through a foil cover so it popped out the little window. Her bras and girdles and a nest of stockings. He had been looking for pot. He had asked her if she'd tried it and she'd said no. But he didn't trust her. He trusted her but he felt compelled to check.

He had not thought of his daughter's bras and stockings and girdles as the undergarments of a young woman but when he found the pill packet he felt the sexual static like electricity and flicked his hand out of the drawer as if burned.

The pill, you think the pill is the problem, Patterson said.

Young women, Hernandez said. They have turned against their fathers.

Patterson's daughter had turned away from everything he and Delores had tried to give her. He thought of the little girl she had been. How she would stand on a chair in the kitchen and fall forward into his arms. How tightly she held on to his neck. How she leaned against him while he talked to his wife in their small kitchen. She needed to be leaning on him or climbing on him as soon as he came home from work. She loved showing him her printing, a little scribbler full of letters, nonsensical rhymes about rain or talking dogs. She played the piano for him, her legs swinging hard under the stool, banging out "Hot Cross Buns."

A drop of sweat inched down Patterson's cheek. The crowd sent out a small complaint, a collective yell toward the bull. The crowd didn't want to see the animal acquiesce. If some part of the bull was timid or polite, or willing to compromise, the crowd wanted that part cut out and served on a plate.

Hernandez spoke unaccented English. Or if there was an accent, Patterson could not detect it. The man's eyes were almost black and Patterson could see a wily intelligence.

Patterson always made a point: engage the eye of the contact; hold the eye. It was a sort of flirting.

They were both essentially untrustworthy men; they were savvy to the ways of trust and saw it was predicated on a flimsy belief system. Trust was an unwillingness to think things through.

It was a collapse in the ability to reason, an intoxicating sentimentality. The ornate work of giving in.

His little girl: he thought of her in the plastic swimming pool they'd bought for her birthday, he thought of her kicking her legs and clots of mown grass on the surface, she was what? — five or six — and the chocolate cake on the patio and her little friends from next door.

Two *banderillas* wagged from each of the bull's shoulders. Then the animal got frisky again. It was dying. It charged and the hooves danced up and kicked out and the matador draped the animal's head and hop-stepped. The bull disappeared in the red flash and came back.

Patterson would meet Slaney and bring him to a bank where he would withdraw forty thousand dollars and Hernandez would be waiting on the sailboat along with the rest of the soldiers and he'd accept the bribe.

They need provisions and fuel, Hernandez said. The men have already repaired the sails.

I'll be there to oversee the exchange, Patterson said. Hernandez stared hard at the bull. He didn't answer.

I'm down here to keep an eye, Patterson said. We got them on three counts if they make it back to Canada. These kids will never see the light of day.

We will meet again on the sailboat, then, Hernandez said. He turned to shake Patterson's hand.

What Patterson admired was the way the animal jackknifed all that weight, turning from the cape to charge it again. The momentum behind each buck and shudder.

He loved that the fight was fixed. Every step planned and played out. Always the bull would end up dead.

It was the certainty that satisfied some desire in the audience. The best stories, he thought, we've known the end from the beginning.

You're Coming with Me

Slaney came down the stairs of the hostel and Roy Brophy was standing at the common room window watching the surf. He was wearing new jeans and a rope belt and a white cotton shirt with a Nehru collar.

Brophy was looking out at the sailboat. The new sails were up and the sun on the white canvas was very bright and the sea was full of sparkle.

Roy, Slaney said. Patterson turned around.

Doug, how the hell are you? The men shook hands. Patterson gripped him hard and he met his eyes. Slaney's hair was longer, curly and black, and his eyes looked bluer because of the tan and he'd lost weight.

Heard you had quite a trip, Patterson said.

Quite the wind, Slaney said. Not something I'd like to try again, let me tell you.

She's looking pretty good out there now, Patterson said. They both turned toward the boat. Patterson had a jocularity, Slaney thought, that was a notch too upbeat. The handshake had gone on for a second too long. The man was perspiring.

Thanks for coming down, man, Slaney said.

No sweat, Patterson said. I'm happy to help. I know how things work down here. I have to look out for my investment.

They serve a half-decent breakfast here, Slaney said. You want something?

I'm ready to hit the road. It won't take us an hour. You guys are planning to sail tomorrow, right? We go to the bank and get the money and the authorities are waiting on the sailboat for us the next day. We hand over the money; they count it. You guys are good to go. I don't foresee difficulties. We want to get you guys back to Vancouver, start turning a profit.

That sounds good, Slaney said.

Sound good to you? Patterson asked.

That sounds fine.

They thought it was the potholes before they realized a flat. They rolled into a garage on the side of the road. Slaney jacked up the Jeep and removed the tire.

There were chickens running around in the gravel outside and a clothesline with a few rags on it. There was a child on a weathered stoop with a doll. The little girl had on a faded red dress and when the Jeep came up the drive in a cloud of dust she stepped back inside the house and watched them through a screen door. She stood in the shadows of the hallway but one knee, covered in the red skirt, was pressed against the screen. A man in a white undershirt took the tire from Slaney without a word and dunked it in a trough of water and slowly turned it, holding the tire upright with just the tips of his fingers.

Three men appeared from the fields behind the house. They gathered around the tire and watched and didn't speak much.

Whatever they said was in Spanish. Brophy stood with his hands on his wide hips, his back to the men, looking at the wall of tools.

Look at that, Slaney said. A jet of bubbles rose in the water near the tire's rim and the man lifted it out and held it up to his chest and Slaney could see a piece of green glass jammed in the rubber. The man brought it over to a work counter and Slaney and Brophy went outside to share a joint.

You have a family? Slaney asked.

I've got a daughter and a son, Patterson said.

And you got a wife, Slaney said.

Wife and kids, Patterson said. I'd say you're about my daughter's age. Give or take.

You're a contractor, Slaney said.

I'm a contractor, Patterson said. Almost twenty-five years.

I just want to know who I'm dealing with, Slaney said. He could hear a bell tinkling nearby. It sounded clear and eerie, a tiny warning bell. Something was rustling in the dirt on the other side of the garage.

I'm here to get your money and make sure it goes through the proper channels, Patterson said. I'm acquainted with the people down here.

You're a friend of Barlow's, Slaney said.

I'm close to retiring, Patterson said. But a little extra wouldn't go astray. I have expenses. Friend, I would say no. Not a friend. I figure a man has one or two friends his whole life, if he's lucky. That's if he's lucky. My brother is my friend. My wife is my friend. Barlow I would call a business acquaintance. I met Barlow because somebody gave me his name. Somebody knew I had some capital I wanted to invest. I called him up.

You called him up, Slaney said.

I called him up, asked if he wanted to get together, Patterson said. He took a long drag on the toke Slaney passed him and dropped it into the dirt, pressed down on it with the toe of his shoe. A goat had come around the corner of the garage. It looked at Slaney with its yellow eye, the vertical black pupil. The goat opened its black-lipped mouth and baaed at them. Then it trotted away, the bell piercingly sweet.

Your friend Barlow is a good cook, nice people he hangs around with, he's got a nice girl. They're nice people. They had me over. Singing and talking, it was a very nice evening. A young man, intelligent, doing his university, seems ambitious, and I think to myself, Okay, maybe. I'll take a chance on this guy.

You're in it for the money, Slaney said.

I know Hernandez, Patterson said. This is a couple of days' work for me down here. Take a few days. This is money should my daughter decide on a university education. I see her as maybe a lawyer.

The man in the white undershirt walked past them with the tire then and Slaney went back to the Jeep with him and they had the tire back on in a few minutes.

Patterson peeled off some money from a wad he had in his pants pocket and the man looked at it and took a blue elastic band off his wrist and put it around the bills and put them away.

Slaney and Patterson drove along a dirt road for fifteen minutes more. The only thing they saw on the road was a barefoot man on a horse with a rope that was tied to the horns of a dusty white ox that plodded behind.

They found the bank and parked in front of it. The beach was a short walk away. The Jeep was hot to the touch and Slaney was sticking to the seats. He closed his eyes for a moment.

He was thinking of Hearn's girlfriend with her hand pressed flat against Brophy's chest. How she had shoved Brophy into the corner and interrogated him.

She had not trusted Brophy either. But Hearn wanted the trip to be a success. He wanted it so badly he was willing to talk to a guy who phones up cold, out of the blue. A guy he's never heard of.

I'll be at the beach, grabbing a bite to eat, Slaney said. Want me to order you something?

No, I'm careful about the food here. I'll find you when I get out of the bank, Patterson said.

I'll be here, Slaney said.

Don't worry, I'll find you.

Slaney sat where he had a view of the beach and a view of the front doors of the bank.

The timbers that held up the thatched roof of the little restaurant were painted jaunty blue and the counter along the back wall was tiled in blue and white. A man was cutting the heads and tails off fish he was pulling from a bucket on the concrete floor. He slapped each fish down on a counter of sheet metal slathered in blood and guts and each time he brought the knife down a cloud of flies rose and settled. After every fish tail he scraped the cleaver blade over the skim of red water on the counter and sluiced it into the bucket below.

The ocean was greenish and the sand was as white as could be and a woman with a beautiful body in a white bikini stood up from her towel. Her hands swatted at her ass, brushing off sand, and she pulled on a scuba mask and fitted a snorkel into her mouth. It made her eyes bulge and her mouth look surprised and dumb. She put on flippers and walked toward the ocean like the flamingos Slaney had seen in the zoo, picking up her knees. Slaney ordered a beer and some beans and rice and fish.

He reminded himself to have a good time. He had never liked the idea of heat but it had got inside him on the last trip and it had unlocked a slow longing for salt and cold drinks. The desire for something was on the tip of his tongue, a word or belief, something half articulated that he realized he could wait for; whatever it was, he didn't have to force it.

Slaney had cleaned off the tin plate with a tortilla and pushed the plate aside and he'd finished his beer when Brophy came out of the bank and walked down the hill to the beach with a duffle bag. The afternoon enveloped Brophy in a rippling jello of heat, and he appeared warped and elongated in the waver, the duffle bag dragging one shoulder down. When he spotted Slaney, he lifted a finger in a weak salute. Brophy's shirt was soaked through and sticking to him and he looked cold and white like raw fish.

Drink? Slaney asked.

I'd like to get going, Brophy said. Slaney stood and counted out some money and tucked it under the plate and he looked out at the ocean.

There was a commotion on the beach. Someone was screaming. A woman on the beach was crippled up and bent with the effort of making herself heard. Begging and pointing toward the water. Flinging her arm out toward the horizon, grabbing at people.

There was a swimmer a long way out. Slaney could see someone's head, a silhouette, far away, or it was a buoy. He gripped the wooden railing that separated the restaurant from the beach and leapt over it, and ran to the edge of the water. He yelled over his shoulder to Brophy to come help.

Somebody's drowning out there, let's go, he shouted. He'd taken off his shoes as he ran and when he got back later the shoes were still there, but far apart from each other. He remembered taking one shoe off, because he'd had to hop-hop with his foot in both hands before he could toss it. The other one must have come off by itself.

He'd taken off his T-shirt too. He would have no memory of doing that.

Another man with a lifeguard ring was ahead of him and got to the drowning woman first. This man and the woman were going under together and whatever they said was under-water. She must have been shouting, You're coming with me. And he must have shouted, No, you're coming with me.

But the language was bubbled and came out silvery and wiggling and broke apart before it got to the surface. On the surface there was just the sucking up of sky and foam and the language went in backwards and garbled and on the surface there was love and desperation and a war of save me, save me.

She was the kind of strong that could hoist a car over her head if she wanted, but what she wanted, with all her might, was to drown the guy who got there first.

The guy was speaking Spanish. Slaney didn't hear it but he formed the impression it was Spanish. He was from there and handsome, these were Slaney's impressions; and he also had an animal strength, just like the woman, and if they ever made love, the two of them, children would burst out of her forehead and all that was wrong would be okay. But they were not making love, there was so much hate it boiled the water.

She threw her arms around and she sank back down and was gone from them for long stretches so they could only see her white bikini like a glimmer of light in the murk and the blooming flower of her hair.

She was going to stand on the Mexican guy's shoulders to keep her chin out of the water whether he liked it or not. She had the authority of a person who refuses to see reason, or is lit up with a reason all her own. She wanted the Mexican guy to be standing on the shoulders of another man, possibly Slaney, and for there to be more men all the way to the bottom. All she really wanted was a lungful of air.

The guy had a family, Slaney thought, he had that look, or that was another one of the impressions formed later, on the drive back. Like Slaney, the guy had ended up in the water without ever considering what he was doing.

They had not thought, None of my business. They had not thought, What about if something happens out there, or that she deserved what she got for being so bloody stupid, for wandering out so far. And they had found themselves in an awkward threesome where she had laid down the law: she would get what she wanted any way she could. The claw marks on Slaney's back were something when they got out.

And the Mexican guy, too, was bleeding from the corner of his eye. She had taken pieces out of his face with her fingernails.

Slaney popped her in the jaw. It was her jaw or her temple and he was not careful. No decision was made. It was done before he knew it. He could not remember it but he knew it happened, the way you know something someone tells you. He knew it second-hand. He would never have believed it if he hadn't been told by a reliable source. He was the source. It was exactly the right measure of violence. He'd never hit a girl before. He had time to think that.

She was still wearing the mask and the water was slosh-ing inside the glass window and her eyes were screaming but — and this he could swear to, this was something he'd never seen before and did not want to see again — he saw the eyes roll back in her head. First a fluttering of one eyelid that looked flirtatious. A nerve with a mind of its own in her eye-lid. The ecstasy of giving up. He saw that.

That's what he hadn't wanted to see. It was a bad preced-ent. If giving up felt that good he might like it. That's what he thought. He never wanted to try it. Giving up was all or noth-ing. The woman had given up.

The Mexican guy was swimming away and Slaney lost sight of him from one wave to another. There, not there. He was swimming out toward the horizon and Slaney found he was yelling over the waves and he had to prop her up, and really, the situation was boring. They were almost done and where did that bastard think he was going? The guy came back with the ring. He had gone to get the ring.

She had knocked the ring out of his arms and he'd got it back and Slaney had her in a loose headlock, face up, and his other arm linked into the ring.

Then there were two other men. And it was just as well because Slaney was done and the Mexican guy was done too. The other two guys lifted her out of the waves and when they did Slaney thought to put his feet down and saw he was up to his waist. The hardest part was the last few waves that drove him into the upside-down sand and he crawled out on his hands and knees.

He lay there and waited to breathe. When he pulled himself

up, the woman broke out of the thick crowd that had surrounded her. The other man had gone. The Mexican had
been swallowed up in a separate crowd that had gathered. The
woman came over to Slaney and put her arms around his neck
and rested her head on his chest. He put his hand on her heart.
He was feeling the heartbeat. It was so off-kilter and bewildering. Her skin was bewildering and a strand of her hair and the
way she pressed against him and her crazy little beating thing
of a heart under his hand. That was just an instant, of course.
Then it was over and she went back to being whoever she was
and Slaney looked for his T-shirt.

Brophy was standing in the sand in his black socks. He held
his shoes, a finger hooked into each heel. Slaney picked up his
clothes as they headed back to the Jeep. He remembered he had
to pay for the meal, and then he remembered he had paid already.

You want a beer? Brophy said.

No thanks, I'd like to get moving, Slaney said.

I have a heart condition, Brophy said. I couldn't leave the
money. My heart is bad. I would have just been in the way out
there. You would have had to rescue me.

Let's go, Slaney said. I don't want to be out in the dark with
all this cash.

There was only that brute thing, Slaney thought. There was
only the pop he'd given that girl and the way she had allowed
him to keep her alive and how important it had been for her
to succumb.

They drove back to the hostel. Brophy said he'd like to help
Slaney with the boat, if they needed help on board, but he
couldn't do heavy lifting. Slaney invited him in for a drink
and he bought a couple of beers from the maid and they sat
out on the deck of the hostel in wooden lawn chairs.

He'd had a clogged artery a while back and his arm would tingle, Brophy told him. He'd wake up; the arm would be asleep. There would be pins and needles. This was his right arm, hanging off his shoulder. He'd spent a weekend drinking at his brother's stag and then the wedding and he'd turned grey.

The colour of that there, he said. He tapped the grey weathered wood of his armrest with his finger. Everything went funny. It had a funny aspect.

My vision, he said. He swayed a hand in the air. My son came to get me at the airport and I told him. My arm, I said. Brophy touched Slaney's arm as he said it.

I told him I'd been throwing up, and I broke a sweat right there at the luggage thing.

The carousel, Slaney said. Brophy was stirring the air with his finger. He nodded. Waiting for my luggage.

He was the one that said a heart attack, Brophy said. He called it. My son called the damn thing.

Slaney had the suitcase of money for the Mexican authorities tucked in under his chair.

What he thought was this. He believed the story about the heart attack, but it had a different cadence than everything else Brophy had said. He was thinking: the heart attack is true, but everything else has been a lie.

They were relying on the Mexicans to be corrupt. It was a hell of an assumption. It was easy for Hearn. Hearn was in Vancouver. Hearn was getting ready for the life after his life of crime. As if there wasn't a tide of events to swim against. It was a merciless quality in Hearn. He didn't respect those who doubted themselves.

Hearn was a contemptuous bastard to those who had doubts.

Brophy was talking about his condition. He said there were

things he'd had to give up because of his heart. He spoke about diet.

You wonder if it's worth it, Brophy said. Slaney took a quick peek at him then, glanced over. Because this statement had come from a deep place, a peeling down of facade. Brophy wasn't aware that he'd said it out loud.

It was a tone of disappointment. The guy was deflated. He was sick and unsure of himself. Why hadn't Hearn checked him out? It wasn't Hearn with a yacht full of weed parked under the noses of the Mexican authorities, owing for fuel and supplies.

Slaney felt the teeter-totter inside him shift. He was dropping from trust to doubt. If he had to pinpoint the moment. There had been a moment and it was when Brophy spoke about it all being worth something.

He had spoken with the authority of a man who had suffered. He was a broken sort of man, Slaney decided. He had been broken not by something big, but the grinding of a thousand small things to which he himself had agreed. He had made concessions.

Brophy had gone into the bank and he came out with the money. His shirt was buttoned up in the heat. You wonder if it's worth it. Slaney knew that every lie commingled with the truth.

But you could not spend an afternoon with a man who had suffered a heart attack, who had come near death because he could not control his cholesterol, and not experience some minor revelation. Something would be revealed and Slaney could already see it. This guy wasn't what he said he was. There would be double-crosses, for which Slaney had to allow; there was a double-cross in the works. But the nature of it mattered.

Hearn didn't know the guy. But it was a question of how deep the double-cross went. It was a question: should he grab the bag of money and run down the beach with it? Should he tell Ada?

It was because Slaney had saved the drowning woman. Slaney and the Mexican and the other men. But it had been Slaney who did the thinking out there. He'd knocked her out and saved all their lives.

It was instinct or he had thought about it. A sharp jab to the jaw. Brophy was drowning too.

What kind of man stands on shore and watches a woman drowning? A man with a bad heart.

Brophy was talking about his daughter. The daughter had lost faith in him. That was the story. Some distancing had occurred. She'd become frustrated with him. She'd left. Walked away.

He was telling about the wild spirit in his daughter. It was a quality Brophy had admired when she was a child. He talked to Slaney about her as a four-year-old. He said about her gymnastics. He said triple somersaults. It was something he'd tried to encourage.

She doesn't understand responsibility, Brophy said, tossing the beer bottle into the bushes beside the deck. But he didn't go on about his daughter after that.

Patterson had intuited a new quiet in Slaney. He knew he'd said something wrong but he could not imagine what it was. He was afraid the smallest thing might cause the kid to give up now. Patterson had thought nobody could give up after coming so far, but maybe the opposite was true. Maybe the kid had come too far. Maybe he'd feel like it was time to turn back. Slaney might give up and leave Carter and Ada Anderson and get the hell out.

I suppose I should get going, Brophy said. Slaney drank down the rest of his beer too. He stood up and got the bag of money from under the chair and hefted the strap over his shoulder.

Slaney thought of the goat they'd passed on the drive back from the beach. The Jeep had dipped down in a rut and bounced up and they were passing the garage where they'd had the tire fixed. The white, white goat was eating a screamingly red blouse. It lifted its head and shut its eyes against the dust they were kicking up.

It came to Slaney then. The revelation he'd waited for, drinking his beer in the bar. The revelation that had hovered over his fist like a butterfly, his innermost thing, while he drank his beer and watched the woman put her mask and snorkel on, while he watched her awkward walk over the sand in her flippers.

He wouldn't return to the port where they were waiting.

Where Hearn was waiting; where the transport trucks were waiting; and the caves were waiting and the men and whatever Brophy had in store for them, the dogs and the sirens and the guns and the cuffs.

He'd alter their course at the last minute. He'd explain it to Carter once they were on the sailboat and Carter would see the wisdom. The wisdom ran like this: Let them all wait.

Maybe You Thought a Vacation

Patterson approached Ada when she walked into the bar.

Hello, Roy, she said. I'd heard you were here. Lovely to see you again. I'm just looking for Cyril.

Patterson told her he'd had a few drinks with Carter, sent him back to the hostel about an hour ago.

I must have missed him, she said.

Why don't you have a quick drink with me, Ada, Patterson said. He pinched the sleeve of her peasant blouse near the cuff and gave it a playful little tug.

I don't know, Roy, she said. Cyril's probably in a bad way. I should get back to the hostel.

You guys are setting sail tomorrow, Patterson said. I have to talk to you. He took her by the wrist now.

Hey, she said. She flicked her arm free but she followed him to the back of the bar where there was an empty table next to the back door. The door was ajar and a band of harsh sunlight fell over the floor. She could hear the chickens outside clucking and step-stepping, the ruffling of wings. Someone was out there scattering feed, speaking in Spanish, cooing and cajoling.

Sit down, Ada, Patterson said. Just long enough for a little chat. I want to make you an offer. He raised his hand to the bartender and she came to the table with two beers and two glasses and they waited for her to wipe the table and lay down the coasters and place the beers.

I thought you might have died in that hurricane, Patterson said. I wished I'd had a chance to say something to you before you left.

We're fine, Ada said.

Do you know that man is married? Patterson said. He suffers from mental illness. His wife and children are worried sick. He's had breakdowns before. The stress here can destroy a man like Carter. My guess is you're seeing symptoms of another nervous breakdown already.

Who are you? Ada asked. My God.

You could be a confidential informant, Patterson said. This is what I'm offering. You don't appear in court. Nobody knows you said a thing. Your identity is never disclosed. I am a father too. I have a daughter your age. I think of your father. I'm telling you there's a way out of this for you. This is an offer.

She stood up and gripped the back of her chair with both hands. She looked as if the chair were alive with a current or spirit and she were struggling to keep it from flying through the air and smashing against his skull. He saw the same girl who had been playing the piano that night at Hearn's. The feral, grounded voltage of emotion.

Hear me out, he said. A rooster came through the door then, black and rust, a white speckled throat, an angry and inquisitive strut.

Maybe you've been coerced, Patterson said. Maybe you didn't know the implications. You're a young girl. Your whole life ahead of you. I want to tell you how moved I was listening to your music. I won't lie; it was unsettling. You have a gift. Maybe you have a responsibility to it. I don't know what you have.

The rooster stood still, its wattles a grotesque red, quivering and wrinkled.

Maybe nobody told you there were drugs, Patterson said. Perhaps the men hadn't told you the whole story when you set out. You thought a vacation in Mexico. You didn't know what was happening.

I knew, Ada said. Of course I knew. She became limp, her shoulders drooping, and she let go of the back of the chair and sank onto the seat.

If you don't want to think about yourself, think about Carter. That man won't last very long in prison.

Patterson kept talking. He told her it would be easy to cast her as an innocent bystander. He took a long drink of his beer.

Everyone involved will be going to jail for a very long time, Miss Anderson, he said. If you co-operate with us, things will be different for you. Carter, too. That's a promise. Please, drink your beer.

No, thank you, she said.

Carter's a very ill man, he said. Right now, if you co-operate, we see a much lighter sentence for Carter, and you go free. Maybe you go back with your father, pursue your career, forget all this ever happened. You're just a kid here. Your whole life ahead. It's really Hearn and Slaney we're after. Or whatever you choose to call them. And believe me, they're as good as caught already.

She put her elbows on the table and held her forehead with her hands. She stayed that way for a long moment. Then she looked up at him. How calculating and innocent. How reckless. He thought indomitable and tender. He didn't know what to think. He had her. That's what he thought.

All I'm asking: If Slaney decides to walk away, you let us know. If there's a change of plans, you let us know. You make a phone call. If you're blown off course, you let us know. You dock somewhere; you make a call. You get to a phone. You call us.

If you don't want to do this for yourself, you do it for Carter. The bartender had come around the side of the bar with a broom. The bristles were neon pink nylon and she swished it at the rooster, ushering it toward the back door. It hop-skipped and swerved around a chair, through the door into the obliterating sunlight. They could hear it crowing outside.

A Visitor in the Night

Someone had come into his room. He'd woken when the door closed. There was a bedside lamp and he switched it on. The lamp had a red shade and cast a glow.

Ada stood at the foot of his bed hugging her army surplus knapsack.

The room was doubled in the black glass of the window and spread on forever over the ocean. The white lines of surf from the beach below moved over her reflection.

She was digging in her knapsack and she tugged out the wrinkled bundle of a negligee. It was white, free-falling layers of gauze and lace, and there was a satin ribbon gathering the neck. She shook it out, holding one puffy sleeve between her finger and thumb. She flicked it twice to get rid of the wrinkles.

Are you drunk? Slaney asked. Where's Carter?

Carter is drunk, she said. I want to sleep with you, David. I'm going to put on this nightgown and get in bed with you. I want you to hold me. Then I'm going back to bed with Carter and I don't want to talk about it. Not ever.

You don't need that nightgown, he said. But she went to the bathroom, and then stood in the doorway, wearing it. The gown fell to her knees and it was see-through. It floated around her naked body.

Do you like it? she asked. I was saving it for a special occasion.

I think this is pretty special, he said.

Ada lay down beside him. Slaney ran his hand over her belly and lifted the filmy gown up slowly so the ruffles and frills at the hem pooled over one hip and between her legs.

He felt her ribs and the slope of her hip bone and he ran his knuckles over her nipples. He watched her breasts rise and fall. Then she moved her leg over him and they kissed. At first he hardly touched her, except to kiss. Then he touched her everywhere he could. He took his time.

He smeared up the gauzy veils of the gown and parted her legs and put his mouth on her and touched her with the tip of his tongue. It was like they had all the time in the world. She held his hair in her fists and twisted it. She was breathing short, shallow breaths and her thighs were trembling and she arched up into him and the sound she made when she came was a fast breath of surprise. Then she was straddling him and he held her ass with both hands and the nightgown tumbled in folds over his wrists and he lifted her down onto him and he was inside her. The bed smacked and smacked and he said, Let me see your face.

She tucked her hair behind her ears. She looked into his eyes. They looked at each other for a long time.

Then she braced herself with one hand flat against the wall over his head.

She looked as though someone were speaking to her and she had to listen very hard. Her eyes closed and she nodded now and then and she began to rock harder against him and faster.

Open your eyes, he said.

No.

Open them. I want to see your eyes, he said. Open them, come on, please. She opened her eyes but they fluttered and then they were closed tight, and there was a beautiful expression he hadn't seen on her face before.

She was astonished or succumbing or, he realized, coming,

maybe three times, maybe four. She spoke a few words and it was a phrase from a prayer.

Afterwards they lay side by side not touching at all. It was too hot to touch. He couldn't handle the cotton bedsheet. She started to giggle.

What's so funny? he said.

No, she said.

Tell me, he said. He ran the back of his finger over her breast, put his lips on the gauze over her nipple and felt the rough texture of it with his tongue. She was trembling, now, with giggles.

Tell me, he said. He rolled over on his elbow and looked at her. She was pressing her fingers to her eyes as if the laughter were leaking from there.

You won't get away with it, she said. David. You are going to get caught. I came to tell you something. They'll be waiting for you.

They can wait, he said. We won't be there.

Where will we be? she asked.

Where they'll least expect us.

The next morning they hired a local guy to row them out to the boat. The man named Hernandez was on board already with several soldiers. They were all armed and standing at attention. Brophy was there already too and he introduced General Hernandez.

Carter was in high spirits; he liked the new sails.

Craftsmanship is superb, he said. He offered everyone a drink. The soldiers ignored him.

You have fuel and supplies, Hernandez said. No one will bother you in these waters.

Brophy nodded to Slaney and Slaney handed Hernandez the duffle bag with the forty grand. Three soldiers took the bag below deck to count the money and they all waited in the hot sun with their heads bowed, silent, as though in church. The soldiers came back up again with the duffle bag and nodded to Hernandez.

Everything is in order, gentlemen, Hernandez said. We will leave you now. I wish you a safe journey and good luck with your endeavours.

Very nice, Carter said. Thank you, sir. A pleasure doing business.

The soldiers disembarked, climbing into the two speedboats that were waiting below. Brophy was the last to go down the ladder. He wished them luck. He'd shaken hands with Carter and Ada.

You take care of that little girl you have there, Brophy told Carter. She's a fine girl.

Slaney took Brophy's hand in his and shook it firmly. He gripped Brophy's elbow with his other hand. He held him there for a long moment.

Thanks, man, he said. Thanks for everything.

Let's get out of here, Slaney said. Then he told Carter they had to change course.

We were set up, Slaney told him.

What are you talking about? Carter said.

We were set up, Carter. We can't go back to Vancouver. They're going to be waiting for us. They'll confiscate the boat. Throw us in jail. We can't go back.

Carter put his hands over his ears and stood for a long moment staring at the deck.

What's happening, Ada, he yelled. Ada? What's happening

here? But she was looking out over the rail of the boat at the water and didn't turn to him.

I want to head back to Newfoundland, Slaney said. Let's go home, Carter.

We'd have to go through the Panama Canal, Carter said. Ada turned to Carter then with her arms crossed tightly over her chest.

The boat handles differently with the extra weight, Ada said. The line handler in the canal will know as soon as he steps on board.

We pay off the line handler, Slaney said. Pay off Customs. Use the twenty-five thou left from the deal with Lopez.

Cyril, it's so risky, Ada said. They're on to us, David already told you that. I don't think we should keep going.

It takes thirty hours to get through the canal, give or take, Carter said. We'd have to skip the line or you can end up waiting forever just to get in. Once you're in, you just sit pretty and the line handler takes you through. I don't know, Slaney. They could lock us up down there and nobody would ever hear from us again.

The whole country is propped up with drug money, Slaney said. It won't be hard to find the right line handler.

Listen to me, Cyril, Ada said. We could just dump the cargo.

It's a couple of million dollars, Slaney hissed at her. He flung his arm out, pointing toward the cargo below deck. We can't give up now, he said. We're almost there. Ada, I didn't want you involved. But you're here. You wanted to be a part of it. Now you've got to see this through.

Ada put her hands on Carter's face.

Look at me, Cyril, she said. Look at me. I am asking you for this. You said you'd give me anything I wanted. This is what I want. I want you to listen.

Honey, Cyril said. It was as though he'd just noticed her. He took her hands off his face and pressed them between his own. He rubbed them vigorously as if they were cold and he had to warm them.

Tonight, when it's dark, Ada said. We could toss the whole lot of it overboard. We could just sail home. They know about the cargo, Cyril. It's too risky to keep going now.

But Carter was staring hard at the deck, his hands held out before him, gently slicing them through the air, as if marking off the miles, calculating the route. Then he was wringing his hands together, muttering with his eyes shut tight. He'd forgotten all about Ada. Then his eyes flew open and he grabbed her shoulders and drew her into his chest. He held her like that in a hard grip.

Ada, he said. This is the real beginning for us. This is the test. We're going to sail through it. We're going to make it. I want to believe you're with me. I want us to do this together.

You can do this, Ada, Slaney said. We're through the worst of it now. Clear sailing ahead. There's no way they can catch us. They think we're on the way to Van-fucking-couver.

I feel like a drink, Carter said. Anybody else feel like a drink?

I'd have a drink with you, Slaney said. Come on, Ada. Let's drink to the trip.

Let's turn this baby around, Carter yelled. He raised a triumphant fist in the air.

I'll get the bottle, Ada said.

So you're in? Carter said.

I'm in, my love, she said. It might be crazy, but I'm in.

I knew it, Carter said. I knew I could count on you. This is why I fell in love, David. Look at her. Just look.

Where we headed, Captain? Slaney asked.

The Caribbean has a strong east-to-west current, Carter said. We'll be up against the trade winds.

We want to avoid sandbars near the Turks and Caicos and the Bahamas, and those waters are lousy with coastal patrols, Slaney said. We learned that the hard way the last time around.

So we head northwest first, Carter said. Get ourselves to Cuba, and then head northeast.

That's the route Hearn and I took the first time, Slaney said. That'll get us there.

Then the Gulf Stream carries us home, Carter said. But we move now, before the sea gets rough up there. We have to beat the bad weather.

They sailed all day and the weather was beautiful. Ada finished reading *Tender Is the Night* and when she was done she threw it over the side.

They went ashore in Panama to get supplies and split up on the dock. Ada hired a horse-drawn cart to take her to the market. Slaney and Carter hung around the dock in a filthy bar until they found the line man they needed and negotiated a price. And Slaney went to place a call to Hearn. Tell him to meet them in Newfoundland.

Hearn, he said. Get yourself a plane ticket to St. John's. There's been a change of plans.

Rings
within
Rings

Eternal Return

Big white spots spangled out blue auras and they were blinded. Slaney had a glowing orb hanging in the centre of whatever he looked at, and in the periphery the water sparkled with moonlight and the cliffs rose up to the sky.

They were off the coast of Trinity Bay, Newfoundland. Four vessels surrounded Carter's sailboat and the cops yelled into bullhorns, baritones with echo and hiss. The cops said they had Slaney surrounded.

Come up on deck and stand with your hands over your heads.

There they were, Slaney and Ada and Cyril, and it was over. Everything was over. The army was waiting. They had brought out the army and the RCMP and there were boats with guns trained on them and the lights.

He saw Ada's face, wet with tears, floating in his peripheral vision and that was the last he saw of her for a long time.

He could not believe he had returned to this. He had wanted to go home; this was not home. There was no returning. Or there was the opposite: an eternal return.

The ground rocked with a phantom sea swell and he wanted to lie down. Nothing was solid underfoot. It was so unlikely that existence should ever exist, but it did, and then it did again. They had been caught. And caught and caught and caught. Time was not linear: it looped, concentric rings within rings, and he had been surrounded.

A dog trotted up to him and sniffed at his jeans and panted and drooled and it was like the dog recognized him, knew who Slaney was. The dog dug in his front paws and growled and snapped his teeth and let off a volley of barks.

It was dark now and Slaney could see the cops rounding up the crew Hearn had put together to unload the cargo, but he couldn't see who they were.

Flashlight beams sliced through the crowd and someone cuffed his hands behind his back and gave him a gentle shove forward. He searched the faces in the crowd on the hill for someone familiar. He half expected his mother. He was looking for Hearn.

Slaney and Carter were headed for one car and Ada was already in another.

Hearn shouted to him. A ragged yell. He called out: Hey. It was a shout that came from the guts and Hearn's body was stiff as he yelled it, leaning into the call. He made a stumbling run toward Slaney but his hands were cuffed behind too and the cops held him back. Hey, Hearn yelled. Hey. Hey. He wasn't saying Slaney's name. Hey, Hey you. Hey. It was a berserk cry. And Slaney would think about it later, full of recognition and maybe love.

There was Hearn. They had Hearn. His orange hair like a fire in the red light that swung around on the roof of the cop car.

Then they pushed Hearn into a car and Slaney watched the car reverse up the gravel hill and it turned at the top and he watched the tail lights go down the road.

Brophy was there. He saw Brophy talking with an RCMP officer and he had a cup of coffee and Slaney called out to him.

Brophy looked up but Slaney noticed the delay. He hadn't responded to the name right away. The name had taken a moment to register. Brophy smiled and waved at him. Lifted his Styrofoam cup in Slaney's direction. A kind of toast.

Slaney realized he wouldn't need the name Douglas Knight anymore.

Over the weeks that followed he came to understand about the satellite technology and that the boat had been followed all the way down. And that he had been followed across the country from the beginning.

The revelation was something of a relief. How could they have beat that sort of omniscience? He learned that they had even let him go from prison so that they could follow him to Hearn, and the humiliation blazed through him.

What he had felt as freedom had not been freedom at all. The wind and the water and the stars. None of that. He had not been free. Slaney had always been caught. He had never escaped. He'd just been on a long chain.

Brophy raised the white Styrofoam cup in his direction and drank a last sip and crushed the cup in his fist and Slaney knew they had his innermost thing. They had crushed it at last.

Slaney and Hearn were each charged with three counts: the conspiracy to import marijuana, importing marijuana, and possession of marijuana for the purpose of trafficking. Seven years for each count.

They were to be an example for the country.

302

Ada got off. Carter went to jail for eight months and when he got out he went back to his wife.

Hearn had been granted bail against all expectation because of a new appointment to the bench, a good Liberal who had practised tax law for twenty years and hadn't seen the inside of a courtroom until he was sworn in. The judge liked the look of Hearn and decided not to consider the merit of the Crown's case. "I'm not considering merit," he said, and Hearn was out on bail. Not the case for Slaney. His judge decided that the Crown's case had quite a bit of merit.

A few weeks later Hearn was at the restaurant in the Newfoundland Hotel, lunching with his lawyer.

The Mistakes

Patterson strolled out over the snowy grounds with Alphonse beside him. They'd put on rubbers over their shoes and Alphonse was wearing a beaver fur hat that Delores had given him for Christmas and black leather gloves and a fine wool coat.

That's a fine hat, Alphonse, Patterson said. You look spiffy.

I love you, Alphonse said. He took Patterson's hand in his and he stuttered and the words burst out of him, finally, emphatic and true: You are my friend. Why were you gone so long?

I'm sorry about that, Patterson said.

I forgive you, Alphonse said.

They'd eaten turkey in the facility's cafeteria for Christmas Eve. They'd worn paper party hats and a musician had been hired to play the piano and there were carols.

Alphonse didn't want his cranberry sauce touching his potato. That had been the only bad moment. Alphonse began to raise his voice about it but Patterson calmed him down right away.

He took the cranberry sauce off Alphonse's plate and put it on his own. And Alphonse clapped his hands with real joy when the pudding was set aflame.

After the meal they walked. There were big, delicate two-ply snowflakes, like in the ads for toilet paper. The black tree branches were rimmed in white. The case was over and filed.

Patterson thought of Hearn in the mouth of the cave where they had arrested him. A year later and he was still thinking of it. The white crests of the waves moonlit, the round beach stones chinking and tumbling as the waves withdrew.

Things are changing, Brophy, Hearn had hissed at him from the back seat of the squad car. You're going to be left behind, man. Do you even know what I'm talking about? You're going to be left behind, man. Everything is changing.

Patterson had heard about the development in Hearn's case on the news last week. Hearn had got off on a technicality. They'd put a bug in a lamp on a restaurant table and the waitress had alerted Hearn's lawyer.

She'd jotted a note on her menu pad and torn it off and put it on the table for the lawyer to read.

Hearn and the lawyer having lunch before court, both of them wearing suits.

The waitress put a note on the table and Hearn's lawyer took out his glasses and perched them on his nose and read the note and put it in his shirt pocket.

Then he stood up, surprising even Hearn, and tore the lamp's plug out of the socket and the wire snapped up like a whip, and with his other hand he turned the whole table over and they left the restaurant with the lamp.

The RCMP had violated solicitor–client privilege. It was an abuse of process. The judge felt the state had behaved egregiously. They revered the solicitor–client thing, these judges. Patterson knew that. They were always going on about it. A punk running drugs and the judge saying the cops were egregious.

Or justice will be denied to one and all, the judge said.

The judge on his high horse.

Case dismissed. The Crown knew it was serious shit, they didn't even appeal. O'Neill had ordered the bug in the restaurant. O'Neill got the dressing-down.

Cyril Carter's wife had done a television appearance the month before. She'd had a microphone clipped to her lapel. They had a glass of water on a table and an arrangement of flowers. They had an advertisement for Cream of the West Flour and they spun a wheel and the viewers could win something: a cookbook featuring recipes for flour.

I felt stirred up all over when I met him, Carter's wife said. Patterson had watched the interview leaning forward, his elbows on his knees, his hands clasped in front of him. Delores had set up the two folding TV trays and they'd eaten in the den so they could watch together.

The wife had been honest. She was asked a question, she answered. The cameras bore through her.

Forgive me if this is hard to believe, she said. But it was chemistry. That man looked at me and I was in love. All he had to do was look.

The wife had taken him back and nursed him through the subsequent breakdown.

The girl had called Patterson from Panama. Patterson had known right away what Carter had seen in her. What had turned his head. There was something trustworthy and feral in her. She had pulled through for him. The girl had said Slaney was going to change their course. They were going up the Caribbean coast, heading to Newfoundland. Patterson had to admit it was a bold move. He never would have found them if not for the girl.

Cyril is too fragile for prison, she'd said. Cyril won't survive it. They'd let her go after the big arrest at the cove and she'd flown to Ontario. Ada Anderson had just begun work on a doctorate in musicology at the University of Toronto.

Patterson had turned the TV off before the interview was over. He and Delores watched the dot of light in the centre of the screen, the only thing left of the picture, fade away.

Twentieth Anniversary

You find yourself standing like this, Ada said. She was holding the phone book at arm's length. She had glasses hanging on a cord around her neck and she put them on. She had thought a pizza but he said he didn't want it. She was flustered and blushing.

I'm not here for pizza, he said. She closed the book and let it hang by her side and put one hand on the bookshelf.

A snack, then, she said. She went into the kitchen. He heard the fridge.

Closer things, I'm fine, she said. She was taking jars out of the fridge and getting the cups and saucers. He moved without a sound to the door frame because he wanted to see how she was in the kitchen when she didn't know she was being watched.

And things in the distance, she said. But the middle distance is blurry. Slaney said he had reading glasses too.

I don't remember you much of a reader, she said. He had forgotten this about her; she could be callous. She was capable of saying anything. There were small wrinkles around her mouth and a slackness under the eyes, but she was the same. If he just focused on her mouth he forgot what she had looked like when she was young.

But when she broke out the smile. She smiled inappropriately. He had forgotten that about her too. He could never predict it. She could smile when she was sad and it wasn't insincere. She was the sort of woman, he thought, everything she felt came at her from a great distance.

Any sudden change of expression, the age fell away from her face. Or the young face from twenty years ago was what fell away, and he involuntarily adjusted to this new, older face, and he couldn't remember the younger one and it left the impression she hadn't changed. Her body was not that much different, she looked slender. She was more or less the same. He told her so.

Oh my, she said. Her hands went up and touched her cheeks. He watched her hands, a hesitation before every gesture, then deft action.

She was working a metal bucket from a bread maker. Elbows jutting up, the metal handle wrapped with a pot cloth and she shook the loaf onto the counter. It came out with a *thunk* and the smell of fresh bread wafted around and she tried to remove a metal part in the bottom of the loaf and shook her fingers because she'd burned them. She turned toward him with her fingers in her mouth. She was sucking three of her fingertips. They were looking at each other like that and she turned her back on him.

Listen, he said. I don't want anything to eat. His heart had been beating hard as he approached the front door and clapped the brass knocker, a lion with a loop through his jaws, but now he felt a lassitude. The low slanting sun lit up her hair, her white blouse; a tiny metal buckle on her sandal near the ankle burned white. She ran the water and put her fingers under.

I didn't want you to go to any trouble, he said. She had written him in prison just before he was released. She had asked him to come. She wanted to talk about it, he'd thought. Or ask him what had happened in prison. They had shared something. Maybe she wanted to remind him of that.

I didn't let it define me, she said.

Something in you, though, he said. She turned the water off but she was still holding the tap, as if whatever she had to say next could be turned on, flow out.

Or she had been arrested by the thought: it was a part of her, the audacity of what they had tried.

Yes, she said. Something in me. It was a wild adventure. Before it went sour. Nothing has compared to it. She took up the dishtowel and unwedged the metal skewer from the bottom of the bread and flipped the loaf upright and turned to him, unleashing the smile.

Fresh bread, she said. He sat down in the living room and she followed him with a tray, two mugs of tea. She had left the bread.

Twenty years, he said. This was how she had been living: a brass door knocker, the sunlight, a baby grand piano with an embroidered shawl draped over the top.

He had been deprived of everything for twenty years. The

thought knocked but he shut it down. He had promised himself he would not let them have what was left. He would not allow the rest of it to be poisoned with bitterness. But sometimes it roared up like a sea monster.

What I found astonishing, she said. How easily people believe a lie. Isn't it something?

I thought about you, he said.

There's a beat and then you see they believe it, she said. Whatever it is. The truth starts to lose currency.

Do you play these days? he asked.

I teach theory, she said. I play now and then. I play for myself.

She sat on the edge of the chair, her hands on her knees, and drew a deep breath and held it. She let the breath out with her eyes closed. There was the ridiculous golden light, liturgical and autumnal, touching everything glass and metal.

The studs on the leather chair she was sitting in and the bevelled strip on the mirror behind her. A cat padded into the room and sat in the middle of the carpet. Its whiskers were lit up.

I'd like to meet your children, Slaney said.

Not a chance, she said. He put down the cup.

They don't know anything about it, she said. I haven't told anyone. Then she mentioned that the cat had no eyes. Glaucoma and eventually the pressure behind the eyes, even after a couple of operations.

They were removed?

The pressure got to be too much, she said. And when she said that, he knew. He knew unequivocally. He'd thought he needed to know, but now he saw it didn't matter very much. She had told Patterson about him changing course. He had known it all along.

She finds her way though, don't you, girl, Ada said. The cat turned toward her voice and he saw the face. He saw there were no eyes, just as she had said, but he didn't believe it. If the lids were stitched together, he could not see it for the fur. There was a black patch of fur where one of the eyes should be and a golden brown patch over the other. It was a calico cat, expectant and cringing. The tea scalded Slaney's throat.

Is that weak? she asked. He remembered this too: she could become prim in an instant. Because you could have let it steep, she said.

You had them removed, he said. The cat had found Ada's legs and was butting its head against her shin and winding through and between.

I got the cat after the eyes were removed. Somebody left it at a shelter.

Slaney wondered if she would have allowed the operation if it had been left up to her. He thought she would have risen to the need. She could act when she faced helplessness in others; pity provoked her, woke her up. It was independence and self-reliance that left her unsure and brought out the coldness in her.

I'm divorced, she said. He wasn't surprised; it would always be harder for her to leave a relationship than stay in it and she would always do the hardest thing.

I've remade my life, she said. Are you done with the tea? Because I want to put it away if you're done. A spoon clattered to the floor on her way out of the living room. She stopped and spoke with the tray in her hands.

You know it was me, she said.

I didn't know, he said. I didn't come here for that.

Yes, you knew, she said.

The cat leapt up onto the arm of the sofa, its back hunched.

It was digging its claws into the fabric and pulling it up. The *pock*, *pock* of the tight brocade.

She must have tossed everything on the tray into the sink; there was the crash of china. Then the tray hit the wall and clattered on the floor.

She came back out and sat opposite him on the same couch. She dug a toe of one foot under the strap of her sandal and flicked it off. She reached down and unhooked the other sandal strap and kicked her foot free. She drew her knees up. She was wearing jeans and a faded green T-shirt and a silver chain with a flat polished stone. She worked her toes under his thigh.

You turned me in, Slaney said.

Yes I did, she said. I told them. They said I would be a confidential informant and not go to jail and my name wouldn't be mentioned in court and Cyril would get a lighter sentence, or no time at all. I called them from Panama while you and Cyril were looking for the line man. I told them we had changed course. I said we were going to Newfoundland.

You did it for Cyril, he said.

I did it because I was afraid, she said. I was afraid for Cyril and I was afraid for myself.

He pressed his thumb and fingers against the bridge of his nose. Then he put both his hands over his face. There was a rose garden outside and he heard a bicycle bell.

It hadn't been Hearn, as he had wondered and sometimes believed. She was digging an elbow into the couch, and she levered herself up out of it and went into the kitchen, put on the kettle again. She came out and leaned on the door frame, her arms wrapped around her waist.

I know I'm not in any position, she said. I've been putting money away for you. I put away ten percent of every paycheque for the last twenty years and I invested it. It's a fair sum now, but not enough, of course. I'm not saying that. I want you to accept it.

Oh, he said. It was a long time ago. Do you want me to forgive you? I forgive you.

He would have said anything to get out of there. Jennifer had developed cancer while he was in prison and she had passed on. She'd had three children and she'd sent him Christmas cards for years. A family portrait on the front, and in this way he'd watched her family grow.

He had nobody. What had he been thinking? Why had he needed to know? It was not Hearn. That was the more important thing.

I'm sorry, Ada said.

Okay, he said. He found he couldn't move himself to get off the couch. He wanted to get out before her children came home. Or whoever she had.

I'm sorry, David.

It's okay, he said.

Please take the money, she said. She turned so her back was flat against the door frame and she tilted her head back and dragged the corners of her mouth down. Her old mouth. But it went young with the crying. Her shoulders were lifting and falling. She slid down to the floor. He got down on the floor himself and walked over to her on his knees. He put his arms around her. He gathered her onto his lap, her knees and arms and her wet face in his shirt.

Will you take the money? she whispered. Please.

The Return

Slaney could see Windsor Lake and Hogan's Pond and Mitchell's Pond and Hugh's Pond and the Bell Island ferry was crossing the tickle very slowly and he could see the two white ragged ribbons of wake behind it. The ocean had small wrinkles all over and there were the dark shadows of the clouds moving across the surface and the plane turned and he could see all of Portugal Cove and Torbay, the cars were zipping up through, and then they began the descent into St. John's.

He had been given his mother's ancient blue suitcase when he was released from prison and he'd bought himself some new clothes and he was wearing jeans and a white shirt and a suit jacket.

The St. John's airport looked fresher to him, more airy; the place had been painted since he'd last been through. It was 1998 and he was home for good. They were on the cusp of the new millennium and he was finally home.

He came down the escalator and his heart was beating hard and he saw her shoes and legs and her blue raglan and then her hands clasped to her lips and there she was. His mother: she threw open her arms when she saw him. He hadn't seen her since her last visit to the prison, seven months ago, and she looked even more frail and stooped than she had then.

She held him close to her and they stayed that way for a moment and then she took a step back and smoothed down the wrinkles in the arms of his jacket.

Is that all you have with you? she said. That ancient little suitcase? And he said it was. He said they had let him take it on the plane and it meant they didn't have to wait at the carousel.

She spoke about the parking and she said she had a ticket and she had to remember where she put it and she would have enjoyed a little party to celebrate his arrival but she respected he might want to have a quiet afternoon.

Quiet is nice too, she said. Quiet is lovely.

I have a chicken, she said. And I made a trifle and I thought we'd have a drink of wine. I don't know if it's any good but Father Murphy said it's a nice wine for the price.

You might want to go out later in the evening, she said. Of course you can come and go as you please.

She drove him back to the house she'd bought in a new sub-division after Slaney's father died. She showed him the room she had furnished for him. An eiderdown and a black and grey bedspread with a print of sailboats, a small bookcase, and a bedside lamp with the plastic still on the shade. He said it would be perfect. She stood in the doorway and he sat on the bed and bounced it a little.

Thank you for coming to get me, he said.

Oh, David, she said.

They ate at the dining room table and she didn't let him help with the dishes and afterwards they watched *Jeopardy!* and *The Price Is Right* and an old rerun of *The Love Boat* and they spoke to each other during the commercials.

I'm going to buy a piece of land around the bay, Mom, he said. Not too far, somewhere with a view of the ocean. I have some money a friend put away for me. A bit of land, grow a few potatoes.

What do you want to live out there for? she said.

He had been formed by what they'd gone through back in '78, Slaney thought. It had been the making of them. They had been brazen. Nothing that came after would ever hold that kind of abandon. He thought of that old-fashioned word: adventure.

Adventure had leaked away from the world and everything like adventure, he thought. Slaney and his mother went to bed at the stroke of eleven.

In the morning Slaney headed in to the university. Streams of students had entered the hall all at once and they looked impossibly young, making noise, hurrying, their hair flapping over their shoulders. He was standing in the middle of the hallway and they rushed past him in both directions and were gone. They looked more like children than what he had imagined university students to look like.

Hearn had written to him for a few years, but Slaney hadn't answered. For a while Hearn sent Christmas cards with just his signature. Then he fell out of touch.

Slaney found the office in the English department and the door was closed. Hearn's name was on a plate that slid into a brass fixture. *Dr. Brian Hearn.* He wondered if Hearn was on the other side.

Acknowledgements

Thank you to Steve Crocker for advising, supporting, reading, and just for being Steve Crocker. Thank you to Eva Crocker for reading so many drafts, for the great talks about literature, and for all her insight. Thank you to Theo Crocker and Emily Pickard. Thank you to my big extended family for being so encouraging.

Melanie Little is amazing. Thank you, Melanie, for demanding that this story be the very best it could be. I feel profoundly lucky to have had the opportunity to work with you. I am eternally grateful for your vision, artistic integrity, deep intelligence, and commitment. Thank you, thank you, thank you.

I am forever indebted to my publisher, Sarah MacLachlan, for her experience, her commitment to publishing, her unrelenting hard work and the joy she brings to it, her encouragement, and her faith in books. I am grateful for our long friendship, her unlimited generosity, and her sharp-eyed reading of many drafts of this novel. Thank you so much, Sarah.

Thank you also to Elisabeth Schmitz for her enthusiasm and keen eye and commitment. Thank you so much to Clara Farmer.

I would also like to thank Heather Sangster for her perfect copy edit, Allyson Latta for her fierce proofread, and Alysia Shewchuk for the beautiful cover. Thank you to Kelly Joseph and Jared Bland for helping with the birth of this baby.

These guys made for smooth sailing: Kent Christian, Robert Decker, Michele DuRand, Gord Koch, Robert MacLachlan, Coady Montgomery, and Paul Snelgrove. Many thanks.

There were early readers for this book to whom I am most grateful. Nan Love went the extra mile. Thank you, Nan. Thank you to my cherished sister, Lynn Moore, for her legal smarts, her generous reads, and big heart. Great big thank-yous to Claire Wilkshire, Lawrence Mathews, Mary Lewis, and Michael Winter. And thank you to the Burning Rock.

And thank you so much to the whole team at Anansi. I am very grateful to Laura Repas, Matt Williams, Gillian Fizet, and everyone else at Anansi who makes the production of a book a great big giant gift. Thank you all for caring so much about literature.